THE AUTUMN MURDERS

Robert Gott was born in the small Queensland town of Maryborough in 1957, and lives in Melbourne. He has published many books for children, and is also the creator of the newspaper cartoon *The Adventures of Naked Man*. He is the author of the William Power series of crime-caper novels set in 1940s Australia: *Good Murder*, *A Thing of Blood*, *Amongst the Dead*, and *The Serpent's Sting*. *The Autumn Murders* is the third book in the Joe Sable detective series, following *The Holiday Murders* and *The Port Fairy Murders*.

The AUTUMN MURDERS

ROBERT GOTT

SCRIBE
Melbourne • London

Scribe Publications
18–20 Edward St, Brunswick, Victoria 3056, Australia
2 John St, Clerkenwell, London, WC1N 2ES, United Kingdom

First published by Scribe 2019

Typeset in 10.5/15pt Janson by the publisher

Printed and bound in Australia by Griffin Press, part of Ovato

Scribe Publications is committed to the sustainable use of natural resources
and the use of paper products made responsibly from those resources.

9781925713466 (paperback)
9781925693591 (e-book)

A catalogue record for this book is available from the National Library of Australia.

scribepublications.com.au
scribepublications.co.uk

For my parents, Maurene and Kevin. Always.

Before *The Autumn Murders*, there was *The Holiday Murders* ...

IN LATE 1943, the newly formed Homicide department of Victoria Police in Melbourne finds itself undermanned as a result of the war. Detective Inspector Titus Lambert has seen the potential of a female constable, Helen Lord. She is twenty-six years old, and, as a policewoman, something of a rarity in the male world of policing. Lambert promotes her on a temporary basis to work in Homicide, alongside a young, inexperienced detective, Joe Sable.

On Christmas Eve, two bodies — of a father and son — are found in a mansion in East Melbourne. As the investigation into their deaths proceeds, Military Intelligence becomes involved. An organisation called Australia First has already come to the attention of the authorities through its public meetings and its pro-Hitler, pro-Japan, and stridently anti-Semitic magazine, *The Publicist*. A local branch of the organisation's enthusiasts has been trying to form itself into a political party, but they are essentially dilettantes. What they feel they need is muscle, and they find it in the person of Ptolemy Jones — a fanatical National Socialist. Jones has gathered about him a small band of disaffected men, susceptible to his dark charisma. Among these is George Starling, who calls himself Fred, a man in his late twenties who is dedicated to Jones.

Soon, Military Intelligence joins with Homicide to find the killer. Detective Joe Sable, for whom the atrocities in Europe are awakening the dormant sense of his own Jewishness, is given the task of finding his way into Australia First. He does so with the help of Constable Helen Lord and

Group Captain Tom Mackenzie, an air force officer who is also Inspector Lambert's brother-in-law. But the operation goes horribly wrong, and both Sable and Mackenzie are badly injured.

The Holiday Murders ends with the death of Ptolemy Jones, and with the sense that this case has not yet run its course. It has damaged the lives of everyone involved in it. George Starling, previously overshadowed by Ptolemy Jones, remains at liberty, and he is determined to avenge Jones's death and to step out of his shadow ...

And then there was *The Port Fairy Murders* ...

SERGEANT JOE SABLE, of the Melbourne Homicide division, has returned to work, having suffered severe injuries in the course of an investigation into National Socialist sympathisers. The investigation has for Joe, who is Jewish, focussed his attention on what is happening to the Jews in Europe under the Nazi regime. Inspector Titus Lambert, the head of Homicide, is worried that Joe has returned too soon.

When a known Hitlerite, John Starling, is found dead at his property near Warrnambool, a town six hours south-west of Melbourne, Inspector Lambert, Sergeant David Reilly, and Constable Helen Lord make the long trip there to investigate. They're interested because John Starling's son, George Starling, is a known acquaintance of the brutal Ptolemy Jones, the man who tortured both Joe and Group Captain Tom Mackenzie, Lambert's brother-in-law. Both Joe and Tom were working for Military Intelligence at the time.

In Melbourne, two men are savagely murdered, and Joe's flat is burned to the ground. Now homeless, he is billeted with the wealthy businessman Peter Lillee, who lives in a grand house in Kew, along with his sister, Ros Lord, and her daughter, Helen Lord. Inspector Lambert organised the billet, and Lillee was happy to oblige. Here, Joe should be safe.

In a decision that will put both their lives at risk, Joe and Helen are sent to Port Fairy, a small seaside town near Warrnambool, to investigate the bizarre double murder of a brother and sister. Nothing about the case is straightforward, but nothing is as dangerous as the menacing George Starling, who has become obsessed with finding and killing Joe Sable, and whose shadow falls as far as Port Fairy.

I

Late March 1944

GEORGE STARLING WAS often angry, but he'd never felt anger like this before. Usually, his anger subsided to allow him some breathing space — some time to think clearly. This time, there was no relief. He was shaking with it: possessed by it; invigorated by it. He'd come so close, so close, so close. He'd had her there. He'd run his hand up her thigh and seen the intoxicating fear in her eyes as he'd played around her lips with his stinking filleting knife. It had come to nothing; and worse than that, much worse than that, he'd had to run away. He'd never run from anything in his life. As a child he'd endured his father's beatings, and had met his verbal abuse with silence, rather than give him the satisfaction of seeing his son cringe. But that night in Port Fairy, it had been run or die.

Well, he had no immediate plans to die. He had plans for other people to die — and his list was growing. Sitting at the top was the Jew policeman Joe Sable, and just below him was that fucking ugly bitch of a policewoman Helen Lord. Just knowing their names and being able to say them out loud kept the furnace of his fury fuelled. Joe Sable. Helen Lord. Joe Sable. Helen Lord. He'd find them, and when he did, he'd cut out their tongues, so they couldn't scream, and he'd take them slowly, slowly to their deaths.

Starling picked up his filleting knife and examined the blade. It still smelled of fish guts. Gutting fish was a job he'd never have to do again. He had £5000, taken from his dead father's house, and a motorcycle. He had no petrol rations, but money trumped rations, and where it didn't, a filleting knife was an eloquent persuader.

Joe Sable and Helen Lord had seen his face. This troubled him. He imagined that a description of him would have been circulated among police stations, and a police artist had doubtless worked up a likeness. All the police had to do was show this to his landlord in Port Fairy to determine its accuracy. He could grow a beard. He knew this would take only a few days — his beard shadow was dark and heavy — but it wouldn't do as a disguise. They'd be expecting that.

Starling had come to the place he'd come to since childhood. It was a remote and secret place. In all his years of coming here he'd never seen another person. It was a cove, a few miles from his father's house in Mepunga. Burning that house down had been a moment of keen joy. It was called Murnane's Bay — he had no idea who Murnane was or how it was that a bay was named after him. He'd smashed the sign that said 'Murnane's Bay' a long time ago. As far as he was concerned, it was Starling's Bay. It was a small, inconsequential gap in the coast on the south-western edge of Victoria. The descent to the beach was steep and along a single narrow path worn by wallabies or bandicoots, made reasonably accessible by his own repeated visits. Getting down to the small arc of sand and rocks had never been easy. The bay's inaccessibility secured it for him as his private demesne. Helen Lord would be surprised that he even knew that word. She probably didn't know it herself. Well maybe she'd find out that he was a lot smarter than she was, a lot smarter than Joe Sable, a lot smarter than all of them.

His motorcycle was hidden in scrub above Murnane's Bay, and he was sitting down below, beneath an eroded overhang at the back of the cove. The sand was dry here and he knew that the waves never reached this far up the beach, not even in the wildest weather. He'd sat here many times, frightened and exhilarated, as storms had broken over the Southern Ocean. Once, he'd been joined by a shivering, wet wallaby, too afraid of the thunder and lightning, he presumed, to be afraid of him. He'd just turned seventeen at the time, and the wallaby was the first truly wild thing he'd ever killed. He'd killed it simply because it was afraid and had thought it had found shelter. The electric charge he experienced as he watched the wallaby die under his hand would never be matched later by the muted pleasure he took in hunting, or in the small cruelties he inflicted on domestic animals.

Starling laid out on the sand the things he'd need for a week-long stay at Murnane's Bay. He had food, a length of canvas, fuel, and an English translation of *Mein Kampf*. He'd dipped into it a few times and had found it dull, repetitive, and uninspiring. Perhaps here, in isolation, he'd find something in it to reinvigorate his interest in National Socialism.

Starling had bought himself decent clothes — better than decent. He had three suits, good socks, good shoes, and flash underwear, and in a very short time he'd come to admire their capacity to disguise him. He'd also come to enjoy the feel of expensive cloth against his skin. For Starling the sensation of fine woollen trousers against his legs, and the perfect fit of his beautiful grey fedora, offered an erotic charge that had taken him by surprise. He'd always had contempt for the rich cunts who wore clothes like these. His contempt for them had grown. How easy they were to fool! They paid deference to a suit, and were blind to the hard, dangerous body it covered.

His clothes now, however, were something of a problem. He had nothing ragged or cheap to change into. He'd taken off his shoes and socks when he'd reached the beach, and they sat neatly beside him now, alongside his suitcase, which had been an extravagant but essential purchase. He took off his suit coat and trousers and folded them into the suitcase. Despite the heat of the day, the breeze coming off the ocean had teeth, and he left his shirt on while he stood for a moment and gathered his strength for what he intended to do. He would need a week after this, and at the end of that week he'd be ready, and implacable.

He removed his shirt and underwear and put them in the suitcase, which he closed and placed against the rocky wall behind him. Among the items he'd unpacked, he located a bottle of carbolic. He again picked up the filleting knife. He splashed the blade with carbolic and walked to the water's edge. He paused there, concentrating on the chill of the waves as they curled around his toes. He followed the cold as it moved up his legs, into his belly, and across his chest.

He put the blade against the skin under his eye, and in one swift, fierce movement sliced open his flesh, down past his nose to a point just below his mouth. He made no sound, and, for a moment, he wondered if the edge of the knife had bitten. Blood began to pour over his chin and into the thick hair on his chest, and a searing pain engulfed him. Still he made no sound.

He threw the knife behind him, safely away from the tug of the waves, and again opened the bottle of carbolic. He cupped some in his free hand and took it to his face. As it hit the open wound, he uttered a small sound. He recapped the bottle, stood it in the sand, and walked into the ocean. The wound bled extravagantly into the stinging, salty water. George Starling floated on his back, tasting blood and brine as the Southern Ocean lapped over his ruined face. The pain, now, was intense, and he began to slip into an ecstatic state. As the blood poured out of him, he wondered at his own strength, and at his genius. The wound would heal with the help of sea water and carbolic, and his face would be dramatically scarred. People would see and remember the scar. What they wouldn't see was the face behind it: the face that Joe Sable and Helen Lord had seen; the face that every copper in the state would be on the lookout for.

HELEN LORD DIDN'T have a gift for friendship. At school she'd made no enemies, but a close friendship came late, in her final year. When she'd first arrived at the Methodist Ladies' College at the age of twelve, she hadn't been particularly impressed by the imposing building that greeted her. Her uncle's house was, to her eyes, its equal. She'd been prepared to hate MLC, but she'd made a vow to herself that Uncle Peter, who was footing the bill for her education in this establishment, would never hear her complain. As it happened, she sailed through her schooling without incident. She was clever, and she liked most of her teachers and tolerated those who she knew to be less accomplished than she was. One of these, a Miss Ferrier, was retained, surely, out of loyalty and pity. She was elderly, deaf, and if she'd ever been a good teacher, the beneficiaries of her abilities would have been middle-aged by the time Helen sat in her class.

If Helen had ever been excluded from a party or a sleepover, she'd never felt the sting, because she hadn't been aware of it. She was immune to social slights because she was uninterested in the private lives of her classmates. She would never have been accused of stand-offishness. She joined in games and conversations, but the truth was that her classmates liked her more than she liked them.

At the beginning of sixth form, a girl arrived who decided in her first week that Helen Lord's friendship was worth cultivating.

Her name was Clara Dawson, and, without meaning to exactly, she intimidated both students and staff. The intimidation wasn't ugly or aggressive. It was simply because she was brilliant. There was a certain haughtiness that sprang from this, but it was accepted as natural and earned, and no one despised her because of it. Girls wanted to be in her company. The girl whose company Clara Dawson sought out was Helen Lord. Helen was someone you could have a decent conversation with, and Helen's forensic dissections of her classmates' idiosyncrasies, and her speculations about their futures, were endlessly entertaining. Helen discovered for the first time the joy of unguarded friendship. She could talk to Clara in a way that she'd never been able to talk to her mother. And Clara was witty. She made Helen laugh.

At the end of matriculation, both Clara and Helen graduated cum laude. Clara chose medicine at Melbourne University, and she was so demonstrably brilliant that she joined the handful of women accepted into the faculty. Helen's talents lay elsewhere. She had no interest in medicine, or science — there had been some suggestion that she might pick up a position in the CSIR — and although journalism was vaguely attractive to her, the idea of languishing on the women's pages put her off. There was teaching, of course, and she'd had six years of mostly excellent teachers to guide her, but she knew that she had no aptitude for teaching. She wouldn't be patient with dull students and she didn't believe she could confect a continuous interest in her students' work. She joined the police force to the astonishment of almost everyone who knew her.

Only Clara knew that Helen's father had been a policeman, so she'd been less surprised than anyone else. What had surprised Clara was Helen's willingness to stick it out. There was no prospect of promotion — a fact made manifest to all policewomen by there being no uniform. Policemen wore uniforms because adjustments to rank could be sewn onto shoulders. A female constable would remain at that rank for the duration of her career. Helen might not have stuck it out if Clara hadn't been there to listen to the daily humiliations she was forced to endure. Clara assured her that things weren't much better in hospitals.

'I'm constantly reminding careless, incompetent male doctors that I'm not a glorified nurse, that I'm not going to run screaming from the room at the sight of some cantankerous old bastard's withered cock, and that my opinion on most matters is more useful than theirs. Naturally I've been quietly relegated to the female wards.'

Variations on their respective complaints were a part of almost every conversation, but it created a collegiate determination to persist, however ugly some encounters were. Clara didn't come often to Peter Lillee's house. She said she never felt comfortable there, that it was like having afternoon tea in a museum, or some terribly respectable public building where you didn't feel able to smoke or say 'fuck', both of which Clara liked to do. She rented a room in an all-female boarding house in East Melbourne. It was a large room, with its own kitchen. She shared the bathroom with two other women, one a nurse, the other a teacher.

On the day after Inspector Lambert had suspended her from duty — Helen was resolute in interpreting this as him telling her that she wouldn't be returning to Homicide — she and Clara sat talking over what had happened in Port Fairy. It was a rare afternoon off for Clara, a break she'd pay for in a brutal run of night shifts.

'I can't tell you what it felt like to be touched by George Starling, Clar. He ran his hand all the way up the inside of my thigh.'

'You have quite a severe concussion. You should be at home.'

'I have to tell you something, Clar. I did something awful, and I can't tell anyone else. I can barely bring myself to say it out loud.'

'I'm all ears.'

This was the right response. Any show of deep concern would have silenced Helen. She wasn't looking for sympathy.

'I gave Joe Sable up to George Starling. Just like that.'

'What do you mean you gave him up?'

'Starling wanted to know where he was, and I told him.'

Helen caught herself on the edge of tears. This was the first time she'd uttered this confession. Clara, who knew Helen too well to imagine this was all there was to it, said, 'Oh right. You want me to believe that this Starling creature casually asks you where Joe Sable is, and I presume he does that so that he can go kill him, and you just cheerfully give him directions. Your concussion isn't that bad, Helen. I think you might be leaving out a few details. So, let's go back a bit.'

Clara stood up, opened a window, and lit a cigarette. She sat down again and threw her legs over the arms of her chair.

'And I want all the details, Helen. Don't leave anything out. Remember what I said about old men's cocks. I'm unshockable.'

Helen laughed. She knew what Clara was doing, but she was grateful, and it worked. She could talk about this here and nowhere else.

'I've told you about George Starling.'

'Yes. Not the kind of boy you want to bring home to meet mother, unless you want your mother done away with.'

'He took me into this room, Clar, in Port Fairy. I think it was his bedroom. It stank of sweat and rotten fish. I wanted to vomit. I was groggy because he'd punched me.'

'Bastard.'

'He touched my face, and then he slapped me.'

'Jesus Christ, Helen.'

'Then he put his hand up my skirt.'

'Did he touch your genitals?'

The question shocked Helen briefly, but Clara was a doctor, so it wasn't a prurient question.

'No. He didn't get that far. He threatened to rape me — well, he said that that was what he was going to do, after he'd made me watch him kill Joe.'

'What a prince, Helen. What a fucking prince.'

'He tied my legs.'

Helen thought for a moment. She hadn't pieced together the sequence of events in the bedroom in Port Fairy until now.

'He had a knife. A filleting knife. He pressed it against my lips — it stank of fish — and said he'd cut out my tongue if I made a sound. Then he asked me where Joe was, and I told him.'

There was silence for a moment.

'I would have told him a lot earlier than that,' Clara said. 'Besides, he didn't get to him, did he?'

'No.'

Clara stubbed out her cigarette, swung her legs round, and sat forward in her chair.

'You know what I don't understand, Helen? I don't understand why you're not a cot case. If that had happened to me, I'd be fit to tie. I wouldn't be sitting here telling you about it as if it was all in a day's work. I'd be curled up in a corner, whimpering and probably incontinent.'

'Incontinent?'

'I don't know why I said that. It was decorative flourish.'

'I betrayed Joe, Clar.'

'You'd been punched in the head, you had concussion, you were terrified, and Starling did not find Joe, so in what sense did you betray him?

'I told Starling.'

'You told Starling what he wanted to hear, and you bought some valuable time. You did not betray Joe.'

'Should I tell him?'

Clara stood up and closed the window. This was to cover the few seconds she needed to answer the question. If she said no, it would be admitting Helen's point that she'd betrayed Joe. She wanted to say no, because this was sensible, but she said, 'You can tell him if you like. You haven't done anything wrong, Helen. Sure. Go ahead, tell him. He'll have the same reaction I did.'

'You've got a lot of confidence in a man you've never met, Clar.'

'He's the man you're in love with. That gives me confidence.'

'I've never said that I'm in love with him, Clar.'

'And yet you are.'

'Is it really that obvious?'

'It is to me.'

'It isn't to him.'

'He's a man, Helen. Men are morons.'

HELEN HAD BEGUN to feel the weight of the resentments she'd harboured since she'd joined the Victorian police force. Along with the handful of other women who'd reluctantly been accepted as sworn officers, Helen had languished as a glorified secretary, called on to clean up the cells when a drunk woman had emptied her stomach or bowels in a corner. The men she worked with had treated her initially as an object of curiosity, and had settled finally on contempt, expressed as derisive and dismissive moues when she spoke, or frank and foul-mouthed attacks. They made much of her plainness — one senior officer had told her in a crowded room, 'Rape is your best chance of losing your virginity, love.' 'Your only chance,' someone had added, and the room had echoed to laughter. She'd stuck it out, meeting large and small daily humiliations with steely silence. This may have disappointed her colleagues, although they never gave her the satisfaction of demonstrating this disappointment, and they never tired of letting her know that she didn't belong. Policing was men's work, and any woman who thought she could do men's work was either a lesbian or up herself, or both. Whichever the case, women spoiled everything, and it was best if their spoliation was confined to the house.

It had taken her completely by surprise when Titus Lambert, the head of the newly formed Homicide division, had invited her to join the depleted group of his officers, on a grace-and-favour basis. Conscious that such an opportunity was purely the consequence of wartime manpower shortages, she'd been suspicious of Lambert's motives, and even as her opinion of him improved and grew into admiration, still this small, hot ember of suspicion and resentment smouldered. Now, having been dismissed from Homicide after the incident in Port Fairy — this was how Helen saw it — she was febrile with indignation. Inspector Lambert had told her that the decision had been made by Police Command and that while he didn't support it, he was unable to argue against it. She'd been instructed to take two weeks' leave of absence. Unpaid.

A week had passed since her dismissal, a week in which she'd managed to avoid discussing the Port Fairy investigation with her mother, and with her uncle, Peter Lillee. There was a mean corner of Helen's heart that allowed a small resentment of him to do battle with her love for him. Peter Lillee's house in Kew was a vast, Edwardian pile, and he'd accepted his widowed sister and her daughter into his life without complaint and had never expressed the slightest indication that he wished they would leave. He'd paid for Helen's education, a financial impost that was for him negligible, and he employed his sister as his housekeeper.

Ros Lord would never have accepted money from her brother without the formality of employment, but their relationship never resembled that between employer and employee. They'd been close growing up, with Ros, two years Peter's senior, feeling protective of him. As they'd matured she'd found that she liked him as a man. He was decent and kind, although she suspected that his success in finance pointed to a ruthlessness he never displayed at home. Ros had fallen in love with a policeman and had followed him to Broome. The separation from her brother had been a lengthy one, but the sanctuary he'd offered her and her daughter after the death of John Lord had been natural, and had been offered without hesitation and without any sense that attached to it was pity or obligation.

Helen sat in the library of her uncle's house and watched as Sergeant Joe Sable lowered himself into a chair opposite her. Joe had recently been on the receiving end of Peter Lillee's generosity. Lillee had billeted and clothed Joe after Joe's flat had been burned to the ground in an arson attack by, it was assumed, George Starling. He'd been embarrassed to have to wear another man's clothes, even though those clothes were of a quality he could never have afforded. He'd been ragged mercilessly at work for the sudden elevation in his dress standards, but in only a few days he'd grown accustomed to the feel of expensive fabrics.

'I know I've said it already, but I think it was lousy of them to take you out of Homicide.'

'No, you don't,' Helen said, with that edge in her voice that made Joe nervous around her. 'You think that's what I want you to say, but it's not what you really think.'

'It is what I really think.' Joe's tone was measured. He didn't want an argument. Firstly, because he was a guest in this house, and tension made an awkward situation even more awkward. Disagreement felt bad-mannered and ungrateful. Secondly, Joe knew that Helen Lord could marshal too much verbal weaponry against him. Even if he felt he was right she would overwhelm him and leave him feeling like a dolt. Helen left his riposte unchallenged for a moment, then she said, 'Much worse happened to you, yet you weren't asked or told to leave the unit.'

'I don't make the rules, Helen.'

'You're just the passive beneficiary of them.'

There was an unmistakeable sneer accompanying this remark.

'Inspector Lambert has taken some heat for seconding you, Helen.'

'So, if he's taking the heat, why am I the one getting burned?'

They both knew the answer to that.

'I'm looking for a place to rent,' Joe said, and the non sequitur did nothing to ease Helen's general level of annoyance.

'No one's asking you to leave, Joe. I resent the fact that you get to keep your job and I don't, even though I'm much better at it than you are, but I don't resent *you* personally.'

If this was supposed to make Joe feel more comfortable, it failed, and, as often in her conversations with him, Helen was torn between wanting to please him and wanting to correct him, and she felt more keenly than ever that her feelings for him were vulnerable to exposure.

'I can't stay here indefinitely, Helen. Your uncle can't be expected to house me forever, and he won't accept rent.'

'Inspector Lambert thinks this is the safest place for you until Starling is caught.' She paused, and in a clumsy attempt at ameliorating her earlier remark she added, 'And I agree with him.'

As soon as Starling's name was mentioned, Joe felt more at ease. Conversations with Helen had always been less fraught when confined to work.

'You haven't really spoken about that night in Port Fairy,' he said.

'He touched my skin. It was like being touched by some sort of disgusting animal.'

'He's like an ape.'

'No. He's an unknown species, and he looks like Rudolf Hess.'

'He does a bit. He should be easy to spot. That police sketch of him has been widely circulated now. Maybe he'll lie low. Maybe we've heard the last of him.'

Helen shook her head. 'Oh, I don't think so. He hates you too much. It's like a canker in him. When he said your name, it made his breath rancid.'

Joe laughed uneasily.

'Who knew being a Jew could be so poisonous?'

'You need to stay here, Joe, until Starling is safely out of the way. Anyway, I imagine finding anywhere to rent is virtually impossible. The Americans have snaffled all the decent places.'

This was true, as Joe had discovered, and prices being demanded for even the most rundown places were ludicrous.

'When the insurance comes through for my flat, I'll buy a place. You're right about the rents.'

Helen was relieved. Despite the confusion of feelings he aroused in her, she found proximity to Joe Sable preferable to distance from him. It made her hot with anger that he was blithely unaware of this, and simultaneously she hoped it *was* simply lack of awareness and not indifference.

DETECTIVE SERGEANT RON Dunnart was prepared to overlook the fact that Sergeant Bob O'Dowd was a fucking Mason. What business did someone named O'Dowd have being a Mason? There were too many Masons in the force, and all of them were arseholes. That was Dunnart's view. He had a deep, Catholic suspicion of them. Not that he practised his Catholicism. He had no time for that Immaculate-Conception, Assumption-into-Heaven shit, and he'd never met a priest who could by any measure be considered an intelligent man. He'd gone along dutifully as a boy and confessed his wet dreams to the dullard behind the grille, but as an adult he'd no more share his private transgressions with a priest than he'd fuck one of them. Still, his inherited distrust of Masons ran deep, and he was one of those officers responsible for the continuing tensions between Catholics and Masons in the force — tensions that had spilled over into violent tussles on more than one occasion.

Under these circumstances, Dunnart wouldn't normally have had anything to do with O'Dowd, except perhaps to thwart his ambitions or provoke a fight. But, having worked with him on several investigations, Dunnart had discovered that O'Dowd was weak and compliant, and that he shared Dunnart's dislike of Inspector Titus Lambert. Dunnart was certain that Lambert didn't like his methods, and he was fairly sure that if Lambert had his way, he would get rid of him. After all, Lambert had seconded a sheila into Homicide. Christ! That had gone pear-shaped, so that was all right, but so much for Lambert's legendary judgement. Dunnart couldn't remember the woman's name. He'd never bothered to learn it.

Dunnart watched from a distance as O'Dowd punched a bag in the gymnasium. O'Dowd needed the exercise. He'd begun to develop a paunch, which Dunnart saw as a symptom of O'Dowd's essential weakness. He had the kind of body that would inevitably surrender to flabbiness, catching up to the general flabbiness of his character. Such a man was useful to Dunnart.

O'Dowd pummelled the bag and, as he circled around it, caught sight of Dunnart. He stopped, his face red and his singlet sticking to his soft body. He walked across to Dunnart, who recoiled slightly at the smell of sweat that came off O'Dowd. Dunnart was fastidious about such things. He was a man who attended assiduously to personal hygiene, and he found other men's indifference to how they smelled both puzzling and disgusting. He'd watched many times, and with a kind of horror, as men exercised vigorously in the gymnasium, and then simply put their uniforms back on, with only the cursory swipe of a towel to mop up the sweat. Did none of these men have wives to tell them they stank? Dunnart had certainly never given his wife cause to utter such a complaint, although early in their marriage he'd had occasion to complain about the odour of her menses. She'd become more careful after that.

'Go and have a shower,' he said to O'Dowd, 'and then we have a few things we need to discuss.'

'Is this about that bloke whose name you found in that dead fairy's address book?'

'His name is Peter Lillee, and I've done some digging on him. He's a rich cunt — a very rich cunt: big end of town, Melbourne Club, the whole shebang. Unmarried, of course. Big house in Kew. And you and I, Bob, we know something about him that he wouldn't like anyone else to know. A man in that position would be willing to finance our silence, I reckon.'

'You sure about this, Ron?'

'Go and have a shower, Bob. You stink.'

MAUDE LAMBERT WASN'T a very good cook. This didn't trouble her husband in the least. Titus Lambert wasn't interested in food. He ate whatever was put in front of him with undiscriminating indifference as to its flavour or the complication of its preparation. Maude's brother, Group Captain Tom Mackenzie, on the other hand, considered himself a dab hand in the kitchen, and to Maude's relief and delight he'd begun to rediscover this ability.

'Tom is recovering,' she'd told Titus. 'He's coming back to us.'

Titus agreed that Tom's appearance and general demeanour had improved greatly over the few weeks since the appalling torture to which he'd been subjected. Often though, he would catch Tom sitting, and sometimes standing, his face expressionless, but with tears streaming down his cheeks. It was a peculiar and disconcerting sight, this immobile face with running tears the only movement on its surface.

Tom Mackenzie's house in South Melbourne was small, smaller even than the Lamberts' house in Brunswick. Titus and Maude had moved here temporarily, primarily to look after Tom, but also because George Starling had found out their address. Titus wouldn't expose his wife to the risk Starling represented. There was no question of Titus remaining in the Brunswick house on his own. If any risks were to be faced, they'd face them together. After so many years of marriage, during which Maude had become an inextricable and essential part of Titus's working life, the idea that any sort of crisis might be managed separately was anathema.

Maude had been surprised when her brother had agreed without hesitation to place himself under the care of a psychiatrist. That decision alone revealed the damage that had been done to him, damage that went far beyond the obvious and distressing physical injuries. She'd been able to nurse those. The dismaying vacancy in his eyes, his silence, and his nightmares had been more difficult to manage. The nightmares especially, erupting in a small house in South Melbourne, had been nerve-stripping and exhausting. Now, though, Tom was returning.

The night terrors had been worrying Titus, and not just because of their debilitating effect on Tom. 'Is Joe Sable waking up at 2.00 a.m., terrified?' he asked Maude. It was just after 2.00 a.m., when he asked this question. Maude had been up, calmed

Tom, and had just returned to bed. She placed her hand on Titus's chest.

'I imagine he must be. He blames himself. And he went back to work too soon.'

Titus felt this as a personal rebuke, and the muscles in his chest jumped. Maude felt the tremor at her fingertips.

'You have to stop blaming yourself, Titus.'

'Have you stopped blaming Joe?'

The question wasn't a spiteful one, and Maude didn't take it as such.

'Yes, and when I did, I stopped feeling wretched. I'm very glad he's not on his own.' She paused. 'Do you think he knows that Helen Lord is in love with him?'

Titus turned on his side to face her.

'Is she?'

'Honestly, Titus, my question was rhetorical. You've seen them together much more frequently than I have. You can't *not* have noticed. You're as bad as Joe, who I'm quite certain doesn't have a clue.'

'Perhaps he's more distracted than unobservant, darling.'

Maude laughed gently and moved into her husband's arms. 'Where men are concerned, that might be a distinction without a difference.'

'You have my full attention.'

Anthony, the porter at the Melbourne Club in Collins Street, opened the door as soon as Peter Lillee had placed his foot on the bottom step to the entrance. He liked Mr Lillee, who was one of the members who didn't feel it was his duty to remind the porter of his place.

'Good morning, sir.'

'Good morning, Anthony. Has Sir Marcus arrived?'

There was the faintest hint of disdain in Anthony's response, so faint that Peter Lillee missed it.

'Yes, sir. Sir Marcus has gone upstairs to the library, I believe.'

Peter paused on the stairs, as he always did, to admire the Streeton landscape, which hung, he felt, too high to be appreciated properly. It was the best of the paintings in the club's collection, although there were many who disagreed and who preferred the dull, dark portraits of celebrated, and dead, members. Most of them were painted by competent, journeymen portraitists, who preserved the dignity of the sitter at the expense of revealing anything of his character. The result was a picture where the rendering of a cuff or a watch chain was more admirable than the face. Peter intended to bequeath to the club the portrait done of him in the manner of John Singer Sargent. Well, it was more than just in the manner of. It was in fact a remarkably skilled copy of Sargent's portrait of Dr Pozzi, with his head being the only point of difference.

Sir Marcus Ashgrove, who'd recently engaged the services of William Dargie to commit his florid features to canvas, was standing by a window, looking down into Collins Street.

'Sir Marcus.'

He turned at the sound of Peter Lillee's greeting. He admired Lillee, or rather he admired his business acumen, and had been instrumental in securing Lillee's current appointment and his acceptance into the Melbourne Club. Sir Marcus's elevation to a knighthood had been the result of his own facility in banking and finance, and he recognised this facility when he saw it in others — and this was by no means a common occurrence. Although he would never say it out loud, he had one serious reservation about Lillee. He suspected him of vanity. Lillee's suits were the best that money could buy, and his hair was too carefully trimmed and combed into place. Sir Marcus was indifferent to his own appearance, and loathed sitting for Dargie. He'd agreed to do it simply to silence the nagging of Lady Ashgrove. The Melbourne Club would inherit it, so that was something. Sir Marcus made a distinction between the small fillip of pride he felt at the thought of his portrait hanging in the club, and personal vanity.

'Lillee,' he said. 'Good of you to see me at such short notice.'

'Not at all, Sir Marcus.'

'I've taken the liberty of ordering two whiskeys. My chit of course.'

They moved to two large chairs in the corner of the library. The whiskeys arrived, and each man breathed in the aroma and took a sip.

'This is the last place in the whole bloody country where you can still get a decent drink,' Sir Marcus said.

'My sister tells me potatoes, of all things, have become scarce.'

'Not in here, Lillee. I had a decent dauphinoise just last week.'

'Is Lady Ashgrove well?'

'As well as can be expected with no household staff to help out. She had me cleaning the bathroom yesterday. I suppose we all have to pull our weight while there's a war on.'

'And your son?'

Lillee asked this question automatically and immediately regretted it, remembering too late that Matthew Ashgrove had been captured by the Germans in 1942.

'As far as we know he's still alive and healthy. The Germans have moved him twice. He's an officer so one hopes they're civilised enough to treat him accordingly. I keep telling my wife that his biggest problem will probably be boredom.'

Sir Marcus made no inquiries as to Lillee's family. He knew he was a bachelor, and was anyway not in the least interested. He'd heard that Lillee lived in a rather grand house, but he'd never visited, and as to his domestic arrangements, well, that was a subject not worth broaching.

'I won't beat around the bush, Lillee. The bloody Capital Issues Advisory people have knocked back a perfectly reasonable investment opportunity, and a lot of people, me included, are unhappy about it.'

'And how can I help you, Sir Marcus?' The question was disingenuous. Peter Lillee knew precisely what was expected of him. As a member of the Capital Issues Advisory Committee he was aware of Sir Marcus's consortium and its request for permission to enter the Wombat State Forest near Daylesford and dig for gold. The job of the Advisory Committee was to grant investment privileges only to projects that minimised personal returns in favour of their advantageous potential to boost the war effort. The Wombat mine, apart from a consequential loss of a large area of forest, was exclusively about personal wealth speculation, although ludicrously the consortium had suggested that the vast amount of timber that would be felled would help alleviate the shortage of wood for heating and cooking in Melbourne. There was a shortage of wood, that was true, and the previous winter had been harsh and uncomfortable for many. Sir Marcus's clear-felling did not strike the Advisory Committee as an exemplary addition to the war effort, particularly as the consortium would profit from the sale of the wood.

'We're not talking about pin money here, Lillee. We've already invested a considerable sum in investigating the viability of the mine. I'm assuming you know what I'm talking about.'

'The Wombat mining lease.'

'Good. So you're up to speed. We started work on that lease back in 1938, before this bloody war got going. I've got serious money tied up in it and so have several other very important people. Serious money, Lillee.'

'I'm not sure how I can help you, Sir Marcus.'

'Don't be obtuse, Lillee. I didn't pull strings to get you into this place for your looks.'

'Looking around the club, Sir Marcus, I'd say looks were never a criterion for entry.'

The waspishness of that riposte unsettled Sir Marcus more than it warranted. It was the delivery, the tone, the ease with which it fell from Lillee's lips. Was Lillee queer? he wondered. Christ, he better not be, or if he was, he better be inhumanly discreet about it. The Melbourne Club tolerated acceptable indiscretions from its members — fraud, adultery, manslaughter — but it drew the line at Jews and perverts.

'I don't care how you do it, Lillee, but at the next Capital Issues Advisory Committee meeting we expect you to go in to bat and protect our investments. Push the wood angle. We need to take down God knows how many trees, so there'll be loads of the stuff.'

'I've read your submission, Sir Marcus. Profiting from the trees and the mine is not in your favour.'

'If there's no gold there, Lillee, the money from the trees might be the only reward.'

'If the removal of the trees and the consequential profits were managed by a separate group who diverted those profits into a war industry, the committee might re-examine the mine lease. I say might. I stress might.'

'Out of the question, Lillee. I didn't get to where I am by compromising. My son is in a bloody prisoner-of-war camp. That's all the sacrifice I'm willing to give to this war, which was entirely avoidable in the first place.'

Lillee raised his eyebrows.

'Read *The Protocols of the Elders of Zion*, Lillee. Educate yourself about who's really behind this war. You *will* argue for us, and you *will* alter the committee's decision in our favour. If you can't do that, I can't guarantee that your position in the club will be secure.'

Peter Lillee's reaction to this took Sir Marcus by surprise.

'Are you threatening to have me blackballed, Sir Marcus?' He said this quietly and with a smile that was entirely at odds with what Sir Marcus saw as a grave situation. 'I've always admired you, Sir Marcus, and it is amazing to me how many years of admiration can evaporate in a matter of seconds. I'd always thought of you as a decent man. Dull, but decent. Your indecency is shocking to me. I have no doubt that you could organise a block to have me blackballed. I could save you the trouble and resign, but I don't think I'll do that. You'll have to work for it. I have no intention of supporting your consortium. On the contrary, I will do everything in my power to prevent it from being successful. So, line up your forces against me, Sir Marcus. I don't flatter myself that I can defeat you, but I won't go quietly, and it will be instructive to see who stands with you.'

Sir Marcus had too much self-discipline to bluster and fume, although that's precisely what he was doing internally. He felt betrayed and appalled that it was he, Sir Marcus Ashgrove, who'd brought this viper into the heart of the Melbourne Club. Getting rid of him wouldn't be too difficult. He wasn't old money, after all. He'd only risen through talent, and that was brass to the gold of inherited, pastoral wealth and position. Blackballing wasn't the only way to drive Peter Lillee out of the Melbourne Club.

2

DETECTIVE SERGEANT RON Dunnart parked the car a street away from Peter Lillee's house. He'd signed out the car with Bob O'Dowd — things had tightened up about vehicle use since petrol rationing had begun to bite — and he was confident that no one would question him too closely about why he needed to drive to Kew. If one of the pen-pushers did demand an explanation, he'd simply say that he was following up a lead in the murder of two queers, which, in an obtuse way, was true. Not that Peter Lillee was a suspect. In fact, if Dunnart could arrange it, he was about to become a victim.

'So, what's the drill here, Ron?'

Dunnart suppressed the slight irritation O'Dowd aroused in him whenever he spoke.

'We find out as much as we can about him before we show our hand. The first thing I want to know is who answers his door when we knock.'

O'Dowd looked doubtful. Dunnart stepped out of the car, and without waiting for O'Dowd he began walking. O'Dowd caught up with him and asked, 'What if Lillee answers the door?'

'He won't. He's at work. But even if he did, it wouldn't matter. We're not pretending to be anyone we're not. We're police officers and we're making inquiries about a spate of burglaries in the area — and yes, I know there hasn't been a spate of burglaries.'

'We're saying we're policemen?'

'Yes, Bob. Yes, we are. The person who answers the door will be a housekeeper, probably a young man who Lillee is keeping house with, if you see what I mean.'

Dunnart's brazenness made O'Dowd nervous. He was of a much more timid disposition. Dunnart, however, had been squeezing queers and low-lifes for years and had never been in danger of exposure. Dunnart knew what he was doing, and going along with him would put money in O'Dowd's wallet.

Peter Lillee's house was extravagantly fenced with elaborate iron railings. The gates were open, and Dunnart and O'Dowd walked down the manicured driveway to the front door.

'Christ!' Dunnart said. 'There must be a fucking army of gardeners to maintain this place. This Lillee clown must know people in high places if he's still employing staff.'

'Maybe he does it himself.'

Dunnart snorted.

'He wouldn't want his hands to get calloused. Rough skin rubbing a smooth cock or arse? Nah.'

Dunnart raised the knocker and looked at it for a moment before he used it to rap on the door. It was in the shape of a mythical creature, a phoenix perhaps, and had been polished to within an inch of its life. He knocked and stepped back.

'Try to look a little less shifty, Bob.'

O'Dowd had become used to Dunnart's frequent snide digs at his expense. He didn't like them, and he was storing them away as fuel should he one day need to convert his current alliance with him into righteous opposition. There was no answer, so Dunnart knocked again.

A muffled voice called, 'I'll get it, Mum!' A reply, less muffled and just behind the door, told the first voice to stay where she was.

'I'm closer. I'll get it.'

The door opened, and Ros Lord stood before the two policemen. She was wearing an apron, and her hair was pinned back away from her face. Dunnart and O'Dowd removed their hats.

'Yes? How can I help you?'

Dunnart produced his identification card and showed it to Ros Lord.

'Senior Sergeant Ron Dunnart,' she said, and looked from the card to him, and then to Bob O'Dowd, who also produced his card.

'May we come in?' Dunnart asked.

'Perhaps you could tell me why you're here.'

Dunnart was taken aback by this. Housekeepers in aprons weren't supposed to backchat. Keeping his temper under control — a measure Ros Lord noticed, and which confirmed for her what she already suspected, that these were men who couldn't be trusted — he said, 'We have routine inquiries regarding a series of nasty burglaries in this area.' He hoped the inclusion of the word 'nasty' would give this biddy a fright.

'We haven't been burgled, and I haven't heard of any burglaries in the area recently.'

Dunnart smiled.

'I think we'd know more about that than you would, Mrs …?'

The question elicited no name from Ros Lord.

'Well, I haven't seen anything or heard anything, so I'm afraid I can't help you.'

'Perhaps there's someone else in the house we could talk to?' O'Dowd asked.

'If anyone here had heard of someone being burgled, I can assure you it would have been the subject of conversation, so, no, there's no one else who could help you. If you'll excuse me, I have work to do.'

As she closed the door each of the detectives was aware that she was committing their features to memory, and each of them found this disconcerting. This had not gone to plan. Outside Lillee's gate, Dunnart turned to take in the house.

'What a fucking bitch,' he said.

'That didn't go as expected,' O'Dowd said, and was more than a little pleased to be able to say so.

'She doesn't like coppers. I wonder why. I hate women like that. She'll get hers, though. I'll see to that.'

'WHO WAS AT the door?' Helen asked.

Ros Lord rubbed her hands on her apron.

'Two policemen.'

'What? Who? Why didn't you ask them in?'

'There was something odd about them. I know a rotten copper when I see one. God knows I saw enough of them in Broome. These two lied to me for a start. They wanted to come in, and thought they could frighten me with some nonsense about burglaries in the area.'

'Did they give their names?'

'Ron Dunnart and Bob O'Dowd.'

'Dunnart and O'Dowd? They're in Homicide. Why would they be investigating burglaries?'

'You know these men?'

'I know about them. I know Inspector Lambert doesn't trust Dunnart. Maybe they wanted to speak to Joe. He must have told them he was staying here.'

'They didn't mention Joe. They lied about burglaries in the area, and I'll wager we're the only house they visited. I'll check on that later. I'll telephone the Davieses and ask if two policemen came to call.'

'They must have wanted Joe, Mum, even if they didn't mention him.'

Ros Lord shook her head. 'No. They weren't here for Joe. You should try to find out something about them, Helen. The man named Dunnart is a very bad egg.'

'It couldn't be anything to do with Uncle Peter, could it?'

Ros caught the slight panic in Helen's voice.

'Why would two policemen want to talk to Peter?'

In a household where personal subjects were easily and regularly broached, the answer to that question would have been explored. However, Helen had always been reluctant to discuss delicate matters with her mother, and although Ros Lord had never discouraged it, they'd fallen over the years into a pattern of unhealthy silence. Helen knew nothing about Peter Lillee's private life. She suspected he was queer, although her knowledge of that world was practically non-existent. She knew about it mainly through the vicious, foul-mouthed references made to homosexuals by the police officers with whom she worked. None of what they said married with her sense of her uncle. Nevertheless, his discretion about his private life was so absolute that she knew he had secrets he felt compelled to protect.

'Perhaps they want his advice on something,' Helen said, lamely.

'Those men would no more come to Peter for advice than they'd fly to the moon.'

If Helen had asked her mother whether Peter was queer or not, Ros would have said, without demur, that she suspected he was. Helen, however, had no clear idea of whether or not Peter and his sister discussed such private matters. She knew they were close, but when it came to her family, her critical faculties — those same faculties that made her such a fine detective — failed her utterly. She didn't so much suspend them as lose the capacity to engage them.

JOE SABLE SAT opposite Inspector Lambert and prayed that he wouldn't begin to cry in the course of their conversation. This had happened once before as the emotions surrounding the torture of Tom Mackenzie and his own torture had overwhelmed him. That had only been a few weeks previously and Joe recalled it with shame. He hated feeling weak in front of Lambert, but he always began from that position because Lambert knew about the physical unreliability of his heart.

'You're beginning to look human again, Sergeant. The bruising is disappearing.'

'I was fortunate, sir, compared to Tom.'

'He's improving too. The human body is remarkably resilient. The mind is more fragile.'

'My mind is fine, sir.' There it was, that childish, defensive response which Joe hated falling into, but of which he was too frequently guilty. Inspector Lambert's patience made him feel worse.

'I wasn't talking about your mind, Sergeant. I was talking about Tom.'

'Yes, of course.'

'However, to be perfectly honest, I suppose I was thinking of you as well. My wife thinks I let you come back to work too soon, and I listen to my wife.'

'With all due respect, sir, Mrs Lambert is wrong. I would've gone crazy if I'd been sitting in my flat with nothing to do.'

'Do you have anyone you can talk to?'

'I have close friends, yes. But I don't see them much as they're mostly in the forces. My closest friend is in New Guinea. I'm not even sure if he's alive or dead.'

'Surely his parents would have let you know.'

'No. They thought our friendship was inappropriate.'

'Inappropriate?'

Joe realised what Inspector Lambert was asking.

'Not sexually inappropriate. Worse than that. I was Jewish. I was amused by that at the time. It didn't interfere with our friendship. I'd never really come up against that sort of thing before, and I just thought it was eccentric. I never had much to do with his parents, so it didn't mean anything. Guy was a boarder at Newman College. His family lived in western Victoria. It doesn't seem quite so amusing now.'

'But you do have someone you can talk to?'

'Yes, but I don't need to talk to anyone. I don't want to talk to anyone. All I want to do is my job. That's all.'

'I'm not trying to annoy you, Sergeant, so try to control your testiness. All *I'm* trying to do is *my* job, and part of my job is to make sure that the people I rely on can be relied on.'

The cold steel in Titus Lambert's voice reminded Joe of the distance in experience and authority that separated them. He lowered his eyes in embarrassment.

'Tell me how Helen Lord is travelling. I imagine she's disappointed and angry.'

'She's both of those, yes.'

'And how much of that is directed at you?'

'Oh, she doesn't think I'm responsible.'

'No, she thinks *I'm* responsible, but you're still here, and she isn't.'

'She has made it clear that she's a better detective than I am. She's right, of course.'

'Self-pity, Sergeant?'

'Self-awareness, sir.'

'Don't underestimate your skills. You're young. What you lack is experience, not talent.'

Joe didn't take this as a ringing endorsement of his abilities. He was conscious of the fact that he had yet to demonstrate any real evidence of a talent for policing. He knew he lacked the intuitive skills that Helen Lord possessed. He supposed he might have the doggedness required to solve most cases, although he felt this was a second-order talent. He used to think he was courageous, but he'd experienced the crippling, destructive power of pure fear at the hands of George Starling, and so he wondered now if his heart would fail him at some critical moment.

'Tell me honestly, Sergeant, are you well enough to work?'

'Of course, sir.'

'Good. I need detectives I can trust, and I can count them on the fingers of a leper's hand.'

Joe knew that Inspector Lambert had a fractious relationship with a couple of officers in the Homicide unit, but he was too new, and too junior, to have been made privy to any of the details.

'A good detective, Sergeant, is not the same as a good man.'

GEORGE STARLING KNEW he'd been lucky. Despite the severity of the wound he'd inflicted on his face, no infection had set in. He'd been careful, and he'd endured the pain of carbolic regularly, as well as what he believed to be the antiseptic wash of cold water from the Southern Ocean. He'd heard, or read perhaps, that some Aboriginal tribes created elaborate, dramatic scarring by packing wounds with hot ash. He was tempted to try this, but thought better of it.

For seven days he remained at Murnane's Bay. He had no mirror, so he kept track of the progress of his wound by feeling the firming of the long scab with his fingers. He let his beard grow, and it grew in quickly. He lost weight, even though he had no weight to lose. The rations he'd brought were meagre, and he didn't supplement them by attempting to catch fish or crabs. He'd developed a distaste for seafood since his recent work scaling and gutting fish in Port Fairy.

Fresh water was his biggest problem. He couldn't rely on rain in March, but he knew there was a farm dam a mile or so from the point where the descent began to Murnane's Bay. He walked to it at night. Getting there on his motorcycle wasn't an option. Conserving fuel was essential, and the noise of a motorcycle's engine might carry across paddocks into the ears of a curious farmer, or a curious farmer's busybody wife, or one of their disgusting children. Starling didn't know for certain whether such a family lived nearby, but the dam belonged to someone, and its edges were trampled by cattle.

He needed the cover of darkness for another reason. He wore no clothes, being unwilling to risk soiling one of his beautiful suits. They would be his best disguise — as he'd discovered, elegant tailoring was as protective against discovery as armour.

He carried the water back to Murnane's Bay and boiled it. It still tasted muddy, and he worried that this precaution was insufficient when he suffered a bout of diarrhoea so severe that he thought he was fouling the ocean with it.

At the end of seven days, he was ready to leave. Early one hot morning, in the last week of March, George Starling took one last swim, stood with his arms outstretched to let the warm wind dry his skin, and, for the first time in a week, dressed. He packed his things, buried his rubbish, and removed all evidence of his fire. His hair and beard felt as if they were encrusted with salt. He needed a haircut and a close shave, and a place where the wound on his face could settle into its final, livid form.

There was someone he remembered from the meetings his father used to take him to: meetings of National Socialists who gathered at various houses in Warrnambool to sing Hitler's praises and discuss the pernicious influence of Jews and Communists in Australia. Most of these people were men, and they either ignored him or joined with his father in humiliating him. There had been a woman, Mrs Pluschow. She was different. She'd married a German man, and they lived just outside of Warrnambool, on the Port Fairy road. Starling recalled that she'd got along well with his father, which was by no means the case with others who came to the meetings. John Starling would have claimed that he didn't suffer fools gladly, when in fact he simply despised most people and made no secret of the fact. However, in George Starling's memory, there was no record of his father having had cross words with Mrs Pluschow. What was her first name? Maria. Maria Pluschow. She'd never been particularly, or especially, kind to George, but she'd never gone out of her way to be unkind to him either. Indeed, on more than one occasion, she'd spoken harshly to his father and curbed what would have developed into a vicious attack on him. His strongest memory of Maria Pluschow was her fierce National Socialism. She wore her hair in braids, pinned close to her head, like a storybook Fräulein. Her broad Australian accent always came as a surprise.

He hadn't seen Maria Pluschow since he was sixteen years old. Sometime in the ensuing ten years, she'd been widowed. His father had told him that. She'd remember him as a fat, shy, silent lump of a boy. If he visited her now, she'd open the door to a thin, scarred, and bearded man, and his appearance might alarm her into calling the police. He had no other options. The more he thought about it, the more he convinced himself that this was a risk worth taking. If she screamed, or turned him away, he'd simply kill her. Weighed in the balance, a decent bath and a shave were more valuable to him at this moment than the life of a middle-aged widow. He started the motorcycle and headed for Maria Pluschow's house.

3

UNTIL WATSON COOPER began killing policemen, his neighbours thought of him as merely eccentric. He was sixty-six years old, tall, thin, and stooped. If Mrs Carstairs next door had known the word, she would have described him to the reporters who asked for her opinion after the tragedy as lugubrious. What she told them instead was that, on the rare occasions when she saw him, he was 'surly looking, like he'd just been told some bad news'. She heard Cooper more frequently than she laid eyes on him. He used to stomp around his house — well, his late mother's house — in the dead of night, barking orders at himself, as if he was marching or square bashing on a parade ground somewhere. The house in Coburg was on a generous block, although its southern wall sat quite close to Mrs Carstairs's northern wall, so sound carried, especially at night when competing sounds were few. She'd become used to the stomping, but she never got used to the gunfire. Two or three times a week, Cooper would wake Mrs Carstairs and his other neighbours by firing his .22 repeating rifle in the backyard at dawn. What was he firing at? Possums, birds, cats? When Mrs Carstairs looked over the fence into his yard, there were no corpses to indicate what his targets might have been.

Watson Cooper knew what he was firing at. Germans. He saw their shadows creeping about the bottom of his garden, near the dunny, and he did what any good soldier would do — he shot at them. When he checked for their bodies, he discovered that they'd always managed to avoid his bullets.

On 28 March 1944, as George Starling began his ride to Port Fairy, as Inspector Lambert questioned Joe Sable about his fitness for work, as Ron Dunnart and Bob O'Dowd drove back from Peter Lillee's house in Kew to Russell Street Police Headquarters, and as Helen Lord began to worry what their visit might mean, Watson Cooper wandered through the rooms of his mother's house, trying to quell the echoing voices that insisted on reminding him that his life had amounted to nothing.

'I'm a soldier,' he said under his breath. Was that laughter? 'I'm a soldier,' he repeated more firmly. This time there was silence. 'I'm a soldier!' he yelled. *If you're a soldier, the streets are full of Germans. They're all in uniform — you can't mistake them. Why aren't you out there, killing them? Why are you leaving that to all the other young men?* Was this voice male or female?

It wasn't his mother, he was sure of that. She knew he'd been no coward. She knew he'd tried to join up, right at the beginning of the war, right then, in 1914. He was thirty-six then, but that wasn't too old, was it? He was fit and healthy, and his eyes were good. 'Varicose veins,' the doctor said. 'Rejected.' He'd tried three times, and each time he'd been told, 'Varicose veins. Rejected.'

The Australian Imperial Forces didn't want him and his bad veins, so he went back to his work as a colour printer. He was good at that. He knew all about inks and the latest processes. He was a soldier, though. He was a printer, but what he really was, was a soldier.

The first white feather arrived one Friday in September 1914. It was wrapped in that week's casualty list. Each Friday, for the remainder of 1914, and for the whole of 1915, an envelope arrived at the house in Coburg, and inside the envelope was a white feather wrapped in the casualty list. Watson Cooper kept every one, and his life became the short walk to his work and the short walk home. He saw his mother, and, until she married and moved out, his sister. The white feathers stopped after Christmas 1915. Perhaps the sender died. The sending of white feathers was women's work.

'Ignore them, love,' Mrs Cooper said. 'She doesn't know about your veins. Still, she ought to be ashamed.'

'She's not ashamed, Mum,' Watson Cooper said. 'She might have lost a son, or several sons. She wants *me* to die of shame, and sometimes, I do want to die of shame.'

'Don't be so silly, Watson. What would I do without you? I'll make us a cup of tea.'

The cups of tea stopped in 1920, when Mrs Cooper died. Watson found her, lying on the floor in the kitchen. It was a stroke, the doctor said, and it must have happened not long after Watson had left for work, because the fire in the stove had gone out, and Mrs Cooper hadn't done the shopping.

With his mother dead, the house became his, and he began to be gripped by a sense of destiny. He wasn't sure what this destiny was, but in preparation for it he needed to limit his contact with other people. Conversations with workmates, shopkeepers, and neighbours were kept to a minimum. He wasn't rude. He was never rude. Any sort of familiarity was simply to be discouraged. He was always well turned out, and it was while he was shaving one morning, over two decades after his mother's death, that a voice said to him, *You should grow a neat moustache*. He wasn't startled by the voice. It was quiet, undemanding, simply making a suggestion, and accordingly, that morning he refrained from shaving above his top lip. After two weeks, he had a good, dark moustache, but he wasn't sure it suited him. People at the printing works said nothing. Perhaps they didn't notice.

Clip it a little, said the voice. *You look like an officer now*, and for the first time Watson Cooper answered it. 'Yes,' he said. 'Yes, I do.'

He began marching through the house at night, following the instructions in his head, and eventually the voice whispered his destiny to him. 'There are leftover Germans, the ones you didn't kill during the war. They're here. You have to do something about that.' It was just a whisper and hard to understand at first. It would take him by surprise and he'd have to stop what he was doing and say, 'What? What did you say?' and strain to hear the reply. Bit by bit the whisper became more confident, until it was easily heard and until finally it began to roar in his ears. 'The Germans! You have to kill the Germans!' He began shooting at their shadows in the backyard.

On that March morning, his carefully trimmed moustache now as grey as the hair on his head, Watson Cooper slung his .22 repeating rifle across his back and walked to the tobacconist. The tobacconist was next door to the greengrocer, and there were many people about, some of whom nudged companions and indicated the gun slung across Watson Cooper's shoulders. 'That's Cooper,' one woman said. 'He's an odd sort of bloke. Harmless. Keeps to himself.' The tobacconist, Mr Blake, handed Watson Cooper a pouch of tobacco and a packet of Craven As. 'That's fourteen shillings.'

'Bill the government,' Cooper said.

'Very funny, mate.'

'This is government business, so that's who you should bill.'

'What's government business?'

'This is.'

'Pay for the smokes, mate, or hand them back.'

With a flurry of disdain, Cooper threw the cigarettes and the pouch of tobacco on the floor. Mr Blake, made nervous by the rifle, even though Cooper made no move to retrieve it from his shoulder, simply said, 'I think you should go home, mate.' Cooper turned and walked into the street. Mr Blake picked up the telephone and asked to be put through to the police.

Watson Cooper stood on the footpath outside the tobacconist shop for a full minute. His stillness drew eyes to him, as did the gun. Several people crossed the road rather than pass close by him. He took the rifle from his shoulder and held it, barrel down, by his side. One witness, an ex-soldier, later said that the smoothness of the movement gave him the creeps and that he knew this bloke was dangerous. Cooper moved to the tram stop a few doors up from Blake's shop. There was a seat there with two women sitting on it. Cooper sat down beside them. Neither of the women had noticed the gun, and continued chatting about the inconvenience of meat rationing.

'They'll be rationing the air we breathe next,' one of them said. Cooper couldn't quite make out what they were saying. He strained to hear them, but a tram passing, and the rattle of a milk horse and dray, drowned out their words, which is why the clarity of the man's voice, quite near his ear, startled him.

'Mr Cooper, isn't it? Could you stand up, please?'

This wasn't the voice in his head. This voice was deeper, and a sweet smell came with it. Soap? Hair oil?

'Mr Cooper?'

He felt a hand rest on his shoulder. It didn't grip him. It just rested there, gently. He was conscious of the two women looking at him now, and he was conscious, too, that they were suddenly afraid. He stood up slowly, and the hand on his shoulder remained there. He turned to face Constable Paul Beckett, who had been told just a few hours earlier that his wife, Anne, had given birth to their first child, a daughter. They hadn't yet decided on a name for her. He'd been given a few hours leave to visit Anne in hospital, and he'd been about to leave the station when Mr Blake had telephoned there. Constable Beckett knew Watson Cooper, and the police station was just around the corner from the shops.

'I know old Cooper,' he said. 'I'll sort it out on my way to the hospital.'

'Mr Cooper,' Constable Beckett said again. Watson Cooper turned around, raised the rifle, and shot Constable Beckett once in the face and twice in the chest. Beckett was dead before his head hit the ground.

'A dead German is a good German.'

One of the women was screaming. He turned the rifle towards her. 'He's dead. You're safe.' He lowered the rifle, puzzled that the woman continued to scream, but that was women, wasn't it. She'd settle down when she realised the German really was dead. He began walking back to his mother's house. No one tried to stop him. He was aware of people getting out of his way, and that they were staring at him. He didn't know why. He entered the house, sat in a chair in the front room with the gun across his knees, and waited for the voice to say, 'Well done.' Instead it said, 'There are more of them.'

News of the murder of Constable Paul Beckett was telephoned to Homicide within minutes of its occurrence. Joe Sable and Sergeant David Reilly were dispatched, and three quarters of an hour later were being brought up to speed outside the Cooper house. There were eight uniformed police there and two CIB men, both of them senior to Reilly and Sable, and both of them sceptical about the decision to create a Homicide unit separate from the CIB. Joe's expensive suit confirmed their suspicion that newly minted Homicide detectives gave themselves airs and graces.

'Have you got people round the back?' Reilly asked.

'Oh Christ! No, we hadn't thought of that,' said Detective Kevin Maher, a lean man in his early forties. 'We were just waiting for you to arrive to tell us what to do. Of course we've got men round the fucking back.'

Reilly seemed indifferent to the rebuke and replied with a steeliness Joe hadn't heard in his voice before.

'So, we're all just standing around, are we, chatting?'

Perhaps Constable Allan Humphries overheard this remark, or perhaps his impatience simply broke at that moment. Paul Beckett had been the best man at his wedding, and he was to be godfather to Paul's baby. Whatever the cause, he simply walked to the front door of the Cooper house, turned the handle, and entered. He instinctively took off his helmet, and it was this movement that killed him. He ought to have unholstered his gun. Watson Cooper was standing in the hallway, and he calmly raised the rifle and pulled the trigger. Constable Humphries collapsed against the door, and Cooper fell upon him and plunged a newly sharpened Bowie knife into his neck.

Humphries's sudden, unauthorised move had taken everyone by surprise, and although both the CIB men and the uniformed men began to move quickly, they weren't quick enough, so that Humphries had fallen back against the door before anyone had reached it. It was Detective Maher who began pushing against it. One violent shove dislodged Cooper from Humphries's body and set him back on his haunches. It also caused his knife to slide through Humphries's neck where its brutal edge found no purchase or resistance and would have decapitated the body entirely if Cooper hadn't let go of the hilt. As it was, Constable Humphries's head lolled to one side, attached only by stubborn tendons and skin.

Cooper was mesmerised by the welter of blood and the strangeness of the head's position, so he remained seated and made no attempt to reach for his gun. There would have been time to reach it, because Detective Maher took a moment to assimilate the grotesque tableau that greeted him, before he fired three shots into Watson Cooper's chest. The noise bounced off the walls and hammered his ears, disorienting him so that it was only as the echoes died away that he became aware of Joe Sable standing at his side.

'He was going to shoot me,' Maher said.

'What with?' Joe asked evenly.

Maher looked to where Cooper's rifle lay on the floor, well away from his body. With a swift, deft movement, he used his boot to move it close to him, and then slid it across the floor to lie between Cooper's splayed legs.

'With that,' Maher said, and the room began to fill with the remaining police officers.

4

GEORGE STARLING RODE the motorcycle into Maria Pluschow's front yard. It was almost midday. He didn't want to sneak up on her. He wanted to remove any unnecessary element of surprise, although when he cut the engine, the barking of a dog from behind the house would have ensured that his approach would have been detected anyway. That was fine, because that he was there at all would be surprise enough.

Either the noise of the motorcycle or the dog's barking brought Maria Pluschow from the backyard, where she'd been hanging sheets to dry. Starling was standing by the machine, one hand on its now silent throttle. Elegant from the neck down and dishevelled from the neck up, he was an unusual sight. She knew immediately who he was. She'd been shown a sketch of him just a few weeks earlier by a rather dull-witted policeman from Melbourne. She'd given this detective short shrift and denied that she recognised the face in the sketch. Now here he was, George Starling, in her front yard. She surprised him by calling out his name.

'George Starling. The police have been here looking for you. They think you might have killed your father. Did you?'

'Unfortunately, no.'

Maria Pluschow laughed, and Maria Pluschow rarely laughed.

'You'd better push that thing out of sight, round the back. Don't worry about the dog. She's chained up. You look like the wild man from Borneo.'

Maria Pluschow's house was uncluttered and maintained at a high pitch of cleanliness and neatness that suggested that its maintenance was her principal occupation. It made Starling feel self-conscious about his appearance — a feeling that was new to him.

'You look truly terrible, George.'

She spoke to him with sudden familiarity, as if she'd known him for a long time.

'I need to clean myself up.'

'Well, first I think a cup of tea will do you good. Sit in here.'

She directed him to the front room and to an armchair with an antimacassar and embroidered sleeves draped over the arms. Starling had no doubt that the embroidery was Maria's. Among the flowers, small swastikas punctuated the cloth. You couldn't buy that in any draper's shop.

On the wall, directly opposite the chair, there was a large print, which Starling had seen before. It was of four naked women and might have seemed out of place, except that he knew its significance. It was called *The Four Elements*, and Hitler had the original in his house in Munich. Starling had no knowledge of, or interest in, art, but he'd seen another version of this picture at a house at Candlebark Hill, near Daylesford. The house was owned by a soft, decadent man named Mitchell Magill, who played, along with his silly companions, at being a National Socialist. He'd loathed Magill and his coterie of flabby, self-indulgent companions. They'd been more interested in art and running around in the nuddy than in confronting the Jewish menace. He supposed that they'd all been rounded up and interned by now.

He couldn't think of them without anger, because he held them partly responsible for the death of the man who'd rescued him, who'd given his life purpose: Ptolemy Jones. Jones was the only person who'd aroused in him feelings akin to love — not physical love, deeper than that — and now Jones was dead. He hadn't thought of him for days. Oddly, this painting inflamed his grief, and in doing so, it also inflamed his hatred of Joe Sable, the man he truly blamed for Jones's death.

'You like that picture?' Maria asked, having noticed its physical effect on Starling.

'I've seen it before, that's all.'

'I'll make the tea.' Maria retreated to the kitchen, sensitive to the tone of Starling's response, which indicated that further inquiry would be unwelcome.

'Who did that to your face?' she called, as she encouraged embers in the stove into flames.

'I did it to myself.'

The easy honesty of his response made them both aware that a strange and immediate domesticity between them had sprung into being. When Maria returned with the tea, and half a dense fruitcake, she sat near him.

'I wouldn't care twopence if you'd murdered your father. He was a dreadful man. He killed your mother, I'm sure of it — and got away with it.'

'I barely remember my mother.'

'That's all to the good. Your father liked to keep one of her eyes blackened at all times. That's how it seemed to me.'

'I wish I had killed him. He didn't deserve to die a natural death.'

'Why did you come here, to me?'

'I remembered you from meetings my father used to take me to. Some of them were here, in this house.'

'What do you remember about the meetings?'

'They bored me. It was all talk. Empty talk.'

'You didn't approve of your father's politics?'

'It was him I didn't approve of. He didn't really believe in the politics. He was all wind.'

'Why are the police after you, George?'

In other circumstances a direct question like this would have curled Starling's fingers into a fist. Coming as it did from a woman who defiantly decorated her walls with an Adolf Ziegler print, he was happy to answer bluntly.

'I killed two perverts and burned down a flat that belonged to a Jew.'

'You are welcome in my house, George Starling. I think this might be what people call fate.'

PETER LILLEE WOULD have been surprised had he known that his name had been jotted down in Sturt Menadue's diary. The news of Menadue's murder, which he'd just been given, was interesting, but not particularly distressing. Apparently, Menadue and a young man named Steven McNamara had been violently killed in a queer club in Little Bourke Street. The murderer had not yet been found. Lillee wondered how much time and energy the police expended on the murder of homosexuals.

'You've met Menadue,' said the man who sat opposite Lillee.

'I don't think so. The name isn't familiar.'

'You met him here, a couple of months ago. He came to supper.'

'Oh? Was he taking instruction?'

'No. He was a cradle Catholic. I asked him to come. He was something of a lost soul.'

'Did you know he was queer?'

'My job is to love the sinner, not the sin, Peter.'

Peter Lillee had no strong objection to queers. He was aware that many people believed him to be one, although he wasn't. He'd known many and generally preferred their company to that of men like Sir Marcus Ashgrove. Outside his professional life, he moved discreetly in circles that might euphemistically be called artistic. Peter Lillee loved artists and was perfectly at home in their louche, chaotic world. These were the two great secrets of his life — his flirtation with what passed for the demi-monde of Melbourne, and the fact that he was taking instruction to convert to Roman Catholicism. The priest from whom he was taking instruction was Father Dougal McGrath, who served at St Patrick's Cathedral, and who, on the recommendation of Archbishop Daniel Mannix, had just been granted the honorific of 'Monsignor'.

'It's not a promotion. It's just a title in recognition of service.'

'So, what do I call you?'

'Oh, Monsignor, definitely.'

Peter Lillee didn't much like Monsignor McGrath. He was too spick-and-span, too groomed. Vanity wasn't a quality a priest should indulge. Lillee wasn't impressed by his intellect, either, but for him conversion wasn't about the mediocre men who held offices in the Catholic Church. It was about the offices themselves and the sense of the sacred that moved through the flawed conduits who dispensed the sacraments. There were elements of the faith with which he struggled. He could accommodate the key articles of faith — the Resurrection, the Assumption of Mary into Heaven (although this required a real suspension of disbelief), transubstantiation, and the others. The sacrament of confession was attractive to him, but he could not imagine revealing his transgressions to Monsignor McGrath. If he was accepted into the church, he would take advantage of confession only in circumstances where he was anonymous, and where the priest was unknown to him.

Monsignor McGrath leaned back in his chair, appraising Peter. They were sitting in the study of the presbytery, which sat close to the cathedral, and which housed two other priests. Archbishop Mannix, who Peter had seen but had never met, preferred to live at his residence, Raheen, in Kew.

'I think, Peter, that you're ready to be brought into the Church.'

'I'm not without doubts, Monsignor.'

'If you told me you were without doubts, I'd know you were lying.'

'Do you have doubts?'

'Of course. Doubts test our faith. We know our faith is strong when it overcomes our doubts. My certainties outweigh my doubts.'

'And the Pope? Infallibility and doubt are contradictory, surely.'

'The Holy Father is infallible only in matters of faith. I'm sure he makes as many mistakes in the course of a day as anybody else. He is a man, Peter. He is God's representative, but he is not God.'

Peter Lillee wished that Monsignor McGrath was a more subtle and able theologian. Their discussions were always unsatisfactory. McGrath was a shallow thinker, but, imbued as he was with the priestly authority to administer the sacraments, he was a tolerable teacher of Catholic doctrine. And that was the thing about Catholic doctrine — it was codified and simplified into a catechism of beliefs and observances that didn't make intellectual demands on adherents. Sometimes, Lillee worried that his attraction to the Church was because of its paraphernalia. High art and vulgarity were a heady mix.

'I think we should set a date for your reception into the Catholic faith, doubts notwithstanding.'

'I want it to be a private affair.'

'It's a celebration, Peter.'

'My faith is private. If I am to be received into the Church, I see no reason why it needs to be bruited abroad.'

Monsignor McGrath nodded in acquiescence.

'Shall we say Saturday next at 3.00, here in the cathedral? I'll perform the baptism and give you your first communion.'

Lillee agreed and was disappointed in his failure to feel elation. Perhaps that would come later. For now, his mind turned to the meeting of the Capital Issues Advisory Committee and his desire to get there before any of the other members arrived. Sir Marcus Ashgrove may well have approached some of them individually. Lillee wanted to avoid entering a room where a discussion may already have begun, or taken place. He made his apologies to Monsignor McGrath and left the presbytery.

Lillee didn't believe that the committee was susceptible to influence, but he was a cautious man, and he was certain that Sir Marcus Ashgrove would attempt to exert some influence. He, Lillee, was the only member of the five-man committee who was not a public servant. He'd served on the earlier incarnation of the committee, the Capital Issues Board. The board had consisted mainly of businessmen until John Curtin's government, in 1941, had thought it wise to remove any possibility of conflict of interest by reducing the representation of the business community to one person. That person was Peter Lillee. The brief of the committee was clear. It was to advise Treasury on those investments which it deemed unnecessary, or which were designed to enrich individuals or corporations in ways which had no bearing on the war economy. Lillee got on well with the four men who sat on the committee with him, and it was rare that there was a disagreement over whether a particular investment was or wasn't approvable for war purposes.

As it happened, this meeting of the committee dismissed Sir Marcus Ashgrove's application in a few minutes. The chairman of the committee, Mr McConaghy, who was also the chairman of the Tariff Board, raised the Wombat goldmine issue not as an order of business, but as an annoyance to which he'd been subjected none too subtly in the Australian Club.

'I think,' he said, 'we need to issue them with a Treasury refusal as quickly as possible.'

'It is in train,' Peter Lillee said. 'We're just waiting for it to come down the line.' He didn't mention his spiky meeting in the Melbourne Club with Sir Marcus.

'The bloke who buttonholed me,' McConaghy said, 'tried to imply they could bring pressure to bear at Treasury level.'

'That's just bluster,' Lillee said. 'These people know perfectly well that this committee was successful two years ago in limiting the ability of goldmining companies to make calls on shares and to open new mines. They have no access to Manpower, so they can't staff their claims even if they wanted to.'

'Good, so let's squash this bloody claim once and for all.'

'It won't help our popularity.'

'Did we have any to begin with, Peter?'

'Well, no. Rich people don't like being told they can't do what suits them.'

'Are you speaking from personal experience?'

Peter Lillee's wealth was no secret to his fellow committee members, but this question wasn't intended to offend, and it didn't.

'As a matter of fact, I am,' he said. 'I'm as guilty as the next man of wanting to get my own way. I'd like to think it wasn't always at the expense of someone else, but perhaps that's pious self-delusion.'

The committee moved on to other matters.

Ros Lord had gone upstairs to bed. Peter Lillee had not yet returned home. He'd telephoned in the late afternoon to say he'd be dining out, which Ros understood to mean that he'd be spending the evening with his friends. She had a vague idea who these friends were, but she'd never met any of them. She knew they were artists, writers, and actors, but Peter had never brought any of them home. She hoped he wasn't protecting her sensibilities in the mistaken belief that she'd disapprove. She was close to her brother, but as with her daughter, there was a point at which closeness surrendered to stifling discretion.

Downstairs in the library — a gorgeous room, the existence of which, in a private house, Joe Sable could scarcely believe, but which he'd already begun to take for granted — Joe and Helen Lord sat listening to a radio drama.

'Do you mind if I turn it off?' Helen asked. 'It's not very good.'

'It's awful.'

'Ron Dunnart and Bob O'Dowd called here this morning.'

'Why?'

'Mum answered the door. Dunnart made up some story about burglaries in the area.'

'Why would Homicide be interested in that?'

'Well obviously, we … they, wouldn't be. Mum didn't like them. She reckons she can smell a bad copper, and they smelled bad.'

'And they didn't ask to speak to you?'

'I don't think they know I live here, which makes this visit even more sinister.'

'Sinister?'

'It felt like that. Inspector Lambert doesn't like Dunnart, does he?'

'No. He thinks he's corrupt.'

'Corrupt? In what way?'

'He hasn't said anything to me. I think David Reilly knows more about it.'

Helen snorted.

'Reilly? Now there's an unimpressive detective.'

Joe didn't challenge her. Any attempt to defend Sergeant Reilly would derail the conversation. He hadn't formed a strong opinion about Reilly either way. Inspector Lambert seemed to like him, or trust him at any rate, so Joe was prepared to give him the benefit of the doubt. Helen Lord didn't believe in giving people the benefit of the doubt.

'I'll have a quiet word with Reilly, if you like.'

Reluctant to acknowledge that Reilly might be of practical use in any situation, Helen nevertheless agreed that this would be a good idea. Joe then settled into what had become a nightly pattern since Helen's enforced leave of absence. The first few nights had been awkward, but Helen's wish to know what was happening inside Homicide gradually allowed her to hear it without resentment-induced deafness. They were both conscious that this exchange of information mirrored Inspector Lambert's discussions with his wife, Maude. For Helen, Joe's willingness to confide in her to this extent was an intimacy that affected her in ways to which Joe was oblivious. He described the shootings in Coburg and censored nothing. Helen would have known immediately if he was shielding her from the worst of what he'd seen, and she would have been furious.

'Watson Cooper could have been taken alive and tried. This Detective Maher executed him on the spot. That's what it comes down to. Cooper's gun was nowhere near him until Maher kicked it between his legs *after* he'd shot him.'

'Coppers don't like it when people shoot other coppers.'

'He's expecting me to say nothing.'

'I'll be the devil's advocate here, Joe. Was there any doubt, any doubt at all, that Cooper was the person who'd killed those two officers?'

'No. No doubt whatsoever.'

'So, if he was tried, what would happen?'

'He'd be found guilty, and, unless he was found to be insane, he'd be hanged.'

'So, the end result would be the same. One dead murderer.'

'Unless the court accepted an insanity defence.'

'In which case he'd be locked up at great expense to the taxpayer.'

'That decision shouldn't be in the hands of Detective Maher of the Coburg CIB. I don't know what to do.'

'Are you afraid of making enemies? If you are, you'll do nothing. If you're not, you'll tell Lambert what you saw and prepare yourself to become one of the most hated men in the force. You blokes are supposed to watch each other's backs, no matter what. How brave are you, Joe?'

'I'm pretty confident that Lambert will back me.'

'So am I, but Lambert won't be there with you in the gymnasium, or walking you home.'

'I understand why Maher did it, but self-appointed executioners are dangerous people.'

'You really see it as an execution?'

'That's what it was. Maher shot an unarmed man. A Nazi puts a gun to a woman's head in Kraków and pulls the trigger. Maher shoots Watson Cooper. What's the moral difference?'

'The woman is innocent.'

'The executioner is guilty. Each of them would defend his actions, or justify it. Cooper is guilty of murdering two policemen. The woman in Kraków is guilty of being a Jew. It makes the killing palatable.'

Helen's heart tightened whenever Joe made reference to what was happening to the Jews in Europe. She'd read the odd report in *The Age* or *The Argus*, but it had sat among a flood of what was considered bigger news, and so it hadn't taken hold. She knew now, though, that the slaughter of Jews was having a profound effect on Joe. She had no way, or she knew no way, of offering solace without revealing her feelings for him, and this she felt incapable of doing. So she remained silent.

THIS MOMENT HAD been inevitable, and Peter Lillee ought to have hurried to it much sooner. He would never have been guilty of such a delay in his professional life, but in his private life he was far less adept at managing the whims and passions of other people. The woman who sat before him now must have known why he'd come, but she wasn't going to make it easy for him.

'Can I get you a drink, Peter?'

The formality of the question belied the fact that Lillian Johnson had been Peter Lillee's lover for two years. Her husband, James, had at first sanctioned the affair. It gave him licence to pursue his own sexual dalliances, but when he discovered the identity of his wife's lover, he'd withdrawn his approval and moved quickly to hostility, and then to demanding a divorce. Peter Lillee had cost him a lot of money in a business venture that had worked out well for Lillee and poorly for him.

The flat in Camberwell, in which Peter and Lillian now sat, was Lillian's, one among several properties she'd inherited. She required neither her husband's nor Peter Lillee's financial support. What she did require of the man who sat opposite her was marriage. Lillian Johnson believed in marriage. It mattered to her. She'd overlooked her husband's early dalliances because she understood that he was weak, in some ways even pathetic. When she met Peter Lillee, she'd found herself susceptible to the same weakness and she'd found a way to accommodate this within her sense of herself. A part of this accommodation was to win from Peter a declaration that this affair would end in marriage, and not a termination that would offer no choice but to return to her husband. That possibility ended anyway when James began divorce proceedings with the bitter intention of naming Peter Lillee as the adulterous cause. She could weather that scandal.

'Lillian.'

'If you're about to launch into some popish nonsense, Peter, please don't bother. I'm really not in the mood.'

'I don't know what to say.'

'I'm not a fool, Peter. I put up with your reluctance to be intimate with me over the past few months because I assumed it was temporary. The idea that you were wrestling with your conscience about whether or not to touch me, as if I was some unclean thing, makes me sick. The thought that your conscience won makes me so angry I want to kill you.'

The even temper with which these words were spoken had an effect on Peter that was more violent than if they'd been hurled at him in a rage.

'No, Lillian, no. That can't be true.'

'Tell me why you're here. Tell me. Just say it.'

'I've been honest with you about taking instruction in the Catholic faith.'

'Are you expecting applause?'

'Understanding, perhaps.'

'You'll never get that from me. I left my marriage for you. I didn't do it on a whim. I did it because I loved you, and because I believed that you loved me. You asked me to marry you. Do you seriously think I would have begun an affair with you just for the thrill of it?'

'Of course not. It was wrong of me to offer marriage.'

'You're already sounding like a martyr. How dare you go into a confessional and beg forgiveness from some grubby, half-wit of a priest for touching me? How dare you reduce me to a sordid temptation, to a threat to your immortal soul?'

'That's not—'

'Have you done penance for your sins of the flesh?'

'Yes, but the penance is for my weakness, not yours.'

'I spent six years at a convent school, Peter. I know all the bullshit, all the ugly, demeaning words to describe perfectly normal human behaviour. I began as your lover, now I'm an occasion for sin, and what makes me sick, what makes me incandescent with rage, is that you believe that.'

'I wasn't expecting this to happen, Lillian.'

'Christ, next you'll be telling me you have a vocation.'

'No.'

'I used to love looking at you. I thought you were the most handsome man I'd ever seen. Now all I see is a milksop. I see all the flaws in your face. Your faith has made you ugly.'

'It wasn't ever my intention to hurt you.'

'I'd like you to leave, Peter.'

'Please, Lillian. I want to explain.'

Lillian stood up and walked out of the living room towards her bedroom. She said nothing further, went into the bedroom, and closed the door quietly behind her.

Peter sat for a moment. He put his head in his hands. When he stood up, he looked around the room and noticed that the two framed photographs of him that usually sat on the mantelpiece were no longer there. The fireplace had been set in preparation for the first cold night of autumn and the photographs had been wedged between two pieces of wood. He retrieved one, wrote 'Forgive me' on its back, and returned it to the fireplace with the words facing outwards.

He left Lillian Johnson's flat knowing that he would never see her again. He felt both wretched and strangely ecstatic. *This*, he thought, *is the exquisite joy of self-denial and sacrifice*. He didn't leave Lillian Johnson with his faith shaken. He left her with a fierce conviction that he was right, and the cruel certainty of that conviction dulled any sense he ought to have had that Lillian's feelings might be of consequence.

RON DUNNART WATCHED from the shadows as Peter Lillee left Lillian Johnson's flat. He'd pleaded an upset stomach and had left work early. He'd found out where the Capital Issues Advisory Committee met and, just a few hours earlier, had been sitting outside the building for a full half-hour without any real expectation that he'd see Lillee come or go.

He was building a picture for himself of Lillee's world. He had a photograph of him, a good photograph. Even so, identifying him in a crowd of people leaving the building was going to be difficult. It was possible Lillee had already left, right under his nose. Dunnart had crossed the street and had stood at the entrance to the self-important building in which men made decisions that affected the lives of other men, like Dunnart. It was the Napier Waller mural above the door that lent the building its air of pompous regard. All that striving, half-naked flesh — and striving for what, for whom? Not striving for Dunnart. No. He'd learned long ago that if he wanted to get ahead, the way to do it was to exploit the vulnerabilities of people whose reputations mattered to them, and who were willing to pay to protect those reputations. He hadn't earned a fortune, not by any means. But he'd earned a tidy enough sum. Peter Lillee though … Dunnart was hoping for big things from Peter Lillee.

As he'd been contemplating this, Lillee had appeared, as if Dunnart had summoned him. There he was, two feet from Dunnart, having emerged into Collins Street with two other men.

Dunnart recognised him, but to confirm the identification, one of the two men said, 'I'll see you soon, Peter.' Lillee then walked with the remaining man a short distance down Collins Street. He stopped at a car.

'Can I give you a lift?'

Lillee's companion said no, that he'd take the train.

Dunnart hadn't intended following Lillee's car, but a taxi passed just as Lillee pulled out into the street, and Dunnart had hailed it, produced his identification, and instructed the driver to follow Lillee's vehicle. He'd been irrationally annoyed that Lillee had taken him as far as Camberwell. He paid the fare, a cost that annoyed him further. Well, he'd get that expense back in spades.

Lillee had gone into a handsome block of six flats. Dunnart couldn't tell which flat he was visiting. The residents here were still taking the blackout seriously, despite its having been relaxed. Not a chink of light escaped. When Lillee entered the block, the gloaming had declined into evening, and by the time Lillee emerged, about half an hour later, darkness had fallen. Dunnart hadn't come this far and waited this long just to watch Lillee go in and out of a block of flats. He hurried towards Lillee's car and reached it just as Lillee opened the driver's door. He waited until Lillee was seated behind the steering wheel, then opened the passenger door and got in. Before Lillee had a chance to express surprise, Dunnart said, 'Detective Sergeant Ron Dunnart, Melbourne Homicide. You and I need to have a chat, Mr Lillee.'

THE MAN WHO sat opposite Maria Pluschow bore little resemblance to the man who'd arrived earlier in the day. Bathed, shaved, and with a neat haircut, which she'd given him, he was almost elegant — although most of the elegance was borrowed from the suit he wore. He looked a lot like a young, hungry Rudolf Hess, which for Maria Pluschow was no bad thing, though Hess couldn't be recalled without bitterness, given his gross betrayal of Herr Hitler.

'Your face still needs more time to heal, George. You can stay here, of course.'

'I can pay.'

'Don't be silly. Blondi and I would like the company.'

The dog lifted its head when it heard its name. It could sense Starling's discomfort, and its muscles tensed. Maria placed a hand on its head.

'She'll get used to you, George. When she knows I trust you, she'll love you.'

The dog settled. Starling had never thought of animals as pets and had never understood how people formed attachments to them. Now, though, as he watched the dog respond under Maria's gently placed hand, he felt an unfamiliar emotion. It was small and fleeting, an inchoate feeling that might have grown into something like sympathy had Starling given it room to swell. He tamped it down, panicked by its strangeness.

'You were a strange boy, George, but I always thought there was something there, something in you. You never said very much, but I always suspected that you were much smarter than your father. He really was an unpleasant man, your father.'

'I hated him.'

'A perfectly reasonable response. Do you remember your mother?'

No one had ever asked him about his family, and if he had been asked, he would have shut the conversation down. Without really understanding why, he answered Maria's question.

'I barely knew her, like I said.'

'She loved you very much, George. I think that's partly why your father killed her.'

'I don't remember any of that.'

'She tried to protect you.'

'She failed.'

There was a moment's silence as those words fell heavily between them. Maria Pluschow looked closely into George Starling's disfigured face and said, 'I won't fail you.'

A wracking sob burst from Starling and, helpless to prevent a volcanic rush of emotion, he began to weep. His shoulders heaved, snot flowed from his nose, and he uttered sounds that were almost animal in their incoherence. Maria moved quickly and sat on the arm of his chair. She put her fingers in his hair and wiped his face with her apron.

'You're home now, George.'

Starling nodded and didn't pull away when Maria leaned down and kissed the top of his head.

'You HAVE TO get out of my car,' Peter Lillee said. 'I don't care who you say you are.'

'Oh, I am who I say I am, I assure you.'

It was too dark for either man to clearly see the other's face. Ron Dunnart recognised Lillee's cologne — Hungary Water. What he didn't smell was fear. Obviously, Lillee thought he was well barricaded behind his wealth.

'This isn't a social call, Lillee. I'll save us both time and get to the point. I know you're a pansy and I know who your associates are. I know it all: all your filthy bum-chums. Now, I'm an open-minded man, Lillee. I don't really care where you put your dick, as long as it's nowhere near me, but you and I both know that having your name dragged through the courts on a sodomy charge wouldn't impress your mates at the Melbourne Club.'

'So that's what you are — a cheap little blackmailer.'

'Oh, I don't think you'll find me cheap.'

'What did you say your name was?'

'Dunnart. Ron Dunnart.'

'What makes you think I'll pay you a penny?'

'You and I both know what your reputation is worth. That house you live in must be expensive to keep up.'

'You've been to my house?'

'Let's just say, I know where you live.'

'Get out of my car.'

Dunnart didn't admire Lillee's failure to be intimidated. It infuriated him. He'd paid good money for a taxi and hung around on the footpath for an inconvenient amount of time. He considered both these things an attack on his dignity, and now Lillee thought he could be dismissed as if he was a nobody. No, no, no. You underestimated Ron Dunnart at your peril.

'Maybe you need some time to think about this, Lillee.'

'Not that it's any of your business, but I'm not a homosexual and never have been, so whatever grubby information you think you have about me, it's baseless. I loathe men like you, Dunnart. How many lives have you ruined?'

'I'm not sentimental about pansies.'

'I feel that way about blackmailers.'

Dunnart felt an unfamiliar stirring of uncertainty. Could he have been wrong about Lillee? Surely not. His name was in that dead pansy's notebook. That's how they contacted each other discreetly.

'You can't bluff your way out of this, Lillee, and I couldn't care less what you think of me. I don't want your good opinion, just your money. How's that for unsentimental?'

'I'm not paying you a penny, but what I am going to do is put a stop to you.'

'Sturt Menadue.'

If there'd been light to see by, Dunnart hoped that Lillee's face might have registered shock at the mention of that name. All

Lillee gave him by way of satisfaction was a tired sigh.

'Sturt Menadue? This is your source? A dead man?'

'So you know him.'

'No, Dunnart. I don't know him; I know of him, and I know that he's dead because Monsignor McGrath at St Patrick's told me. Maybe you should try blackmailing a highly placed priest. See how far you get with that. However, your blackmailing days are over. If I were you, I'd resign my position and crawl out of sight under whatever rock you call home. If you don't resign, I'm going to make it my special project to expose you, and I have the money and the contacts to ruin you. Now get out of my car.'

'Fuck you, Lillee. We'll see who ruins who.'

'Whom, Dunnart … who ruins whom.'

Dunnart spat at the shadowy form beside him, and got out of the car. He didn't slam the door, but reached into his pocket, withdrew his keys, and dragged one, screeching, through the paintwork on the passenger door. Peter Lillee showed no acknowledgement and drove away.

Ten hours later, in the early morning, a man walking his dog along the banks of the Yarra River in Kew came upon the body of a well-dressed man. The body was lying close to the water, so close that the river flowed around one submerged hand.

'Hey, mate!' the man called, hoping that the prone figure was dozing, or drunk. When there was no response, he approached carefully. The body was lying on its front, so its face was obscured. The man nudged it with his boot and leaned in so that he could see the face. The skin was a ghastly blue, and vomit pooled near the mouth. This is not how a man as fastidious as Peter Lillee would have wanted to die, stinking of sick and shit. This, nevertheless, is precisely how Peter Lillee did die.

5

THERE'D BEEN NO difficulty identifying Peter Lillee's body. His wallet was in his back pocket, and a document folder was tucked inside his suit coat. Within an hour of the body's discovery, Inspector Lambert and Joe Sable were watching as the attendants necessary at a suspicious death went about their work. The medical officer had declared Peter Lillee dead, the coroner had been informed and was on his way, and Martin Serong, the police photographer, was carefully recording the scene.

Inspector Lambert never presumed to tell Serong what to photograph. No one was better than Martin Serong at capturing the awful intimacy of death. On more than one occasion, Maude Lambert had noticed a small detail picked up by Serong's camera that Titus had missed. It was contrary to police protocol that Maude should see crime-scene photographs, but early in their marriage Titus had understood that Maude's intelligence and her understanding of human nature, even its darkest manifestations, were invaluable. There was no one in Homicide who was her equal. Helen Lord had shown promise, but Police Command had reprimanded him for seconding her into the Homicide unit. It was true that he'd done this without informing them. She'd been dismissed from Homicide —

a decision he'd been unable to overturn, but which infuriated him. Now her uncle, Peter Lillee, lay dead at his feet. Joe had formally identified the body.

'I'll break this news to Ros and Helen,' Lambert said. 'The house is nearby. I don't want them hearing this from some awkward constable.'

'I'd like to be there,' Joe said.

'Of course.'

Martin Serong approached Inspector Lambert.

'What have we got, Martin?'

'A bit of a mystery, Titus.'

'The doc thinks it might be some sort of poisoning.'

'That would be my first guess, too.'

'Did he take it, or was he given it?'

'I just take pictures, Titus. I just take pictures.'

'He hasn't been interfered with in any way. There are no ligature marks, no defensive wounds or wounds of any kind. Nothing has been stolen. It looks like he came down here sometime last night, took a massive dose of some poison, and died quickly. Cyanide?' Lambert asked.

'Impossible to say without a blood analysis,' Serong said.

'There's no sign of a struggle, no disturbance of the grass.'

'Peter Lillee would be the last person in the world who'd take his own life, sir,' Joe said.

'How well did you know him, Sergeant?'

'I'm wearing his clothes, sir.'

Lambert said nothing, recognising that Joe was trying to collect himself. He waited.

'He's a successful businessman and he moves in privileged circles. He's never shown any signs of stress or depression, or none that I've noticed.'

'What do you know about his private life?'

Joe thought for a moment. 'Absolutely nothing. I know he has friends who are artists, but in the couple of weeks that I've been living with them, no one has visited; at least, no one who I've been aware of. The house is so big it's possible people have called and I just haven't heard them.'

'Rich men have enemies, even decent rich men, and I'm assuming Peter Lillee was a decent man.'

'He was a decent man, sir. What I really can't believe is that if he was going to kill himself this is how he'd choose to do it.'

'So how did he get here? If he didn't take his own life, someone either killed him here or brought his body here, and there are no footprints other than his and the bloke's who found him. I'm not eliminating him as a suspect, but it seems unlikely.'

'Maybe the killer brought the body here by boat.'

'That, Sergeant, is a real possibility.'

Martin Serong said, 'I was waiting until the last minute to do this, Titus, but the time has come.'

He took off his shoes and socks, and then his trousers, and waded into the Yarra River. There was no gentle decline. He sank into stinking mud almost to his waist just two steps from the bank. Despite teetering uncertainly, he took a series of shots before regaining the bank and staring glumly at his filthy legs.

'Water is supposed to wash you clean,' he said.

'Not this water, Martin. You wouldn't want to drink it.'

'That might explain the dead fish. There are three of them, caught in a tree root, quite close to the dead man's hand.'

'Could he have released cyanide into the water, Martin? Maybe he had some in a phial, swallowed some, and dropped the rest into the river.'

'I was careful not to disturb the area near his hand. It's possible he may have dropped something.'

'We need to get someone down here to do a sweep of the mud.

Sergeant Reilly can supervise that. He's due here in a few minutes. We should get to Peter Lillee's house.'

'No,' Ros LORD said. 'No. Suicide. No. My brother would be incapable of such an act.'

Helen Lord was staring at Joe Sable. Her face was expressionless, but he felt keenly that she wasn't seeing him. She was seeing her uncle's clothes. He felt like an interloper and wondered if his presence would be welcome in the house any longer.

'Each of you knows better than most that an investigation into Peter's death will involve great intrusions into your privacy, and his.'

'I need to know what happened to my brother, Inspector. Our privacy is immaterial, and Peter is beyond caring.'

Joe could see the effort that Ros Lord was making to hold herself together. He wanted to say something, to offer some sort of useless comfort, but the feel of Lillee's suit struck him dumb with self-consciousness.

'I'd like to see Martin Serong's photographs,' Helen said.

'I'm afraid that won't be possible,' Lambert said. 'Even if you were still with us in Homicide, you wouldn't be allowed to investigate the suspicious death of a member of your own family.'

'So you agree it's a suspicious death.'

'If you tell me that the idea that your uncle might take his own life is incomprehensible to you, then yes, I'm unwilling to rush to that convenient conclusion.'

'My brother was both a public and a private man, Inspector. I know you'll want to speak to Peter's friends and acquaintances and business associates. The business associates will be easy. He was a member of the Melbourne Club and various committees.'

'Any names you can give us will save us time, Mrs Lord.'

'I know this will seem strange, Inspector, but I really don't know any of Peter's particular friends. I suspect he thought I might disapprove.'

'Why might you disapprove?'

'Well, I wouldn't, but Peter was old-fashioned, almost Edwardian in some ways. His friends were artists, I know that. There are several drawings and paintings on the walls here that were done by his friends.'

'We'll take down those names, of course. Did any of his friends come here to the house?'

'No. Never. You must find that very peculiar.'

'Not at all, Mrs Lord. We all divide our lives into discrete compartments to some extent. I have friends who've never met each other, and I'm sure that's true of Sergeant Sable as well.'

'Yes, sir,' Joe said, without thinking, and immediately wondered if it was in fact true. He had friends outside the police force who'd never met any of his police colleagues, that was true. He'd never wondered until now about Helen Lord's friends. He'd certainly never met any of them, and she'd never mentioned them. His incuriosity about this didn't trouble him greatly, but being obliged to acknowledge it did cause him to feel mild surprise.

'I'd appreciate it, Mrs Lord,' Lambert said, 'if you'd permit us to have a look at Peter's bedroom.'

'Of course.'

'Is it against the rules if I join you?' Helen asked.

'It is, Constable Lord, but I'd welcome your help anyway.'

Helen, who'd been expecting a rebuff, was visibly taken aback. Lambert's invitation demonstrated his trust in her, his trust that she wouldn't attempt to conceal anything incriminating or unseemly.

Peter Lillee's bedroom was twice as large as the largest room in Titus Lambert's house. Indeed, he thought as he stepped into it that it might accommodate his entire house. The walls were hung with paintings and drawings. There were no photographs. Ros Lord, who stayed in the doorway, said that she cleaned and tidied the room daily, but that Peter maintained it in a way that made her efforts unnecessary.

'He always made his own bed, and his bathroom was spotless.'

'We're going to have to do awful things, like look under the bed, aren't we?' Helen said.

'Worse than that, we're going to have to look under the mattress,' Inspector Lambert said.

Titus, Joe, and Helen searched Peter Lillee's room with a thoroughness that disrupted its order, however careful they tried to be. Early in the search, Helen withdrew an elegant suitcase from a wardrobe. It was locked. She placed it on the bed, assuming that the fact that it was locked was significant. Its weight suggested that it wasn't empty. At the end of the search, which had revealed nothing beyond the fact that Lillee's tastes in everything from socks to shaving soap were expensive, the three of them stood looking down at the suitcase.

'It's an Alzer, Louis Vuitton,' Joe said. 'My parents had a couple of them, which I inherited. They were destroyed in the fire.'

'Valuable?' Titus asked.

'They're the type of suitcase you pass down to your children. Ridiculously expensive.' He added, because he thought this last statement might sound like a rebuke to Lillee's extravagance, 'But they're sturdy and elegant. If I could afford it, I'd replace the ones I lost.'

Helen missed this attempt at mollification because Joe's initial comment hadn't struck her as being anything but accurate.

'Where would you put the key if you didn't want anyone to find it?' Titus asked.

'Behind, under, or in something,' Helen said. 'We've looked under and in everything already.' She went to one of the pictures on the wall and moved it, so she could see its back. Nothing. She tried another, and another. The key was taped behind the fourth picture — an exquisite Dobell pencil-sketch portrait of Lillee.

'Why that drawing, I wonder?' she asked. Under other circumstances, Joe might have suggested that the tone she used when she said the word 'drawing' didn't quite catch the mastery of the portrait.

The suitcase snapped open with the satisfying click of a well-tooled lock. Titus took each item out of the case and placed it on the bed. There were three photographs of a woman, two of them casual and one of them a formal studio portrait. On the back of the studio portrait were the words, 'To Peter, with love, Lillian'. There were several letters, a catechism, rosary beads, and a small crucifix. A bronze Christ depended from a plain, polished-wood cross. There was nothing else in the suitcase. Each of the letters was from Lillian Johnson, and a cursory read revealed that the relationship between her and Lillee had been intimate. On the inside cover of the catechism was a dedication to Peter Lillee from Monsignor McGrath of St Patrick's Cathedral.

'Does any of this mean anything to you?' Inspector Lambert asked. Helen said she had no idea who either of these people was and that she had never heard her uncle mention them. Ros Lord, who'd remained outside the bedroom throughout the search, came in to examine the contents of the suitcase. No, she'd never seen or heard of Lillian Johnson, and Monsignor McGrath was a complete mystery.

'Had your brother converted to Catholicism, Mrs Lord?'

'Certainly not. He never expressed any interest in religion. In fact, I always thought he was rather hostile to it.'

Helen chose a letter and read it through closely.

'Uncle Peter was engaged to this Lillian woman. Did you know about this, Mum?'

'Good God,' she said, 'I had no idea.' She paused. 'And I'll be frank with you, Inspector, I didn't think my brother was much interested in women.'

'It seems he was interested in at least one woman,' Helen said.

The search and the contents of the suitcase had distracted Ros and Helen from the news of Peter Lillee's death. Now the awful reality of it hit them both. Ros Lord sat on the edge of her brother's bed and began to weep. Helen moved to her, sat beside her, and drew her mother's head to her shoulder. Inspector Lambert and Joe Sable withdrew to the corridor outside the bedroom.

By EARLY AFTERNOON of the day on which Peter Lillee's body had been found, Inspector Lambert had drawn up a comprehensive list of people who needed to be interviewed. He wasn't going to wait for the autopsy and toxicology results. His instincts told him that this wasn't a case of suicide. Misadventure perhaps. Murder possibly. He had the names of artists, business acquaintances, and the people listed in Lillee's address book. At the top of the list were Lillian Johnson and Monsignor McGrath. Lambert had an aversion to the cathedral and the priests who staffed it. That interview would be done by Sergeant Sable. Lambert would visit Lillian that afternoon.

Watson Cooper's murder of Constables Beckett and Humphries had affected the mood at Russell Street Police Headquarters. In the gymnasium, men praised Senior Sergeant Maher's courage in facing Cooper and shooting him dead. Knowing that Joe had been there, they wanted details from him. They noticed his reluctance to join in the general praise of Maher and put it down to what many of them considered his stand-offishness.

Joe wasn't popular either inside or outside Homicide. There was a feeling of resentment that he'd been promoted too quickly — more quickly than manpower shortages within the force warranted. There was also a sense that Inspector Lambert favoured him, and Lambert himself had made enemies among his fellow officers. There was also the inescapable fact that Joe Sable was a Jew. This was a minor mark against him and not nearly as problematic as being a Catholic or a Protestant, depending on which side you stood.

Joe had never felt unpopular, largely because he'd never taken much interest in his colleagues. He never thought about them as friends, or potential friends. He'd been resistant to the forging of bonds among fellow officers, a resistance that was unusual and alienating. If he'd formed close bonds with his colleagues, his decision to talk to Inspector Lambert about what he considered to be the murder of Watson Cooper by Sergeant Maher would have been more difficult. Lambert had just told him that he was sending him to interview Monsignor McGrath when Joe said, 'I need to talk to you, sir, about Watson Cooper.'

Lambert put down his pen.

'Go on.'

'I believe, well, I *know* that when Sergeant Maher shot him, he was unarmed. There's no question about it being self-defence. It wasn't. It was murder.'

'That is a very serious allegation, Sergeant. Tell me exactly what you saw.'

'When I entered the room, Watson Cooper was sitting with his back against a wall. He looked as if he'd fallen there. Sergeant Maher raised his gun and fired, I think two rounds, into Cooper's chest. There was a rifle, Cooper's rifle, on the floor near Maher's feet. Maher's first words to me were, "He was going to shoot me." It was after he'd said these words that he kicked the rifle towards Cooper.'

'You can't unsay this, Sergeant. You're accusing a fellow officer of murder, and you'll get no sympathy or support.'

'Yes, sir. I know that, and I know that most people will think that Maher did everyone a favour by killing Cooper, but it looked like an execution to me.'

Titus Lambert looked at Joe and felt both sympathy and pity for him. He felt, too, slightly sick at the thought that he, Lambert, should bear some responsibility for the stresses and traumas that had visited Joe since his arrival in Homicide. He'd been advised against accepting someone so young, but he'd seen something in Joe Sable that had impressed him. He was inexperienced, it was true, but he had the kind of integrity that Lambert wanted in the people he worked closely with. Time would cure the inexperience, and although the integrity would be tested, Lambert believed that Joe wouldn't fail the test. What Lambert hadn't counted on was that this young officer would suffer torture in the course of an investigation, or that revenge would be taken upon him and would make him homeless. Lambert could only imagine what it might feel like to lose everything in a fire. When George Starling set fire to Joe's flat — and Lambert had no doubt that Starling was the culprit — he destroyed every personal and family object that Joe owned. Photographs, letters, things left to him by his late parents, everything of real and sentimental value had been destroyed. Joe wore another man's clothes and lived in another man's house, and tragedy had reached into that house, too. Now this. Well, he'd been right about Joe's integrity, but Joe was going to pay a high price for it, and Lambert knew that he couldn't protect him from the worst of what was to come.

'I know, Sergeant, that what you've told me is the truth, and not just the truth as you see it, but the *truth*. When this investigation gets under way, you'll be accused either of lying outright or of having misinterpreted something that you saw. I know very little about this Senior Sergeant Maher, but one thing I'm sure of is that he's not going to roll over and admit to shooting Watson Cooper in cold blood. He's going to say that you're lying. It will be your word against his.'

'I understand that, sir.'

'How many people here know where you're living?'

'I think only Sergeant Reilly, so unless he's mentioned it to anyone, he's the only one.'

'He won't have mentioned it. Reilly isn't given to gossip. I want you to keep your living arrangements under your hat.'

Lambert didn't need to elaborate.

'All right, Sergeant. The process will begin. Meanwhile, I want to know what Peter Lillee's connection to Monsignor McGrath is — or was. The cathedral is a short walk up the street. McGrath is expecting you. I telephoned ahead.'

As JOE WALKED towards St Patrick's Cathedral, he thought of his friend Guy Kirkham. He hadn't heard from him for many months. He knew he was in New Guinea, and he assumed that he was still alive. He'd explained to Inspector Lambert that Guy's family disapproved of their friendship, and although he'd always known, because Guy had told him, that their disapproval was on account of his being a Jew, he'd dismissed their anti-Semitism as irrelevant and silly. It'd had no effect whatsoever on his friendship with Guy, whose relationship with his parents was fraught for other reasons. Guy had declared, over one cataclysmic lunch, that he was an atheist. Joe hadn't been there — Joe had never been invited to lunch — but Guy had described vividly the ensuing paternal rage and maternal tears.

Guy had had no intention of joining any of the forces. He wasn't a pacifist, but neither, as he'd declared, was he a martyr. The government, blithely indifferent to his feelings, conscripted him in 1942, and because conscripted men couldn't be sent to an overseas theatre of war, he, along with his fellow 'chocos' as they were derisively called, had been sent to New Guinea. New Guinea was technically overseas, but it was an Australian dependency, and so conscripted men could be sent to defend it and to halt the Japanese advance south.

From reports in the newspapers, Joe knew that the New Guinea campaign had been vicious and deadly. He sometimes felt guilty that he'd been unable to keep Guy at the front of his thoughts, and recently he'd slipped from Joe's thoughts altogether. Now, though, as Joe approached the cathedral, Guy's frequent railings against the Church in which he'd been raised came to mind.

Guy had characterised the priests who he was supposed to revere as dull-witted and mediocre. The only priest Joe had ever spoken to — Father Brennan in Port Fairy — had done nothing to challenge Guy's assessment. Guy had dismissed the Mass and all its sacraments as hocus-pocus used to distract a gullible and tractable congregation. Guy was the only of Joe's friends who was a Catholic, so it was Guy's vision of the Church which Joe accepted as accurate. He'd never been inside any Catholic church, although he was familiar with their gaudy interiors from Italian paintings. He assumed that the cathedral, despite its Gothic exterior, would be a riot of baroque or rococo extravagance within.

When he stepped through the main door, the cathedral's interior restraint surprised him. What also surprised him was the immediate effect the space had on him. He wasn't overwhelmed by it, but he was uplifted by it in a way that stunned him. It had nothing to do with religion and certainly nothing to do with Catholicism. This was, for Joe, an aesthetic response, a joyous rush of wonder at the majesty of architecture. He'd had this response before, to art and to music, and he never confused it with the spiritual claims for it made by priests, vicars, and rabbis. He shared with Guy an irritation that churches tried to corral such feelings and name them as evidence of God's largesse.

He began to walk up the nave towards the main altar. A priest appeared from behind one of the great pillars, which looked to Joe like bundled rods of stone rising towards the distant, unadorned ceiling. The priest approached Joe, smiling. They met halfway up the nave.

'You are Detective Sable?'

'Monsignor McGrath. Am I pronouncing that title correctly?'

McGrath laughed. 'You're not a Catholic, then, Detective. Although to be truthful I knew that when you came into the cathedral.'

'That's very Sherlock Holmes of you.'

'The clues weren't very subtle, I'm afraid. You didn't dip your fingers into the holy water and bless yourself, and you didn't genuflect before walking up the nave.'

'I'm sorry. I should have brushed up on the rules.'

'They're not rules really. Just observances.'

McGrath steered Joe back towards the front door of the cathedral.

'We should speak outside, I think,' he said.

Once outside, McGrath took Joe to the northern side of the cathedral and indicated a seat, in full sun.

'Does the sun bother you, Detective? I'm inside too much and take every opportunity to enjoy it.'

McGrath's even tan struck Joe as putting the lie to this statement, and he noticed how carefully McGrath arranged his spotless soutane when he crossed his legs.

'How should I address you?' Joe asked.

'Oh, Monsignor is fine. Are you Church of England?'

'No, I'm Jewish.'

'Oh, I see.'

Joe wasn't sure what this response meant, and he ignored it. 'I believe Inspector Lambert passed on to you the news of Peter Lillee's death.'

'He did. I was profoundly shocked.'

'We found your name inside a catechism that you'd given to Mr Lillee. His sister and niece are at a loss to explain this.'

'It isn't a mystery, Detective. Although perhaps it is to his family. I had no idea that he hadn't shared his news with them.'

'News?'

'Peter had been taking instruction from me for many months.'

'Instruction?'

'Peter was about to be baptised into the Catholic Church. We'd set a date. He was a very private man, but I didn't realise just how private. Perhaps he wasn't close to his sister and niece.'

'They lived in the same house. They were very close.' Joe saw no reason to add that he, too, shared that house.

'Inspector Lambert gave me no details about Peter's death, but if the police are involved, I'm assuming it wasn't a heart attack.'

'Mr Lillee's body was found on the banks of the Yarra River in Kew, not far from his house.'

'I see. And the circumstances are suspicious?'

'There were no signs of violence and no evidence that there was another person present when he died.'

'If you're suggesting suicide, Detective, you can rule that out. Peter was committed to his faith, and suicide is a grave sin in the eyes of God and in the eyes of the Church. He would no more take his own life than I would.'

'What do you know about his private life?'

'Very little. We never spoke of it. All our meetings were confined to instruction in the Catholic faith.'

'Why do you think he wanted to become a Catholic?'

'Wanting to join the one, true Church doesn't require an explanation.' McGrath smiled at Joe as though this statement were a theological lay-down misère.

'We'd welcome you, Detective. After all, Jesus was a Jew, wasn't he?'

'He was. He wasn't, however, a Catholic.'

Monsignor McGrath laughed.

'That is unquestionably true, Detective. We like to think, though, that he got the ball rolling.'

McGrath's obvious enjoyment in this repartee was getting under Joe's skin. It was as if, being dead, Peter Lillee had squandered McGrath's interest in him.

'Do you know anyone who might want to harm Mr Lillee?' Joe asked in a tone that signalled an end to banter.

'Murder? You think this was murder?'

Joe wished that Helen Lord was with him. She would have extracted more from this smug priest than he could. Thinking of her, and the questions she would have been unafraid of asking, he quelled his nerves and asked, 'Could Mr Lillee have been meeting someone late at night, down by the river?'

'Are you insinuating a homosexual assignation?'

'I'm asking if you think this might have been possible.'

'Again, Detective, Peter Lillee would not have endangered his immortal soul by indulging in such sinful behaviour.'

'Isn't that what confession is for?'

'No, Detective, it isn't. Confession is not, despite what non-Catholics think, a get-out-of-jail-free card that licenses bad behaviour.'

Joe had never heard the get-out-of-jail expression, but surmised its meaning.

'Why do you think Mr Lillee might have been down by the Yarra so late at night?'

'I have no idea. Perhaps he was walking to clear his head. He has … had … heavy responsibilities, and I imagine that sometimes a late-night walk might be a way of winding down.'

Monsignor McGrath couldn't disguise the irritation in his voice.

'I don't believe I can help you any further, Detective. If his sister or his niece — was it? — if either of them wishes to speak with me, she is most welcome to do so. I'll say a Mass for Peter, and a rosary. Please let them know that. It may be of some comfort.'

Joe was certain that neither Ros nor Helen would be comforted by such an empty gesture. He thanked Monsignor McGrath and left.

'WE WERE ENGAGED to be married.'

Lillian Johnson stood by the fireplace in her flat in Camberwell. She'd been sitting opposite Inspector Lambert, but she'd felt as if she'd begin to shake uncontrollably unless she stood up and moved about.

'I was so angry with him, Inspector.'

'You broke off the engagement just last night?'

'No. Peter broke it off. Oh, I knew it was coming, and I was cruel, I suppose. I made him say it. I didn't make it easy for him.'

'From what you've told me, you were very close for a very long time. Why did he break it off?'

Lillian sat down, but before she spoke, she stood up again.

'It was ridiculous. It makes me so angry even now, when what I should be feeling is grief. He'd converted to Catholicism, and suddenly, instead of being his lover, I was an occasion for sin, as they say.'

'What an awful expression.'

'Everything about the Catholic Church is awful, Inspector, and I should know.'

'Why did he need to end your engagement? Why couldn't you have been married?'

'Catholics don't marry divorced women, Inspector. We are tarnished goods. We'd been intimate for years, so you can imagine how galling Peter's new-found chastity was. Last night he thought he was being kind and thought I'd admire his commitment to his so-called faith. I thought he was weak and pathetic, and I'm afraid I told him so.'

'Was he upset when he left here last night?'

'I don't know. I went to my bedroom. I couldn't bear to look at him. I hope he was upset, but you know, I suspect he wasn't especially.'

She took the photograph she'd retrieved from the fireplace and handed it to Lambert.

'He wrote that with a cool, steady hand, wouldn't you say?'

Inspector Lambert looked at the image of Peter Lillee, confident and smiling, and turned it over.

'"Forgive me",' he read. 'What do you think he was asking you to forgive? Something he'd done or something he was about to do?'

'It's not a suicide note, Inspector. He's not the type.'

'You said he was weak. Might that imply ...?'

'His weakness was in his dealings with me. His great strength was his sense of himself. You don't get to be as rich as Peter was without having unplumbable depths of self-regard.'

'After he left here, did you perhaps go out and meet him later?'

'You think I murdered him?'

'It's a question I have to ask, Mrs Johnson.'

She was silent for a moment. 'You say he's dead. I can't ... I don't ... He can't be dead. He was sitting where you're sitting just a few hours ago. He simply cannot be dead. If he was really dead, I wouldn't still be angry with him, would I?' She looked at him desperately. '*Would* I?'

Lillian Johnson took a deep shaky breath, but in the expelling of it, she fell to her knees and began to shudder. Her face, already pale, was now pallid. Even her lips had lost their colour. She began to sway, and Inspector Lambert hurried to her and caught her before she fell sideways, unconscious.

Lambert felt her pulse and telephoned for an ambulance. The pulse was strong, but this looked like more than a fainting spell, and Lillian wasn't coming out of it. She remained unconscious, with Lambert holding her hand, until the ambulance arrived.

It was only later, after he'd been told that Lillian Johnson had had a mild stroke, that Lambert realised that she hadn't answered his question about meeting Peter Lillee later in the evening. The doctor who was treating her said that she'd be unable to answer questions for at least a week, but that she was expected to recover well, although you never could tell with strokes.

6

MARIA PLUSCHOW WENT into Port Fairy as infrequently as possible. Before the war, she and her husband had made no secret of their admiration for Adolf Hitler and National Socialism. In the 1930s, this was seen by most people as merely eccentric, although they'd never had much time for Mr Pluschow, who was, after all, foreign. He also spoke with a thick accent, and nobody understood what Maria, whose real name was Mary, saw in him. Despite her being a local girl, once she'd married Pluschow she'd become something of an outsider. This hadn't bothered her. It was only a matter of time before National Socialism assumed its rightful place in Australian politics, and when that happened, Maria would settle a few scores.

Mr Pluschow had died in 1939, which had spared him the indignity of being interned, but it had left his wife quite alone. She had money, but no friends to speak of, unless you counted Hardy Truscott as a friend. She'd known Truscott for many years. He'd been a regular at the meetings of the National Socialists in the 1930s. He lived in Warrnambool, about a forty-minute drive from Port Fairy. She'd kept in contact with him by mail. He was a strange little man: myopic, thickly bespectacled, and bald. He wasn't physically attractive, but Maria was drawn to Truscott's unusual vision for what the Nazis could achieve.

Truscott was a spiritual man, who wasn't interested in dreary politics. He sent Maria books by his great hero and teacher, a man named Alexander Rud Mills, and Maria had read them. One in particular had convinced her that Rud Mills was a sort of prophet: *The First Guide Book to the Anglecyn Church of Odin, containing some of the chief rites of the Church and some hymns for the use of the Church.* She and Hardy Truscott, who'd had a long correspondence with Rud Mills, and who'd been among the small group of people who'd met with him regularly in Melbourne, found in the pages of this book a convincing philosophy to underpin their faith in National Socialism. Rud Mills saw in National Socialism a structure that could disseminate and institutionalise the new religion dedicated to Odin and the other great northern gods. Rud Mills also shared, in an exaggerated form, Nazism's obsessive hatred of the Jews, blacks, and the impure, weakened races that emerged when the Aryan race sullied itself by breeding with inferior people.

Truscott, deeply schooled in Rud Mills's beliefs, guided Maria through the more arcane passages in Rud Mills's book, and he read in his reedy, flat voice from Rud Mills's *Hail Odin!* These poems, which Maria recognised as execrable, nevertheless generated spiritual uplift whenever she and Truscott discussed the redemptive possibilities of Odinism. For her, the mysticism was seductive and utterly convincing, and she believed that she may have found in George Starling an as-yet-untutored acolyte. She'd sensed a need in him beyond his fierce desire for revenge.

She used her petrol ration sparingly; so sparingly that it had been months since she'd made the extravagant journey all the way to Warrnambool. She'd thought about driving to Truscott's house, but remembered that he didn't like unexpected visitors even if those visitors were sympathetic to his beliefs. Years of official harassment had made the unscheduled knock on the door a source of immediate and visceral unease. She decided instead to drive into Port Fairy and to send a telegram to Hardy Truscott from there.

The nosy Parker in the post office, a woman named Bell, couldn't be trusted as far as you could throw her. That was Maria's firm belief, but that applied to almost everyone in the town. She'd learned, and nurtured, a great contempt for Catholic and Protestant alike. Truscott had taught her that Christianity in any form was just a Jew religion, with a Jew as its god, and with a vile and dangerous belief in equality. The idea that a black, or a Jew, or a cripple were 'equal' to a pure Aryan was laughable.

When she entered the post office, there were three people ahead of her, each of them exchanging banalities as they waited. Maria wasn't invited to join them. These women weren't rude exactly, although their studied indifference to Maria's presence was a kind of hostility. There was no small talk when Maria reached the counter. She pushed a piece of paper towards Mrs Bell, and Mrs Bell pushed it back along with a blank telegram. Mrs Bell saw no reason why Maria Pluschow couldn't fill out the telegram herself, rather than expect her to write out the six words.

Maria transcribed her message — 'Dinner tomorrow night. Do come. Maria'— paid for it, and left. Hardy Truscott wouldn't reply to the telegram. He would either show up or he wouldn't — but he always showed up when invited to dinner, because Maria was an excellent cook. On more than one occasion in the past, she'd also allowed Truscott into her bed. This was never a certainty, but had occurred sufficiently often to make it an enticing probability. She was worried that George wouldn't be impressed by Hardy Truscott. He wasn't impressive physically, and he lacked magnetism, but his message was compelling, and it seemed to Maria that George might be susceptible to the glorious power of the old gods, the real gods, the gods who offered hard, strong remedies to the flabby, sentimental faith of the Jewish Christians.

INSPECTOR LAMBERT'S BRIEFING on the deaths of the two policemen in Coburg, and on the discovery of Peter Lillee's body, had left his officers with a good deal to talk about. They noticed that he was oddly muted in the explanation of Watson Cooper's death. One or two of them had already heard from Kevin Maher that Joe Sable might cause trouble, although Maher hadn't been explicit. He certainly hadn't admitted to shooting an unarmed Cooper. All he'd said was that Sable seemed to be up himself, and they took this to imply that Maher thought that Sable might try to claim some credit. Even though they'd never seen any evidence of this in Joe's behaviour, they were willing to accept it as a possibility simply because he seemed to enjoy the protection of Inspector Lambert.

Ron Dunnart, who'd been briefed separately about Lillee's death, and who'd been given a list of people to talk to, was mildly disconcerted by this news. He would have been one of the last people, possibly the last person, to speak to Lillee before his death. He couldn't, of course, declare this. He couldn't declare any knowledge of Peter Lillee at all. He regretted having taken that dullard Bob O'Dowd into his confidence. O'Dowd, because he had the imagination of a simpleton, would assume that he, Dunnart, had had something to do with Lillee's death, which might cause O'Dowd to panic and say the wrong thing to the wrong person. Dunnart was unsure how to proceed. Should he take O'Dowd aside and threaten him? Should he give him the benefit of the doubt and assume that he'd be smart enough to realise that trouble for Dunnart meant trouble for O'Dowd?

Sergeant Bob O'Dowd wasn't just slightly disconcerted by the news of Peter Lillee's death, he was shocked by it. When he heard about it in Lambert's briefing, he felt ill — so ill he thought he might be sick. There was no doubt in his mind that Dunnart had killed Lillee. Blackmail was one thing. Murder was quite another.

He knew that Dunnart would approach him and point out the fucking obvious — that if Dunnart was exposed, he would be implicated too. And Dunnart was such a ruthless bastard that he'd find a way of shifting the blame, of loading it onto O'Dowd's shoulders. Could he avoid telling his wife? He'd never been good at disguising his anxieties from her. She'd know that something was up. He'd been no good at lying to her either, and God knows he'd tried often enough. She always found him out and made his life miserable for a period. 'I can read you like a book,' she was fond of saying, 'and a kiddies' book at that.'

O'Dowd didn't catch Dunnart's eye during the briefing, and afterwards, he slipped away before Dunnart could confront him. He had work to do, but he wouldn't be able to concentrate, so he went to the gymnasium and tried to ease his nerves by punching a bag. His psoriasis, which itched at his wrists, elbows, and ankles, would flare up. That much was certain.

Ros Lord had prepared dinner for Helen and Joe and had automatically made enough for Peter as well. She'd also absently set his place at the table, and when the three of them sat down, the spare setting was strangely comforting, as if Peter Lillee might walk through the door at any moment.

The soup was too salty, and the meat was tough — failures of technique which were rare for Ros. No one noticed. Both Ros and Helen were half numb, and Joe felt crippled by awkwardness at being a witness to their grief. He wanted to tell Helen that he'd told Inspector Lambert about Maher, but that somehow felt petty and self-interested. Sitting at the dinner table with these two women, he felt diminished by their strength. He realised, suddenly, how much he admired both of them, and how little he knew of each of them.

'Dunnart and O'Dowd call here, and within twenty-four hours, Uncle Peter is dead. That can't be a coincidence.'

Joe wanted to say that it could easily be a coincidence, but instead he nodded in agreement.

'Inspector Lambert is sure that no one inside Homicide knows that you and Mrs Lord are related to Peter, and they don't know, either, that I'm staying here for a while.'

'Reilly knows that I live in this house,' Helen said. 'He was in the car when Lambert dropped me off a few weeks ago.'

'Inspector Lambert said that David Reilly wasn't the gossiping type.'

Helen's face assumed its usual moue at the sound of Reilly's name.

'The two policemen who came to our door were bad specimens, Joe.' Ros Lord began to clear the plates away. 'One of them was worse than the other. The man who called himself Dunnart had that bullying quality about him that you see in policemen who think they've been overlooked for promotion. The other one was the second fiddle. Do you think Peter was mixed up in something?'

'I honestly don't know, Mrs Lord.'

'Both of them will be investigating Uncle Peter's death, won't they?'

'I suppose they will be.'

'Lambert needs to know that they called here, and they need to be taken off the investigation. They're both persons of interest.'

'I haven't spoken to Reilly yet about Dunnart. I'll tell Inspector Lambert first thing tomorrow that they came here.' Joe looked from one to the other. 'Inspector Lambert knows that Peter didn't take his own life.' Joe noticed that Helen's eyes widened slightly, and he hurried to clarify. 'I don't mean he's got extra information. I just mean that he trusts your and Mrs Lord's judgement about Peter.'

'Does Inspector Lambert think it might be murder?' Ros Lord asked.

'He doesn't know, Mrs Lord. I'm sorry. If suicide is ruled out, murder isn't the only possibility.'

'Yes, I see. Misadventure. Or something else.'

Joe was reminded that Ros Lord had been married to a policeman.

Helen and Ros took the dishes to the kitchen, and they refused Joe's offer to help. His mother had always insisted that Joe help with the washing up. His father could never be persuaded to do the same. This had been a daily skirmish between them until the great silence had descended on the house and all conversation between them had ceased. Now, though, Joe assumed that Helen and her mother wanted the privacy that this small domestic chore offered. He was left alone in the dining room looking at the rich portrait of Peter Lillee that hung on one of the walls. It was beautifully done, Joe thought. He had looked at it many times and admired it. Peter had thought it entertainingly vulgar. The skill with which it had been painted rescued it from being truly vulgar. The artist, Forbes Carlisle, was someone who might be worth talking to. The rendering of Peter's face wasn't just accomplished. It spoke of someone who knew the sitter well.

Helen returned to the dining room.

'I've never liked that picture. Uncle Peter would never have worn a coat like that.'

Joe turned to face Helen.

'It's more of a dressing gown. I think Peter liked the joke.'

'Mum's relieved me of washing up so you can tell me about the investigation.'

Joe didn't hesitate. He suggested they go into the library, where he told Helen about his interview with Monsignor McGrath and how unsatisfactory it had been.

'He seemed to think that converting to Catholicism was the most sensible thing in the world.'

'So he didn't see it as being a symptom of something that might be troubling.'

'God, no. If anything, he saw it as proof that Peter was healthy and wise.'

'And wealthy of course.'

'Yes. I left that out deliberately. I'm pretty sure Monsignor McGrath wouldn't lavish such personal attention on a poor man.'

They spoke for two hours, ringing changes on things already said and speculating with small variations on aspects of the case, at the end of which each of them was exhausted. Helen felt reassured that Joe would keep nothing from her and that he wouldn't make the patronising assumption that either she or her mother needed shielding from whatever a close examination of Peter's private life might expose.

'I've promised Mum that I'll tell her everything.'

Joe thought this was reasonable. He didn't know that such a promise represented a significant change in the relationship between mother and daughter.

'There is something you need to know, too, Joe. If Uncle Peter was murdered, Mother and I ought to be suspects, which means you're guilty of a gross breach of professional conduct in talking to me about the investigation.'

Joe hadn't thought about this, and it made him feel queasy.

'I don't understand,' he said.

'I'm just telling you that Lambert wants you to stay here so you can keep an eye on us.'

'No.'

'Listen to me, Joe. You should *not* tell him that you're keeping me up to speed. He's testing you. When you see him tomorrow, he won't ask you outright, but he'll be listening for clues that you've breached protocol, and he'll be very, very disappointed if he thinks that you have. The thing is, of course, that you have.'

Joe felt ambushed, and his confusion was obvious. Helen reached across and put her hand on the back of his hand, a gesture she'd never made before.

'I'm not trying to upset you, Joe. I'm just telling you that Lambert is good at his job, and he wants you to be good at yours. If he thinks you're giving me information I shouldn't have, he'll know your inexperience is a liability and that he shouldn't have pushed for your promotion. Lots of blokes in there resent your promotion. You do know that, don't you?'

'Why are you saying these things to me?'

'Because you're my eyes and ears inside Homicide, and I need you to keep your position there.'

Joe stood up and walked to a wall crowded with small drawings. He kept his back to Helen as he tried to marshal his emotions. Without knowing quite why, he felt humiliated.

'Joe, I'm sorry, but you ought to have known that Mum and I would be persons of interest.'

He knew she was right, but still he said, 'Why?'

'Because both Mum and I know what is in Uncle Peter's will.'

He turned around.

'Uncle Peter was a very wealthy man. Mum stands to inherit ten million pounds in cash and assets.' She paused. 'And Uncle Peter left two million pounds to me. So you see, we'd have good reason to get rid of him if we were that way inclined. And we'd have to do it before he married Lillian Johnson, wouldn't we?'

'You didn't know about Lillian Johnson.'

'We could be lying, Joe. We're not, of course, and it is terrible that she's now in hospital. Should we visit her? I don't know what to think about Lillian Johnson. It doesn't feel like she actually exists.'

'Well, she exists all right, but you and Mrs Lord might be as big a shock to her as she is to you.'

Helen sensed that Joe was holding something back.

'You're not telling me everything, are you, Joe?'

'On the night before Peter died, he'd called off the engagement.'

'Why?'

'He was about to be accepted into the Catholic Church. That made his relationship with her impossible.'

'She's not Catholic.'

'Not practising.'

Helen considered this for a moment.

'So she might have been angry enough to kill Uncle Peter. God, I'd like to meet her. I'd like to find out more about her — and before you say anything, Joe, I know that isn't possible at the moment. I hadn't thought of her as a suspect until now. I hadn't thought of her at all. But suddenly she's more than just a name on a letter.'

MAUDE AND TITUS Lambert were astonished by the plate of food that Maude's brother, Tom, put in front of them. It was a rabbit stew, but Tom had made it so flavoursome that it even made an impression on Maude's and Titus's indifferent palates. The stew represented much more than good cooking. It was proof that Tom's recovery from the violent torture to which he'd been subjected just a couple of months ago was occurring more rapidly than anyone might have hoped. The physical evidence of that torture could still be seen, although his body was healing well, and the only thing that still bothered him was a cigarette burn on his thigh, which had become infected and stubbornly refused to heal. The nightmares continued, but his confusion about what had happened to him had gone, and now he was able to stitch together the events of that terrible night into a coherent whole, where previously, disconnected moments would erupt in his mind with terrifying unpredictability. This meal of rabbit made Maude's spirits soar. When she'd first seen Tom in hospital after his rescue, she'd thought she'd lost him. When she looked at him now, she marvelled at his resilience.

If Maude and Titus had been in their own house in Brunswick, they would have discussed whatever Titus was working on over dinner. But while they were temporarily living with Tom Mackenzie, they confined their discussions to bed. Returning to Brunswick didn't just depend on Tom's recovery. Titus was reluctant to move back until George Starling had been captured. Starling had confronted Tom in the backyard of the house, and the risk of him returning was too great to expose Maude to that danger.

'This is delicious,' Maude said. 'I need this recipe.'

'Thanks,' Tom said, 'but let's face it Maudey, you're never going to make this. It's fiddly and time-consuming. You'd fall at the first hurdle.'

'Nonsense, Tom. I'm not that hopeless.'

'It's not about skill. It's about patience.'

'Try me.'

'OK. Let's just assume that you're willing to break down the carcase into manageable parts. Now, you need to salt the parts so that they're dry-cured.'

'All right. You win. You lost me at dry-cured.'

Tom laughed.

They talked easily about the main stories in that day's newspaper. In a pause in the conversation, Tom said, 'I'd like to talk to Joe Sable.'

'Are you sure, Tom?' Maude asked. 'You went through a terrible thing together.'

'But that's the point, Maude. We went through it together, and I need to talk to him. He must think I'm a bit of a prick. I haven't contacted him.'

'Joe doesn't think you're a prick,' Titus said. 'He wasn't as badly injured as you. He knows you need time to get well again.'

'Even so, I want to know what he thinks about what happened. I want to know if he's all right.'

Titus took a pen from his pocket and jotted down the telephone number of the house in Kew.

'Why is he in Kew? Why isn't he in his flat in Princes Hill?'

As briefly as he could, and because he believed that Tom was ready to hear it, Titus brought him up to date with George Starling's crimes. The fact that Joe was billeted in the same house as Constable Lord meant that Peter Lillee's death couldn't be edited from the account.

Later that night as Titus talked with Maude about Lillian Johnson, and Peter Lillee's conversion to Catholicism, he expressed his concern that he might have over-loaded Tom with grim news. Maude reassured him that if Tom was to talk with Joe, gaps in his knowledge would make conversation difficult, and it would put Joe in the awkward position of not knowing what and what not to tell Tom.

'I think you should ask Joe to come here for dinner tomorrow night. I'll tell Tom in the morning. He'll want to cook. It will be a good way of breaking the ice.'

'Won't they want privacy?'

'You can take me to the pictures after dinner. They'll have plenty of time to talk before we get back.'

Titus saw the sense in this and agreed to take Maude to the pictures, even though he thought most pictures were trivial and a waste of time. They then went over Titus's interview with Lillian Johnson. Maude, as she always did, pressed him for details.

'She was very firm, was she, about the message on the back of the photograph not being a suicide note?'

'Adamant. No one we've spoken to so far believes Peter Lillee would take his own life. Joe said the priest ruled it out as not just unlikely, but impossible.'

'There's all that eternal damnation stuff which is meant to discourage self-slaughter.'

Titus told Maude about Joe's accusations against Sergeant Maher.

'Sometimes, Titus, I think the world is a truly horrible place.'

'It is a horrible place, Maudey, but thank God you're in it.'

Maude laughed.

'The leaven in the lump,' she said.

THE WEATHER ON 30 March 1944 was hot, but not as hot as the previous days. Bushfires, which seemed to have been burning since January, continued to break out and threaten lives. A taint of burning eucalyptus remained in Melbourne's air. People had become so used to it they barely noticed it.

Joe felt something had shifted at the Russell Street headquarters. As soon as he entered, a group of four detectives, who might usually have nodded a greeting, turned away from him. It was subtle, and Joe thought perhaps that he'd misinterpreted what might have been a simple, undirected movement. They couldn't know yet about Maher; but of course they could. Maher might have warned his mates that Sable wasn't to be trusted. Maher must be in the building, Joe thought, and if he was, that would confirm that he was being questioned about the death of Watson Cooper.

As Joe turned into the corridor that led to Inspector Lambert's office, Detective Maher emerged from that office and walked towards him. Maher stopped, and for a moment Joe thought he was going to throw a punch. Instead, he leaned in towards Joe and said, 'You little Jew cunt,' then brushed past him.

Joe was surprised to find that his hands were shaking. The vitriol in Maher's voice had shocked him, even though he'd been expecting an ugly response from him.

Inspector Lambert knew as soon as he entered the office that he'd had a run-in with Maher. He signalled to him to sit down.

'I take it Detective Maher made his feelings obvious?'

'Yes, sir. He called me a little Jew cunt, which I took to mean that he's not happy.'

'I'm sorry, Sergeant. I'm afraid you'll have to gird your loins for a bit. Detective Maher was, of course, almost frothing at the mouth with outrage.'

'What will happen next?'

'I can't promise you a satisfactory outcome. It comes down to your word against his, and he's got a long, reasonably distinguished career behind him, and you're new to the job. I'm sure you're aware that there is some resentment in this building about your promotion.'

'Yes, sir, I am aware of that.'

'Maher believes, or so he says, that you're trying to big-note yourself at his expense. He denies everything that you've said. He claims you were throwing your weight around as if you thought the local coppers weren't up to scratch.'

'That's not true, sir.'

'I know that, Sergeant, but you need to be aware that the investigation triggered by your allegation will expose you to a great deal of unpleasantness, and having met Maher, I can assure you that he'll do everything in his power to wreck your career and your reputation.'

With more bravado than he was feeling, Joe said, 'Even if I could, sir, I wouldn't withdraw my allegation. I know what I saw, and what

I saw was an execution, and men like Maher shouldn't have power over the life or death of anyone.'

Inspector Lambert said that he would do what he could to protect Joe from the worst of what was to come, but he wanted an assurance in return that Joe would tell him the minute he thought any pressure he was under was compromising an investigation. They then turned to the Peter Lillee case. Joe's task that day was to find Forbes Carlisle, the artist who'd painted Lillee's portrait. Lillee had mentioned once that he was employed by the army to paint camouflage at Puckapunyal. Would he still be at that army base this late in the war? Inspector Lambert agreed that Carlisle might know more about Lillee than Lillee's business acquaintances, and he authorised the use of a police vehicle for the long drive to the base, should Carlisle still be there.

Just as Joe was about to leave, Lambert asked him if he could come that night for dinner at Tom Mackenzie's house in South Melbourne.

'Tom is anxious to talk with you. Maude and I will go to the cinema after dinner, so the two of you can talk. We'd appreciate it if you could come. Tom is making a good recovery, and this would help.'

'Of course, sir. That would be wonderful. I've wanted to talk to Tom ever since it happened.'

'I know you have, but Tom hasn't been well enough, until now. Shall we say 6.00?'

'WHERE DOES THE little prick live?'

Kevin Maher downed a neat whiskey after asking this question. He was sitting with Ron Dunnart and Bob O'Dowd in Dunnart's favourite watering hole, the Sarah Sands Hotel in Brunswick. It was 5.00 p.m., so they had a solid hour of drinking before the pub closed at 6.00 p.m. At least some of the drinks would be free. Many of the clientele in the Sarah Sands either owed Dunnart a favour or wanted to stay on the right side of him.

'He used to live in a flat in Princes Hill,' Dunnart said. 'It burned down a couple of weeks ago.'

'Couldn't happen to a nicer bloke.'

Bob O'Dowd didn't want to be here. He knew that Dunnart was keeping him close, that this invitation for a drink was a way of reminding him that Peter Lillee's death meant trouble for both of them. And O'Dowd didn't like this Maher bloke at all. Maher was cut from the same cloth as Dunnart. When he'd told them about Joe Sable's accusation, Dunnart had immediately taken Maher's side. Dunnart didn't ask if there was any truth in the accusation, because whether it was true or not was immaterial. A cop killer was dead. And the cop who'd killed him deserved a fucking medal, not a fucking investigation. O'Dowd was unnerved to be sitting drinking with two men who were capable of, possibly guilty of, murder. He could barely follow the conversation. He felt as if he'd been caught in a rip, or an undertow. He could feel himself surrendering to panic. He'd been an average detective, and that was all he wanted to be. Getting mixed up with Dunnart had been the worst mistake of his life. Lambert would discover Dunnart's connection to Lillee. He'd find out they'd visited the house. O'Dowd's mouth went dry.

'What's the matter with you?' Dunnart asked. 'You look like you're about to shit yourself.'

Dunnart's voice seemed far away, and O'Dowd's head began to swim. He thought he was going to faint.

'I need a piss,' he managed to say, and with a fierce act of concentration, he managed to stand and make his way to the malodorous urinal.

'What's his story?' Maher asked.

'It's a boring story. He's just one of those career coppers who'll never amount to anything. No talent and no ambition.'

'So what's he doing hanging around you?'

'That's just it, Kev, he's hanging around. Can't shake him.'

Kevin Maher had known Ron Dunnart long enough — although it had been a couple of years since they'd seen each other — to know that Dunnart didn't tolerate hangers-on. If O'Dowd was drinking with Dunnart, there had to be something in it for Dunnart. He let it go for the moment.

'Tell me about this Sable prick.'

'I don't know much about him, Kev. He's Lambert's pet. He and this woman were taken under Lambert's wing for some reason. She's gone now, thank Christ. Can you imagine that, a sheila in Homicide? Neither of them would have jobs here if there wasn't a war on. The Japs have got a lot to answer for. Anyway, this Sable bloke got badly beaten up a few weeks back. He looked like shit, but he still turned up for work. Trying to impress Lambert, of course.'

'Lambert seems like a bastard.'

'He is a bastard. Unfortunately, he's good at his job. And he doesn't like me one little bit.'

'So he'll back Sable.'

'Of course he will, but it's your word against his, and no one's going to believe Sable. Trust me, Kev, Sable is a loner. He's got no friends at Russell Street.'

'I'd like to hurt the bastard. He's a Jew, did you know that?'

Dunnart's prejudices had coalesced into a detestation of Masons. Joe Sable's Jewishness was of no matter to him, so he ignored Maher's remark.

'I'd leave Sable alone if I were you, Kev. If anything happens to him, you'll be the first person Lambert will suspect. Don't worry, he's about to become a social pariah.'

'What the fuck's a pariah?'

Bob O'Dowd returned to the table just as Dunnart had begun to improve Maher's vocabulary. O'Dowd was pale, and his forehead was beaded with sweat. Dunnart had no wish to discuss Lillee's death in front of Maher, so he decided to bring the drinking session to an end.

'It's been good to catch up, Kev. Let's do it again some time.'

Maher took the hint. He was happy enough that Sable was about to be ostracised.

'Can't hang about,' he said. 'The wife hates it when I come home stinking of alcohol.' He didn't bother with the social nicety of telling O'Dowd that it had been good to meet him. He simply stood up and left.

'What the fuck's going on with you, Bob? You're sweating like a pig and your hands are shaking.'

'Lambert's going to find out that you killed Peter Lillee, Ron. What happened? Did he make a pass at you or something? Why did you kill him?'

'Don't be a fucking idiot, Bob. I didn't kill Lillee. That goose was about to lay some golden eggs. Why would I kill it?'

'That's what I'm asking you, Ron. Why? I'm not going to say anything. I'm not that dumb. If you get done for this, Lambert's going to pin being an accessory on me. I know that.'

'Well, I'm glad that doesn't need to be explained to you, at least. You've been briefed, so you know there's no evidence of murder, and I'm telling you, I did *not* kill Peter Lillee. His death is a pain in the arse.'

Bob O'Dowd didn't believe a word Dunnart said. Dunnart raised a beer to his lips and watched O'Dowd over the top of it. O'Dowd looked briefly into Dunnart's eyes, but couldn't hold his gaze. He looked down. He realised that he hated Dunnart and that he was afraid of him. He wanted him out of his life, and he decided then and there that he would find a way to do this.

Forbes Carlisle was no longer at Puckapunyal, and the corporal who'd answered the telephone didn't know where he'd been posted, and even if he did, he wouldn't, as he said, be telling it to some bloke claiming to be a policeman. Joe spent the day instead talking to some of Peter Lillee's business acquaintances. He learned nothing from them to suggest that Lillee had any reason to take his own life. He was liked and respected, and he was considered honest to a fault in his financial dealings.

At the end of the day, Joe went straight from Russell Street to Tom Mackenzie's house in South Melbourne. The snub he'd experienced in the morning hadn't been repeated, but as he'd spent most of the day away from police headquarters, he wasn't sure yet if Maher's influence had begun to infect his fellow officers. When he arrived at the house, he remembered that he hadn't telephoned Ros Lord to tell her not to make dinner for him. Titus opened the door to him, and Joe, who felt this small careless act of rudeness keenly, asked if he could use the telephone before he even acknowledged Titus's greeting.

'You haven't rung the Lords have you?'

'No, sir. I just completely forgot.'

'I'll do it for you, Joe. I'm sure Ros Lord will understand. Go through to the living room. Tom and Maude are having a beer.'

Joe was suddenly nervous. He hadn't allowed himself to think too deeply about the torture that he and Tom had endured at the hands of Ptolemy Jones. Joe didn't know what to expect as he approached the living room. Tom was standing, ready to greet him, and Maude Lambert stood up as he entered. For a moment, nothing was said, then Tom put out his hand and said, 'Joe Sable. It's bloody good to see you.'

Joe took Tom's hand and adjusted the strength of his grip when he realised three of Tom's fingers were strapped. The fingers on his other hand were strapped, too.

'It's a bastard doing really basic stuff, but I'm adept at it now.'

'Good evening Joe,' Maude said, and her eyes filled with tears.

'Steady on, Maudey,' Tom said. 'This is a happy occasion.'

Maude laughed and moved towards Titus when he came into the room. Tom stood beside Joe and faced them.

'So, who looks worse do you reckon?'

'You do, Tom,' said Maude without hesitation. 'By a long way. Joe's cuts and bruises have nearly gone away. You still look pretty sad and battered.'

'I look better the more beers you have,' Tom said, 'and Joe hasn't even had one yet.'

There was no awkwardness between Tom and Joe. The only awkwardness Joe felt was the familiar awkwardness he experienced whenever he was with Inspector Lambert. He felt this too with Maude Lambert. How could they find him anything but callow and probably even foolish? He was intimidated by their intelligence and was never sufficiently at ease to express himself coherently. He would have been surprised to know that neither Titus nor Maude found him incoherent or dull.

Tom was apologetic about the quality of the dinner. It was just rissoles and vegetable stew, but they were the best rissoles Joe had ever tasted. Conversation was mostly about the sensational reports in that day's paper about the inquest into the murder of a woman in 1934.

She'd become known as the Pyjama Girl, and the case had never been solved despite the body having been preserved in formalin and put on display. Joe, who'd been a lad of fifteen when the body was discovered near Albury, remembered the speculation in the press at the time. Like everyone else, he'd been intrigued by the lurid details of the towel-wrapped head, the gunshot wound, the evidence of a savage beating, and the rather louche yellow silk pyjamas she'd been wearing. And then there was the macabre decision to put the body on display and invite the public to come to see it in the hope that somebody might recognise the cosmetically improved corpse. Now, ten years after the discovery of the body, an inquest was being held in Melbourne, because a Melbourne man had confessed to the crime. Antonio Agostini had declared that the Pyjama Girl was his young wife, Linda, and that he'd killed her accidentally and panicked and disposed of the body. At this stage in the inquest, however, Agostini's evidence was being contradicted by an opposing claim that the body was that of Anna Philomena Morgan.

As the head of Homicide, Titus knew more about the case than he was willing to reveal over dinner. Maude knew already that Titus was wary of the New South Wales Police Commissioner, William McKay, and that the rush to extradite Agostini to Victoria and to solve this notorious mystery had as much to do with McKay's need to prop up his reputation as it had to do with the truth of the matter. Linda Agostini had been missing since 1934. There was no doubt about that. And as Titus had said to Maude, there was every reason to believe that Agostini had killed her. But was she the Pyjama Girl, or was this the perfect opportunity for McKay to garner publicity? Neither Tom nor Joe pressed Titus for details.

'What picture are you going to see?' Tom asked.

Titus groaned. 'Maude wants to see *You Were Never Lovelier*.'

'A friend of mine saw it,' Maude said, 'and recommended it. Apparently, Rita Hayworth does a brilliant dance with Fred Astaire, and who doesn't like Fred Astaire?'

Maude and Titus left earlier than they needed to.

'Titus knows more about the Pyjama Girl case than he's letting on,' Tom said.

'I'm sure he does, but he's not going to take someone as junior as I am into his confidence.'

'You're a sergeant. That's not so junior.'

'It's a rank I haven't earned, believe me. In my case, it's just a title. I'm the beneficiary of a shortage of men.'

Tom laughed, and Joe noted again his resemblance to his sister. When Joe had first met him in his cramped office at Victoria Barracks, Tom had worn a neat moustache. Now he was clean-shaven, possibly because the vanity of a moustache seemed ludicrous on the swollen face that Tom saw each morning in the mirror, although now the swelling had retreated to his nose, which had been broken under Ptolemy Jones's fist.

'You got a degree in Classics, didn't you, at Oxford?' Joe said.

'Yes. The air force made me a group captain on the strength of it.'

'I don't think they hand out promotions because you've read Herodotus and Thucydides, Tom.'

'No, I suppose not. I was good at my job, but I was bored.'

'I know you don't blame me for what happened, Tom, but I blame myself.'

'You didn't exactly get away unscathed.'

'No, but it was worse for you.'

Now that the subject had been broached, there was no turning back.

'How much do you remember?' Joe asked.

'Most of it. Now. There were those ridiculous people — I don't remember their names — who played at being Nazis.'

'The main one was Mitchell Magill. They've all been interned.'

'But there were two of them who were different.'

'Ptolemy Jones, which wasn't his real name, and George Starling.'

Tom thought for a moment.

'You know, I thought it was all a bit of a game. Australian Nazis. It just seemed absurd.'

'We don't have to talk about this, Tom.'

'Yes, we do. I need to know what happened to me, what actually happened, so I can stop having nightmares.'

'I wasn't there when Jones discovered that you were working for Intelligence.'

'It was at that place at Candlebark Hill, near Daylesford. You'd gone back to Melbourne. I can't remember what happened up there. Why can't I remember that?'

Joe remembered, because Joe had seen the film that Jones had made of Tom, tied up and beaten.

'He knocked you senseless, Tom.' Joe prayed that Tom wouldn't recall being filmed.

'That must have been what happened. The next thing I remember is waking up in a room somewhere. I was naked, and tied to a chair, and my head was splitting. I remember my vision was blurred. Jones was there, and a woman. Jones didn't ask me any questions. He broke my fingers, one by one.'

'Are you sure you want to go on with this, Tom?'

'Yes. He hit me. The woman watched. I think I must have kept passing out, and then once when I opened my eyes, you were there.'

'They bragged about what they'd done to you, and what they were going to do to you, and to me. You were unconscious most of the time. Jones poured hot tea across your shoulders. I don't think you felt it then.'

'No. Afterwards, though, it was agony.'

'They both stubbed cigarettes out on your skin. They did that to me, too.'

'What else did they do to you?'

'They beat me, and Jones stabbed me here.' Joe indicated his shoulder.

'Christ almighty.'

'He's dead, Tom. Jones is dead: safely dead.'

'The other bloke, Starling, he's not dead. I saw him at Titus's house. I didn't dream that, Joe. I know I was fairly out of it, but I did not dream that.'

'You didn't dream it, Tom. He was there. He burned down my flat — well, not just my flat. The flat next door to mine was gutted too, and the other two flats were ruined by smoke and water. A man died in the flat next to mine, so Starling is wanted for murder.'

'Look at me, Joe.' Tom held up his taped fingers. Then he stood up and unbuttoned his shirt.

'It's not a pretty sight, is it?'

Tom's chest and abdomen were a pale canvas of scabs, scars, and puckered flesh where the vicious scald had not yet healed. He took the shirt off and showed Joe his back, which was criss-crossed with slashes in various stages of repair, some livid, some pink. He put his shirt back on.

'I want you to promise me something, Joe.'

'I know what you're going to ask, Tom, and I can't make that promise.'

'I want to help you find Starling.'

'I'm sorry, Tom. It's a police matter. You can't be involved.'

'If I remember correctly, Joe, you and I were working for Intelligence, not the police, when we were up at Candlebark Hill. As far as I'm concerned, I'm still working for them.'

'Tom …'

'I'm no longer incapacitated, so if I want to go looking for Starling, I'll do it — with or without you. And this is none of Titus's business, so don't bring him into it.'

'Where would you start, Tom?'

'I'm starting with you, Joe. You and I have got more reason than anyone else to find Starling. I'm not going to sit back and do nothing. Are you?'

Joe looked closely at Tom Mackenzie's face. There was no madness in it. He suddenly recalled something that the woman had said when he'd come to in the room where Tom sat slumped and injured.

'Ptolemy wanted to scoop Tom's eyes out with a teaspoon,' she'd said. Ptolemy: Starling's hero and mentor.

'All right, Tom. I'll help you. We'll find George Starling. I'll lose my job, but we'll find George Starling.'

Tom nodded. 'Yes, we will.'

7

HARDY TRUSCOTT HAD received Maria Pluschow's telegram while performing one of his several daily rituals in the service of Odin. The knock on his door had annoyed him, but the contents of the telegram caused him to give thanks to Odin. On the night after he'd received the telegram, he set out for her house on the unmade road to Port Fairy. The road was awful, and he was always uncertain of his car, but the lure of food and sex, and the pleasure he got in schooling Maria, made him risk it.

He arrived just after 6.00 p.m. The light was fading, and he could hear Blondi barking at his approach to the front door. Hardy didn't like dogs and he particularly disliked Blondi. Maria reluctantly tied Blondi to a post whenever Hardy called. Blondi and Hardy would never be friends, which made Maria worry just a little about Hardy Truscott. Blondi's judgement about people, she liked to think, was usually spot on.

Maria had told George that a trusted friend was coming to dinner. He was wary and initially said that he'd go for a walk. He wasn't in the mood to make small talk with a stranger. Maria convinced him that Hardy Truscott wasn't just any stranger. He was a man who could inspire others to change the world.

'He's shown me how powerful National Socialism can be. I never really understood how glorious it was until Hardy came along. You would have seen him at some of the meetings your father took you to, but you won't remember him. He was quiet. He didn't like most of the people who came to the meetings. He especially disliked your father. He thought he was a windbag. No one understood Hardy's message. They were too stupid.'

George reluctantly agreed to have dinner with Hardy Truscott, and as soon as Truscott entered the house, he regretted it. What an unimpressive little fellow he was. For his part, when he was introduced to George Starling, Truscott too regretted his acceptance of Maria's invitation. The scar on George's face turned his stomach, and he wouldn't believe that John Starling's son was worth pissing on. Apples didn't fall far from the tree, that was Hardy Truscott's view. Maria didn't miss the tension that rose up immediately between them.

'The coppers came to see me about you,' Truscott said. 'I don't like coppers sniffing around.'

'They came here, too, Hardy. That's not George's fault.'

'Maybe if he hadn't killed his father, they'd mind their own business and keep their noses out of mine.'

'Unfortunately, I didn't kill that bastard. I wish I had.'

That seemed to mollify Truscott sufficiently to prompt a relatively polite question.

'What are you doing here, George?'

'Getting ready for a job I need to do.'

'And what might that be?'

George decided against obfuscation.

'There are two people I need to kill. They're both coppers. One of them is a Jew. The other one is a woman. They're both vermin.'

Truscott thought it best to proceed carefully.

'And how do you plan to kill these people?'

'Slowly.'

Truscott was emboldened to say, 'Take your time with the Jew.'

The mood in the room changed, and over dinner, George found himself explaining his relationship with Ptolemy Jones and the debt of honour he owed him.

'Mr Jones sounds like he was a remarkable man,' Truscott said.

'He was that. He meant what he said.'

Over several hours Truscott gently introduced, in the most general of ways, the basic tenets of Odinism. He linked them to ideas that were familiar to Starling — racial purity and the need to rid the world of the pernicious Jew and the especially pernicious influence of Christianity. He suggested that a man like Jones would certainly have assumed a place in Valhalla. Odin, as the great protector of heroes, would have embraced him. After a few glasses of a spirit Starling couldn't identify, the idea that Ptolemy Jones might have been rewarded in some mystical kingdom moved him deeply. Prior to meeting this strange little man, Odinism would have struck Starling as foolish and childish. Now, though, it made perfect sense, and for the first time since Jones's death he felt an easing of his grief.

Hardy Truscott was pleased to have so easily recruited an acolyte, and he looked forward to introducing him to the arcane rituals that punctuated his day. He was disappointed at the end of the evening when Maria made it clear that she wouldn't be offering him sexual favours. It was George Starling who she took to her bed when Truscott had gone.

On more than one occasion in the past, a prostitute had called Starling an ape when she'd laid eyes on his extravagantly hairy body. She'd paid dearly for the remark, in bruises. Maria didn't call him an ape. She ran her hands over him and clutched at him in a fever of arousal. Starling was an inexperienced lover, and tenderness wasn't in his repertoire of emotions. Maria wasn't disconcerted by his clumsiness. She would school him in sex as Truscott would school him in Odinism. As he lay beside her after lovemaking that had been brutal and brief, Maria looked at his naked body and thought him beautiful. She'd never imagined that such a creature might be sent to her. She closed her eyes and whispered a prayer to Odin.

ON SATURDAY AFTERNOON, the first of April, Ros Lord was told that her brother's body would be released for burial. The autopsy and toxicology tests had been done. Ros, who believed that her brother would have wanted her to, rang St Patrick's presbytery and asked to speak to Monsignor McGrath. McGrath offered his condolences, but regretfully refused her request that Peter be given a Catholic burial. He hadn't been baptised, you see, and sadly it was impossible — unthinkable — to give him a Requiem Mass, 'As I'm sure you understand,' he said. He added that Peter couldn't be buried in the consecrated ground in the Catholic section of the cemetery. His interment would have to be in the Protestant section. Ros Lord accepted these strictures without comment. She was grateful that this telephone call to Monsignor McGrath marked the last time she would ever have anything to do with him or his hateful, punishing religion. It was confounding to her that Peter had been attracted to it, indeed, seduced by it.

The weather was still warm enough to allow Joe and Helen to sit in the garden. It was a conservative, very English garden with only one or two nods to the country in which it sat. A large river red gum dominated a back corner, and in the opposite corner, a lemon-scented gum rose spectacularly and aromatically, its limbs forming small folds near the trunk, like flesh. Helen told Joe about Monsignor McGrath's refusal to give Peter a Catholic burial. He told her all he knew about the investigation so far and produced two photographs, which he placed in front of her.

'How did you get these?'

'There was a packet of photographs on Inspector Lambert's desk. I presume he was going to take them home for Mrs Lambert to look at. I didn't have time to go through them, so I just took two at random. I'm hoping Lambert hasn't counted them.'

'That's incredibly risky, Joe. If Lambert ever finds out, you'll be demoted.'

'It's worth the risk, Helen.'

It was only as he said this that he realised that the sight of her uncle's body might be overwhelming for Helen. He'd looked at the photographs. Neither was a close view of Peter Lillee's face. One was taken on the bank, some distance from the body, and the other was taken from the water. Lillee's body was visible, but again, his features were obscured.

Helen picked up the photographs without hesitation. She looked at each of them closely.

'Martin Serong must have waded out into the river to take this one.'

'He did.'

Helen continued to stare at the photograph taken from the water. She was about to replace it on the table when something caught her eye, and she peered intently at the image.

'Uncle Peter's hand is actually *in* the water. Are those dead fish?'

'Yes. I think there were three of them.'

'Were they collected?'

'Yes. David Reilly organised for the mud near Peter's hand to be sifted, and for the fish to be collected.'

'Lambert thought that Uncle Peter might have dropped a phial of cyanide, didn't he?'

'It had to at least be considered, Helen. The fish might just have died because of pollution in the water, but there might be another explanation.'

Helen took one final look at the photograph and put it back on the table.

'There is nothing in these pictures that suggests anything other than suicide. I know that, Joe. But equally, I know that Uncle Peter would never have committed suicide. He loved Mum too much to do that.'

'And you. He loved you, too.'

'Yes, I suppose he did. I never really thought about it. You don't think that an uncle loves his nieces and nephews in the same way as he loves a sister or brother. Nieces and nephews are sort of surplus to requirements, aren't they?'

'I think Peter probably thought of you as a daughter. You grew up in this house, after all.'

'No. He never thought of me as a daughter. I suppose I never let him because I never thought of him as a father. I had a father, and when he died, well, I wasn't looking for a replacement. And Uncle Peter wasn't looking for a daughter. We never argued. I was never any trouble, but we were never close, and that's the truth of it. I wasn't interested in art or books or the theatre. I was probably a bit of a disappointment.'

Helen had never spoken like this to Joe. He worried that she might start to cry and that he wouldn't know what to say or do.

'He liked having you here, Joe. You could talk to him about art.'

'He was a good man.'

'Was he? He had a lot of secrets.'

'None of them sinister. He was just very private.'

Helen poured the last of her mother's home-made sour lemonade into a glass.

'He didn't trust us enough to tell us some pretty important things about himself. Mum hasn't said anything, but I think she must feel a bit hurt by that.'

Joe had no way of knowing that this expression of Helen's

feelings was without precedent. She never spoke so openly to her mother, and not even Peter's death had allowed them to fall into unguarded conversation. Helen was wary of telling her mother how she felt about Peter's obsessive privacy. Her resentment of his decision to exclude them from the richest elements of his life was only now beginning to settle into something hard and bitter. Her mother may well have shared these feelings, but it didn't sit well with Helen to intrude on her grief by criticising her mother's brother, and so yet again, as so often in the past, she opted for silence. She found, though, when couched in the language of an investigation, she could say things to Joe that she couldn't say to her mother.

'The engagement and the Catholic thing, they're not going to be his only secrets, are they?'

'His business associates haven't revealed anything suspicious. Inspector Lambert is going to talk to people in the Melbourne Club on Monday. Maybe something will turn up there. We know he rubbed a couple of people up the wrong way over some investment schemes.'

Helen shrugged.

'I hate clubs. I wouldn't join one even if I was asked. Not that I'd ever be asked.'

'We're in the same boat there. You can't join the Melbourne Club because you're a woman. I can't join because I'm a Jew.'

'Why would Uncle Peter want to belong to a place like that?'

'He's a businessman. I imagine that's where most of Melbourne's business gets done.'

'It's just one more thing about Uncle Peter I don't understand. He can't possibly have liked those people.'

They spoke easily for another hour and not just about the investigation. They knew so little about each other that even small details assumed the quality of a revelation. Joe had no idea that

Helen had a close friend named Clara. For her part, Helen was surprised that Joe had friends outside the police force.

'You've never mentioned Clara.'

'Why would I mention Clara? You never mentioned Guy Kirkham.'

'Why would I mention Guy Kirkham?'

They both laughed.

It was strange how the sudden realisation that they each had a life of unknown friends and acquaintances was somehow reassuring. For Joe, the surprising existence of Clara made Helen seem more approachable. For Helen, Joe's friendships excited a small spike of jealousy, but she was also glad that he wasn't as lonely as she'd supposed him to be. He hadn't mentioned any female friends, which was a relief, but she wondered if this had been a deliberate omission.

Helen knew that she had a tendency to over-think things when it came to Joe Sable. She couldn't stop herself from going over what she'd said and what he'd said. Was he really indifferent to her? For a black few seconds, she wondered if she'd mentioned her £2 million inheritance in order to attract his attention. She banished the thought as soon as it arrived, but its exile wasn't entirely successful. If Joe now began to show an interest in her, would that be the reason?

Sergeant Bob O'Dowd never took risks. Going along with Ron Dunnart's plan to blackmail Peter Lillee had been a risk and look how that had turned out. His wife, Vera, had known that something was up. Vera always knew when something was up. The psoriasis gave him away. The patches of it on his wrists and ankles flared angrily whenever something was up. He tried to keep these out of sight, but her disregard for his privacy meant that a closed bathroom door wasn't considered a barrier to entry. She would barge in without knocking, and so she'd seen the red patches as he lay in the bath. They'd made love the night before, and she hadn't noticed them then, but the light had been flatteringly low, and besides, she'd been pleasantly distracted. Whatever else she might say about her husband — he was no Clark Gable, and he was a bit dull — she'd never accuse him of not being an attentive lover.

As he dried himself, she'd taken his ointment from the bathroom cupboard, sat on the edge of the bath, and insisted that he raise each leg so that she could apply the cream. He'd brushed off her questions with vague references to a nasty homicide that was troubling him. When she'd finished with his feet, she'd applied the ointment to his wrists. She hadn't questioned him further, but Bob O'Dowd suspected that she hadn't believed him either. The idea that he might be having an affair was absurd. Vera O'Dowd was the only woman he'd ever been intimate with, and when courting her he'd been so shy that he'd made no attempt on her chastity before marriage. Nevertheless, Vera sometimes got it into her head that he'd been sexually unfaithful, and when this happened, it took weeks to convince her otherwise, weeks during which she barely spoke to him.

The threat of being unfairly sent to Coventry again was part of the reason he found himself, in the late afternoon of 1 April, sitting in his car outside Peter Lillee's house. He didn't have a specific plan, just a notion that he needed to find out for certain whether or not Ron Dunnart had killed Peter Lillee. The key to that, he thought, was to be found behind the doors of Lillee's mansion. He needed to talk to the housekeeper, even though she'd been so suspicious of him and Dunnart just a few days ago. He needed to see inside the house. He thought he had a reasonable chance now of convincing that surly bitch that he had a legitimate reason for questioning her, and for looking around the place. He was a Homicide detective. The man who employed her was dead.

'I'm just following up on some details.' That's what he'd tell her. She wouldn't have a clue how homicide investigations worked, so this time she'd let him in. What was he looking for? O'Dowd didn't know. Perhaps he'd find a note written by Dunnart asking Lillee to meet him down by the Yarra River. This was unlikely, but he needed something to link Dunnart to the crime. Could he create this note himself? Could he use Lillee's own typewriter to produce something that linked Dunnart to the crime? Lillee was bound to have a typewriter. All O'Dowd needed was a few minutes alone with it. Would he turn such evidence in, or would he use it to have more control over Dunnart? O'Dowd's hands were shaking, and he knew he wasn't thinking clearly. Why did he feel so desperate? He should turn around and drive home. No. He'd come this far. Who dares, wins. His father had been in the air force and barely a day went by without him saying, 'Who dares, wins.'

O'Dowd got out of his car, put his hat neatly on his head, and took a few deep breaths. 'I'm following up on some details.' He rehearsed this line in a whisper, and walked to the front door. He took the odd-looking knocker in his fingers and let it fall heavily against the metal plate three times. The woman he believed to be the housekeeper opened the door. Ros Lord was surprised to see O'Dowd standing there. She noticed that he was sweating more profusely than the day's heat warranted. She also noticed as he took off his hat that his hand shook slightly. Here was a nervous man. O'Dowd produced his identification.

'I remember who you are,' Ros said. 'Why are you here again?'

'I'm an investigating officer with the Homicide department, Mrs …?'

Once again, Ros didn't provide her name.

'Go on,' she said.

'I'm sure other members of the department have already spoken to you about the death of your employer, Peter Lillee.'

He waited a moment to allow the woman to confirm that this was so. She merely stared at him.

'I'm just following up on some details. If I could come inside, I'd like to ask you some questions and perhaps examine Mr Lillee's papers, if there are any.'

Ros Lord could hardly believe that a man as transparent and stupid as this man was could be employed as a detective. She thought about shutting the door in his face, but realised that his interest in Peter Lillee's death must be outside the official investigation. This had something to do with his earlier visit with the detective named Dunnart. She invited him in.

O'Dowd was relieved that his strategy had worked. His relief didn't last long. He was intimidated by the opulence of Lillee's house. It made him feel clumsy and shabby, and the sensation was exacerbated when the woman directed him away from the main rooms towards what, if he'd known the term, he would have called the butler's pantry. It was a small room with an ironing board and iron, a sewing machine, and a couple of uncomfortable-looking plain chairs. The woman indicated that he should sit in one of these. Ros hadn't chosen to park O'Dowd here in order to embarrass him. She knew that Helen and Joe were in the back garden and that they might come back into the house at any moment. She wanted a few words with O'Dowd before she turned him over to them.

'My name is Mrs Rosalind Lord.'

O'Dowd nodded, but gave no indication that the surname meant anything to him.

'And you are, were, Peter Lillee's housekeeper?'

'No. Well, in a manner of speaking. I looked after the running of the house.'

O'Dowd didn't understand the distinction she was making. Was she Lillee's mistress? Lillee was queer, though.

'I'm sorry, I don't understand. So, you're not his housekeeper?'

'No, Sergeant. I'm Peter Lillee's sister. Lord is my married name.'

'His sister? But you live here?'

'Yes. I live here with my daughter, Helen. Helen Lord.'

Again, O'Dowd gave no sign that the name meant anything to him. He took out a notebook to make a show of asking questions. It was Ros who asked the first question.

'What are you really doing here, Sergeant? Why have you come back without your detective chum? Dunnart was his name, wasn't it?'

'As I said, Mrs Lord, there are details ...'

'You're lying, and I want to know why. What have you got to do with my brother's death?'

The baldness of the question ambushed O'Dowd into physically revealing that he was indeed lying. The colour drained from his face, and he stammered an inadequate attempt at outrage.

'... I-I understand that your brother's death must have come as a shock, but why would you think that I had something to do with it? I'm here to find out what happened to Mr Lillee. Have you accused every policeman who's been here of killing your brother?'

'I'm not accusing you of anything, Sergeant. It was a stab in the dark. I'm sorry if I offended you.'

O'Dowd felt mollified by the apology and failed to see it for what it was — an empty expression that masked Ros Lord's conviction that she'd stumbled on a suspect. She didn't believe that O'Dowd was a murderer — she'd met one or two murderers, and O'Dowd didn't strike her as having the stomach for it — but he was implicated in some way. She had neither the skill nor the authority to go any further, so to back up her apology, and to put

O'Dowd at his ease, she suggested that he come with her to the library, where she would be happy to allow him to go through Peter's desk.

'There's a drawer that was locked when the other policemen were here. I found the key this morning, so you'll be the first to go through it.'

This volte-face ought to have been unconvincing, but O'Dowd's head was still fizzing as his panic receded, and he congratulated himself on manipulating this Lord woman into giving him what he wanted. Dunnart couldn't have done a better job.

Ros took O'Dowd to the library and told him that she'd just fetch the key and that he should feel free to look around. He thanked her and was pleased to feel that he'd reasserted his authority. Ros closed the door behind her and went out into the back garden. Joe and Helen were deep in conversation, and amid the confusion of emotions Ros was experiencing, an uninvited one raised its head: jealousy that her daughter was speaking so freely to Joe, when she'd rarely, if ever, granted her the privilege of such easy chat. Ros tamped down this unworthy thought. She coughed to signal her presence. Both Helen and Joe greeted her with a smile.

'There's someone in the library I think you should both meet. He's a detective from your department, Joe.'

'Not Inspector Lambert?'

'No. Sergeant Bob O'Dowd is here to follow up on some details. That's what he said.'

Helen and Joe stood up quickly.

'He didn't recognise your name, darling.'

'He'd never have bothered to learn my name, Mum.'

'I think he's going to be very, very surprised to see you. He's expecting me to come back with a key to unlock a drawer. He's most anxious to look through Peter's papers. I knew the first time

I met him that he was a wrong'un. He's also a very stupid man, and stupidity can be dangerous.'

'He's here off his own bat,' Joe said.

'I know. I'd like you and Helen to find out why.'

Ron Dunnart had looked closely at all the available evidence in relation to Peter Lillee's death, including David Reilly's and Joe Sable's notes. It was clear to Dunnart that whatever this was, what it wasn't was murder. He'd noted that everyone who'd known Lillee discounted suicide as a cause. Dunnart wasn't so sure. He'd read Lambert's account of his interview with Lillian Johnson. The night Dunnart had bearded Lillee in his car was the night that that relationship had come to an end. Would breaking off an engagement cause a bloke to take his own life? That might depend on the reason for the break-up.

Dunnart was reluctant to give up the idea that Lillee was queer. What if this Johnson woman had discovered the truth about him, and what if she'd threatened him with exposure? He wished he could talk to her, but he wouldn't be so reckless as to talk to anyone involved in the case without consulting with Lambert. The last thing he wanted to do was to give the impression that his interest was personal. This was just another case, and he'd only been assigned to it peripherally. He couldn't be seen to be distracted from the other cases he was working on. His and O'Dowd's visit to the Lillee house was bound to come up, even though it hadn't yet appeared in any of the notes. He needed to pre-empt this discovery by revealing it himself. He'd do this first thing on Monday morning, having taken O'Dowd aside first. The explanation was simple. He'd go into Lambert's office and tell him that he'd just noticed that Lillee's address was one of the houses he and O'Dowd had doorknocked in relation to another investigation. They'd visited several houses that day, he'd say. Would Lambert check? Why would he bother? He might want to know which investigation he was referring to. That was easy. It didn't matter which one. Dunnart was just following up on a tip he'd been given by one of his snouts, and it hadn't proved useful. All it had resulted in was this coincidence. Dunnart was happy with this story, and even O'Dowd couldn't mess it up. Surely.

WHEN HELEN AND Joe entered the library, they found Bob O'Dowd going through some papers that he'd removed from a drawer in Peter Lillee's beautiful desk. He stared at them blankly for a moment. What was Joe Sable doing here, and wasn't that that sheila who'd worked with Lambert for a while? What was her name?

Helen asked, with ominous calm, 'What are you doing going through my uncle's desk?'

O'Dowd couldn't comprehend what was happening.

'Uncle?'

Both Helen and Joe let the silence grow. In an effort to marshal the disordered fragments that were hurtling through his mind, O'Dowd stood up. It was a mistake. He felt light-headed. A voice, his, although it sounded disembodied to him, said, 'What are you doing here?'

Helen walked towards him.

'I live here.'

With a supreme effort of will, O'Dowd rallied sufficiently to grasp the connection between this young woman, who he'd seen at Russell Street, and Peter Lillee. *Helen Lord.* The other woman, Rosalind Lord, must be her mother. Although this made sense, what didn't make sense was Dunnart's failure to warn him of the connection. Unless Dunnart didn't know. How could he *not* know? A sudden rush of anger cleared O'Dowd's head.

'I'm just doing my job, trying to find out who murdered your uncle.'

'Murdered?' Until Joe spoke, O'Dowd hadn't begun to account for his presence. Lambert must have sent him to question Lillee's sister and niece. This was awkward, but perhaps he could co-opt him as a fellow investigator.

'Sergeant Sable and I are following up on leads. Right, Sergeant?' Joe ignored the question.

'Murdered?' he repeated. 'You said Peter Lillee was murdered.'

The tenor of Sable's question made O'Dowd feel as if he'd made a misstep.

'This is a murder investigation, Sergeant, as you very well know.'

Joe and Helen again let the silence grow. O'Dowd's confidence deserted him.

'Mrs Lord is getting the key to one of these drawers,' he said uncertainly. O'Dowd quickly checked something he should have checked as soon as he'd sat down behind the desk. All the drawers opened easily.

'I think we should get comfortable,' Helen said. She indicated the armchairs ranged around the elegant Adam-inspired fireplace. 'Then you can tell us why you lied to my mother and why you're lying to us.'

Us? O'Dowd thought. Oh Christ, were Sable and Lord an item? He moved to an armchair. Helen and Joe did the same.

'You have no authority to be here,' Joe said.

'I'm your senior officer, Sergeant. I think you need to explain your presence before I do.'

Joe could have discomposed O'Dowd by simply saying 'I live here', as Helen had done, but Inspector Lambert had warned him that this arrangement should be known to as few people as possible.

'I'm here,' Joe said, 'because Inspector Lambert sent me here.'

'Likewise,' O'Dowd said.

'The answer to that is a telephone call away,' Helen said. 'Shall I make that call?'

O'Dowd wished he'd paid more attention when Sable's and Lord's names had come up in conversation at Russell Street. Helen Lord's name hadn't stuck. They weren't popular, he knew that, and Sable was about to become the most hated man in the force. They were seen as Lambert's favourites. That much he did know.

'No,' O'Dowd said softly. 'Don't make that call.'

'Do you know who murdered my uncle?'

The question was so unexpected that O'Dowd received it with the force of a punch. His answer stunned each of them. Perhaps O'Dowd himself was most stunned by it.

'Yes,' he said. 'Yes, I do.'

8

Guy Kirkham chose King's Hotel in Russell Street for two reasons. It was close to the police headquarters where his closest friend, Joe Sable, worked, and it sported a glorious Art Nouveau stained-glass window near its entrance. The purity of that window and its neighbour window had been spoiled a little by vulgar stencilling between them that read, 'First Class Accommodation for Boarders and Country Visitors'. That was sufficient to warn anyone that whatever promise those windows once hinted at, King's Hotel had reached a point where it could no longer live up to it. Flash hotels did not encourage boarders. Still, it suited Guy Kirkham.

He ought to have contacted Joe weeks ago, as soon as he'd been demobbed, only he couldn't face telling him why the army had seen fit to release him from service. He'd been invalided out, not because he'd been wounded, but because he'd started screaming in the middle of the night. It had been unnerving for the men who'd slept near him, and during the day he'd found himself falling deeply and suddenly asleep. It wasn't sleep exactly. It was more like short bursts of unconsciousness. Then it had happened once when he'd been driving a Jeep in Port Moresby. Private Harry Compton had been in the car with him. It was such a short trip, and they should have walked, but Private Compton had had an infected toe and had asked Guy to drive him over the uneven ground between their tent and the hospital tent. Guy had gone over it a thousand times in his head. If only he'd said no. But Harry was in pain and Harry had begged him to use the Jeep. Guy had agreed. And then he'd fallen asleep at the wheel.

The Jeep hadn't even been going very fast, but it'd hit a pothole and over-turned. Guy was unhurt. Harry Compton's neck was broken. Harry Compton was twenty years old. He'd never slept with a woman. Now he was dead.

As far as the army was concerned, Guy Kirkham had killed Harry Compton. But Guy's father was rich and connected, so Guy had been invalided out, with the shameful diagnosis of mental incompetence. The screaming had been real, and the narcolepsy had been real, but the army had been relieved of any obligation to fund Guy's treatment by Mr Kirkham's guarantee that the Kirkham family would assume full responsibility for Guy's rehabilitation. It was an unorthodox arrangement, but the Kirkhams had enough money and influence to ensure that it happened. He'd be safely tucked away on the family property near Natimuk, in the north-west of Victoria — a small settlement, a long way from Melbourne. Guy had been released into his family's care. His family, however, hadn't been prepared for the man who'd turned up on their remote doorstep.

Telling his son to 'buck up' didn't silence the screams that woke the Kirkham household on his first night back home. Mr Kirkham prescribed fence building and mustering as the best treatment for what he dismissed as 'the collywobbles'. Mrs Kirkham had no opinion on the matter. She was frankly ashamed of her son, even horrified by his condition, as if she were a Spartan woman who believed that her warrior boy should return holding his shield proudly, or lying on it, dead.

Guy volunteered to move into an empty farmhand's cottage at some distance from the main house. The sounds of his nightmares carried eerily over paddocks and dams, causing nightjars to shift uneasily on their perches, and found their way, faintly, into his parents' bedroom.

After a few weeks on the Kirkham station, Guy's compulsion to escape saw him pack a bag and leave. He left a note explaining that he was heading for Melbourne. In the note he lied and said that he'd be staying with Joe Sable, even though he'd as yet made no contact with him. He believed he had no need to discuss his decision with his parents. They might make some feint at asking him to stay, but Guy judged it more likely that they'd threaten to cut him off financially and be secretly relieved that he was off their hands. He took one of the family cars, drove to the Horsham train station, left the keys with the station master, and headed for Melbourne.

It took Mr and Mrs Kirkham twenty-four hours to discover that their son had gone. It was the silence during the night that alerted them. They found the note. They weren't disturbed by it. Mr Kirkham was annoyed by the inconvenience of having to retrieve the car. Mrs Kirkham's only comment was that if Guy preferred the company of that Jewish boy to his own family, well, that was his look-out.

Guy had enough cash in his wallet to secure a room at King's Hotel for several nights. He didn't choose the most expensive room. The room he left his suitcase in was sparsely furnished and smelled of stale cigarette smoke. He had to share a bathroom and toilet with the other rooms on his floor, but these facilities were spotlessly clean. They were certainly a step up from the stinking pit toilets in Papua New Guinea.

As it was Saturday afternoon, Guy assumed that Joe wouldn't be working. Unless he'd started stepping out with a girl, in which case he might be at the pictures, Guy guessed that Joe was probably at his flat in Princes Hill. Joe had been the first of Guy's university friends to buy his own place. The house Joe had inherited when his father had died was far too big for a young man with no interest in gardening or maintenance. It had been Guy who'd encouraged him to sell it and buy the flat in Princes Hill. It was a spacious two-bedroom flat in a block of four. The block's name, Rosh Pinah, was Jewish and seemed like a good omen. Guy could never remember quite what it meant. The house had sold for a tidy sum, and Joe had bought the flat outright for £750. The profit from the house sale, along with a considerable inheritance had meant that Joe could afford the luxury of esoteric studies at Melbourne University, without the pressing need to work. The war, of course, had changed all that. To everyone's amazement, Joe Sable had become a policeman.

Guy hadn't seen Joe for about two years and as neither of them was an assiduous letter writer, he hadn't heard from him either. He was confident, though, that when Joe answered the knock on his door to find Guy Kirkham standing there, he'd be thrilled. Their friendship ran deep. It was more than a shared love of art and books. They could speak easily to each other about their families, their ambitions, and their politics. Guy knew all about Joe's unreliable heart. Indeed, Guy was the only one of Joe's friends and acquaintances who knew of this physical weakness, and that Joe found it shameful. The only thing they didn't speak about was religion, and not because it was a sensitive topic. It was simply that neither of them considered it a subject worthy of discussion. Their respective faiths were of no consequence to either of them. Once, after too much wine, Guy told Joe that his mother had christened him 'Guy' because one of her great heroes was Guy Fawkes, in her opinion a Catholic martyr, who ought to have been canonised centuries ago.

Guy walked up to Princes Hill. Walking cleared his head, and when he walked his thoughts turned to the novel he wanted to write. He'd told no one about this ambition. The story had come to him one night in New Guinea, and ever since then he'd turned it over and over in his head. He hadn't yet put a word down on paper. He was eager to talk to Joe about it. Joe would understand this compulsion.

The time passed quickly as Guy moved his characters about and listened to their conversations. He turned into Pigdon Street and walked towards Arnold Street where Rosh Pinah stood on the corner.

He stared in disbelief at its ruin.

Two of the flats, one of which was Joe's, had been gutted by fire, and the remaining two had been so damaged that they were uninhabitable. Rosh Pinah was awaiting demolition. Guy was gripped by a fear that Joe had died in this fire. He sat on the edge of the gutter and breathed deeply. He thought he was going to be sick. Instead, he slipped into sleep.

He woke to a hand shaking him by the shoulder. There was an elderly woman kneeling beside him, and she was asking if he was all right. He sat up, groggy and aware that his cheek was bleeding. He must have hit the ground hard. There was no sign of vomit, so at least he hadn't been sick.

'I'm fine,' he said. 'It's just the heat, I think. I must have passed out.'

'You passed out all right. I saw you from my window. You just keeled over. I thought you must be drunk. We get a few drunks passing through here. Mostly Yanks, and you don't dress like a Yank, so I thought I better come out and check. I couldn't smell any alcohol on you, so I felt your pulse. I was a nurse once upon a time. Your pulse was strong, and you were breathing normally, so I thought, well, he's fainted, hasn't he?'

Guy didn't take in anything the woman said, and if she'd walked away, he wouldn't have been able to describe her features. She was a voice, a form, and a faint smell of soap.

'That cheek needs to be cleaned,' she said. 'Come along. Hop up, and I'll take you inside. You could do with a glass of water, too. Perry's the name. Mrs Perry, and Mr Perry is inside, so it's all right and proper.'

Guy allowed himself to be helped to his feet. Mrs Perry must have been well over sixty. She was a strong woman, dressed to do housework. Her grey hair was constrained by a scarf, and her clothes obscured by an apron. She put her hand on Guy's arm and led him into the house that sat opposite Rosh Pinah. The air inside was stuffy, and the only sound was the peculiar rasping of someone's laboured breathing.

'Mr Perry was hit by the gas in 1917. Just lately he's gone downhill.'

She was matter-of-fact and indicated the bedroom from which the frightful sound emanated.

'We're doing the best we can. Now, let's get you cleaned up.'

While she went to the bathroom to get some disinfectant and some cloth, Guy approached the bedroom. The door was ajar. The curtains were open, and the room was flooded with light. A man lay on the bed, in just his pyjama bottoms. There was a strong smell of sweat. The man's eyes were open, and he managed a smile as his chest rose and fell like broken bellows. Guy walked to the bedside.

'I'm Guy Kirkham. Private Guy Kirkham. I fell over outside.'

This seemed an absurd thing to say, but Mr Perry nodded as if it made perfect sense. Mrs Perry entered the bedroom.

'Private Kirkham, is it?'

'Yes. I'm on leave. From New Guinea.'

'Sit on the edge of the bed, Private Kirkham. I'll clean you up here. Paul won't mind a bit, will you dear?'

For a moment Paul Perry's breathing eased, but a coughing fit returned it to its ghastly rhythm. Mrs Perry swabbed Guy's cheek and declared that a bit of gravel rash never hurt anyone.

'What were you doing, if you don't mind my asking?'

'I'd come to see a friend of mine. Joe Sable. He lived in Rosh Pinah. What happened?'

'Oh, that was terrible. The fire brigade took forever to come. They were all out fighting the bushfires. By the time they got here, well, it was all too late. The poor man died.'

'Joe died?'

Mrs Perry saw the terror in Guy's face.

'No, no. Not Mr Sable. His neighbour, the teacher, he died in the fire. We thought our place was going to go up as well. We had to go out into the street, didn't we, Paul? And Paul was that sick, but we had to go outside.'

'How did it start?'

'Apparently it started in Mr Sable's flat. A cigarette maybe. Young men are so careless.'

'Joe doesn't smoke.'

'Oh well, I don't know how it started then. I didn't mean to blame Mr Sable. He's a very nice young man. Always polite. Always asks after Paul, and if there's anything he can do. He's a detective you know. That made me feel that little bit safer knowing there was a detective across the road. I suppose that's silly, isn't it, but there it is.'

Mr Perry's breathing eased again, and he dozed. Mrs Perry signalled to Guy that they should leave the bedroom. He followed her to the front room.

'I'll get you that water.'

There was a large, framed photograph sitting on an easel in a corner of the room. Guy had seen dozens of similar photographs in his friends' houses. This one was of Paul Perry, in full uniform — the Light Horse — taken in a studio. Every soldier who could afford it had taken himself off to a studio in 1914 and had his photograph taken. Every young man looked handsome in these photographs, Paul Perry especially so, or perhaps Guy was just acutely aware of the contrast between this beautiful soldier and the poor, broken, wracked bastard in the bedroom. When Mrs Perry came back into the room with a jug of water and a glass, Guy's eyes betrayed him as tears stung them.

'Sit down, Private Kirkham.'

'My name is Guy.'

'Guy.'

Guy wasn't embarrassed by his tears, and he didn't automatically apologise for them. He drank some water, and Mrs Perry waited for him to speak.

'We are a dreadful species, Mrs Perry.'

'Once upon a time, I would have said that the world is full of good people — and there are good people, of course there are — but when I listen to Paul trying to take a breath, I find no consolation in the goodness of others. Someone else's kindness doesn't stop my husband's agony.'

Guy bowed his head. He had nothing to say, and silence was better than trite expressions of sympathy, which Mrs Perry wouldn't have wanted to hear.

'Can you tell me what happened to Joe Sable, Mrs Perry? Do you know where I can find him?'

'No, I'm sorry. I know he's alive. I saw him the day after the fire. He'd been in a fight, I think, some time before the fire. Oh, he was a sight, all bruised and bandaged. I didn't ask him what had happened. It was none of my business. If he'd wanted to tell me, he would have. I imagine you'll catch him at work, Guy. That's a lovely name. Guy. I believe he works at police headquarters in Russell Street.'

Guy had an urge to ask Mrs Perry if he could stay the night with her and Paul. It was ridiculous, and he didn't ask. It was just that he couldn't face the idea of walking back to King's Hotel and sitting alone in his room. He had no choice, though. He thanked Mrs Perry for the water and her ministrations and stepped back out into Pigdon Street. As he passed the front window, he saw Mrs Perry standing in front of the photograph. There was no expression on her face, no expression at all.

GEORGE STARLING SAT in a wicker chair in Maria Pluschow's backyard. He was shirtless, with his face turned to the last of the Saturday afternoon sun. He'd come to enjoy the sun on his skin. It felt elemental and restorative. He hadn't embraced the *nakenkultur* of that effete Mitchell Magill and his idiot friends, but he was sure the sun was helping his face to heal.

Maria Pluschow watched Starling from her kitchen window. Blondi was beside him, and from time to time, Starling would idly drop his hand and stroke the dog's head. Maria's heart swelled at the sight of this, and she was convinced that she and Starling had begun a journey together that would lead to greatness. This was her reward for embracing what was demonstrably the true religion. More ancient than the worship of the Jew Jesus, the worship of Odin and the pantheon of Nordic gods had ignited in her a fervour that was close to ecstatic.

She made a pot of tea and took it and two cups out to where Starling sat. She moved a chair to be near him. They drank the tea in silence, and Maria began to intone one of the prayers she'd memorised from Rud Mills's book.

Starling turned his head to look at her. With the sun full on her face, she looked older than he'd noticed before. Lines were beginning to form around her lips, and two deep lines were etched between her brows. She wore no make-up, and her braided hair couldn't disguise the fact that she was a farm woman, educated certainly, but like every other woman Starling had known, she was dull-witted. The prayer, delivered in her flat, ugly voice, struck Starling as absurd and childish. He'd been drunk last night and susceptible to Hardy Truscott's blather. He'd flicked through the book Truscott had left and had found nothing in it that interested him. The idea of worshipping Odin, which had seemed so plausible and consoling last night, now seemed idiotic and infantile. It embarrassed him to recall how enthusiastic he'd been about it.

Now, the sight of Maria's lips, moving as she prayed, stirred in him the familiar friend that if allowed to grow unchecked, would flower into the pure ecstasy of rage. He closed his eyes and settled it down. He needed Maria Pluschow, and she'd been good to him. She was a fool — well, she was a woman — and she'd swallowed Truscott's guff whole. The only thing he had in common with Truscott was his understanding of the fact that the Jews controlled America, and Australia too, of course. Lighting a bonfire and dancing around it — which was a ritual described in the book — wasn't going to redress that, and neither were prayers uttered in the backyard of a house on the road between Port Fairy and Warrnambool.

Truscott was under the impression that he'd found a pupil. Starling decided, as he sat there in the sun, that he would test Truscott's mettle, and he'd test Maria Pluschow's, too, while he was at it. He had no intention of following them. He'd offer them the chance of following him.

He reached down and stroked the dog's head, and as he did so he remembered Ptolemy Jones telling him that SS officers were each given a dog to train and bond with, and that, as a test of their pitiless loyalty, they were required to shoot it on command. Jones had thought this an admirable way of separating the weak from the strong. Blondi yawned. Maria looked at Starling and smiled. He smiled back at her.

SERGEANT BOB O'DOWD told Sergeant Joe Sable that he wished to make a statement in relation to the death of Peter Lillee, and that he wanted to make that statement to Inspector Lambert. It was Saturday afternoon, but Joe had no hesitation in telephoning the inspector at Tom Mackenzie's house. This wasn't something that could wait until Monday morning. O'Dowd couldn't be given time to change his mind.

O'Dowd drove Joe to Russell Street. He didn't say much, and Joe didn't make small talk. What do you say to a man whose life is about to change forever? Joe had little respect for O'Dowd, but he had some empathy with how he must be feeling. Joe knew what it was like to make a statement about a fellow officer.

At Russell Street, Joe and O'Dowd waited in Inspector Lambert's office.

'What were you doing at Lillee's house?' O'Dowd asked. There wasn't any real conviction behind the question. The silence had finally made O'Dowd uncomfortable.

'I was doing my job.'

O'Dowd nodded, having no further interest in the matter. Sable had been assigned to the investigation, so of course he was at the Lillee house. If O'Dowd had been able to think clearly at this moment, he would have wondered at his run of bad luck, but his mind was a soup of worry and regret. And chief among his regrets was his involvement with Ron Dunnart. Perhaps, though, all this was a blessing. He'd be reprimanded for going along with Dunnart's nasty blackmailing scheme, but as nothing had come of it, he could abase himself before Lambert and demonstrate his penitent's credentials by stitching up Dunnart. O'Dowd knew, he just *knew*, that Dunnart had killed Lillee, and he knew, too, that it hadn't been an accident. Dunnart didn't get involved in accidents.

There was a problem. There was no firm evidence of foul play — no bruising and no wounds. Somewhere in the notes, someone had speculated that the body might have been brought to that spot in a boat, which might explain the minimal disturbance around it. 'I don't know', wouldn't be a satisfactory answer to Lambert's inevitable question, 'How did Dunnart kill Peter Lillee?' O'Dowd needed Dunnart to be taken into custody, and to ensure that this happened, he was going to have to play a dangerous game and lie. Having set his foot on this path, he couldn't now withdraw it, and O'Dowd knew that if he accused Dunnart of murder, and the accusation was so flimsy that Dunnart would remain at liberty, he, O'Dowd, would end up as dead as Peter Lillee. What he needed was a powerful and convincing lie, and it was as Inspector Lambert entered the office and took off his hat that O'Dowd thought he'd found it.

Inspector Lambert listened to O'Dowd and left the note-taking to Sergeant Sable.

'I am prepared to make a statement, sir.'

'Why, Bob? Why are you doing this?'

'Because I'm not a bad man, Inspector. I'm not a good man, either, but I'm not a murderer, and I'm not going to stand by and let Ron Dunnart get away with it.'

'I thought the two of you rubbed along pretty well.'

'Dunnart thought that, too, sir, but it was all an act, and he didn't realise that I saw right through him. He thought I was dumb. He was wrong.'

'You've worked together on several cases, haven't you?'

'Yes sir. Dunnart was always in charge of course, or thought he was. I just want a quiet life. I just want to do my job and go home to my wife. The job has never been enough for Ron. I've known about some of the things he gets up to, but he's never involved me in any of them.'

'What sort of things?'

'Blackmail is his main thing. He calls it a nice little earner. He squeezes small-time crims, pimps, prostitutes, but his best source of extra cash is fairies. I don't know how it works exactly. He's never trusted me enough to tell me that.'

'But he trusted you enough to tell you he was blackmailing these people?'

'No. Not until recently. I'm a Mason, you see, and Ron Dunnart hates Masons. I was surprised that he wanted anything to do with me at all. I suppose he thought I was weak and that I'd do his bidding like an obedient dog. In some ways, he was right.'

Lambert was watching O'Dowd closely and listening for the false notes in what he was saying. He took the self-serving and self-pitying tone for granted. Owning up to being weak wasn't going to be enough to convince him that O'Dowd was telling the truth.

'When did he take you fully into his confidence?'

'It was when those two fairies were murdered.'

'Those men have names, Sergeant.'

'I don't remember their names.'

'Even though you worked on, and are ostensibly still working on, this case?'

'Well ...'

'Sturt Menadue and Steven McNamara, Sergeant. Those are the names of the two men whose murder you have been charged with investigating. Those are the names of the two men whose families are waiting for justice.'

'Yes, I remember now, sir.'

Lambert's disgust unsettled O'Dowd. Dunnart had warned him that Inspector Lambert was soft on queers. This would at least ensure that Dunnart's blackmail of Lillee would appal him.

'One of the fai— one of the men, Mr Menadue I think, had a sort of diary with names and addresses in it. Ron flicked through it and found Peter Lillee's name. He'd heard it somewhere, and he tore the page out. No one was going to notice that. He showed it to me, and he said that we could both earn a bit of extra money by talking to this Peter Lillee bloke.'

'By blackmailing him, you mean.'

'Yes. I wasn't sure about it. I'd never been involved in anything like that, but somehow Ron made it all sound perfectly reasonable. If Lillee was a rich man, he wouldn't miss a bit of money to protect his reputation. I mean, Lillee was the one breaking the law, wasn't he?'

Inspector Lambert opened the drawer of his desk and pulled out a leather-bound diary.

'This is *my* diary, Sergeant.'

He pushed it towards O'Dowd.

'In it, you'll find your name, address, and telephone number. You'll find Ron Dunnart's, too, along with lots of other people who work here. If someone were to find it, or steal it, would it be a safe assumption that you and I are intimate friends?'

'No, sir.'

O'Dowd wasn't so stupid that the point had to be pressed further.

'Why did you agree to go along with Ron Dunnart? Why did you agree to throw away your integrity?'

O'Dowd clasped his hands between his knees, and, without looking at Lambert, he said, 'I stopped feeling like I had any integrity years ago. It got chipped away, and when Ron said, "Here's a way to earn some money," my only qualm was about getting caught. Nothing could have been further from my mind than integrity.'

O'Dowd managed to say this without self-pity compromising its essential honesty. Lambert would pick up the faintest hint of the whinny of that emotion.

'It was just a few extra pounds on the side. I didn't tell my wife about it. It was pin money. All this for pin money. Can you believe it?'

'What went wrong?'

'Ron wanted to see where Lillee … Mr Lillee lived. He really believed that when we knocked on the door, some houseboy would answer, and he'd be naïve enough to let us in. Mrs Lord answered the door, and I knew immediately that the visit had been a mistake. I didn't know who she was, of course. I thought she was the housekeeper. Ron thought she'd be a pushover. She wasn't. She wouldn't let us in, and she knew we were dodgy. That didn't seem to bother Ron. He thought she was a bitch. I was embarrassed, and to be perfectly honest, I thought she might be trouble. We'd shown her our cards, and she'd taken long enough over them to memorise our names.'

'Mrs Lord has a nose for rotten coppers. She's familiar with how they smell.'

O'Dowd didn't let the insult distract him. Until now, he'd told the truth, and so his voice hadn't wavered, his face hadn't flushed, and his hands hadn't trembled. Using this momentum, he propelled himself into the potentially treacherous rip of lies.

'Ron told me he was going to confront Mr Lillee on, I think it was, Tuesday night. He was going to settle the amount he was going to get him to pay.'

'What was your role, exactly? Why did he need you?'

It was odd — until Lambert asked that question, O'Dowd hadn't considered why Dunnart had taken him into his confidence. It occurred to him in an instant.

'I was going to be the money collector. Ron didn't want to have to meet with Lillee each fortnight. That was a risk he delegated to me. He'd organise how much Mr Lillee had to pay, and I'd get a cut. The amount wasn't going to be extravagant. It was to be an amount Mr Lillee could easily afford — an amount he'd think too trivial to bother reporting — but it would supplement our salaries nicely. Ron explained his principles for squeezing people. You squeezed them just hard enough to force some money out of them, but not so hard that they'd fight back.'

'How much did Ron Dunnart hope to get out of Peter Lillee?'

'He didn't say. He was going to play that by ear. As it turned out, the meeting went badly. Ron followed Mr Lillee to an address in Kew. I now know that this was Lillian Johnson's flat. When Mr Lillee came out of the flat, Ron was waiting for him. He thought the flat belonged to a bloke. He'd rehearsed what he was going to say, but Mr Lillee departed from the script. He refused to pay Ron a penny, and he made it clear that he'd be taking this clumsy blackmail attempt all the way to the Commissioner. Ron told me that he thought Mr Lillee was bluffing and so he became very explicit about what he knew Mr Lillee had been up to and mentioned Sturt Menadue. Ron thought that would seal it. He said that Mr Lillee flew into a rage and told him that he'd make sure that he went to prison.'

O'Dowd paused.

'So Ron killed him.'

'How?'

'He was vague about that. He was in a bit of a mess when he told me. I don't think he's ever killed anyone before. I thought he was going to be sick, he was that upset and terrified. He said he'd poisoned him. I don't know how, but that's what he said. He said he'd poisoned him because, at that stage, it was either him or Mr Lillee, and he wasn't going to lose his job and go to jail on account of some rich cunt who could buy a successful conviction.'

'This is an extraordinary allegation you're making, Sergeant.'

O'Dowd turned slightly to look at Joe.

'It's like your allegation against Kevin Maher.'

'I suppose it is,' Joe said, 'insofar as two men are dead.'

'Why would Ron Dunnart confess this to you?'

'He needs an alibi for the night he followed Mr Lillee. If he went down, I'd go down with him. He knew that, and he made sure I knew it, so he told me how it had all gone wrong.'

'Do you think he killed Mr Lillee accidentally?'

'No, sir. Absolutely not. Ron said nothing about self-defence. He said he'd killed him to shut him up. It wasn't premeditated exactly. He hadn't followed him with the intention of killing him.'

'And yet he had some sort of poison with him.'

'I don't know how he did it, sir, and I don't know how he got the body down to the river.'

'Did you help him?'

'Absolutely not, sir. I was home with my wife. I wish I knew more, but all he said to me was that he'd killed him. He didn't say how he'd administered the poison or what he did with the body. He's a very smart man, sir. When he finds out I've betrayed him, he'll kill me. Sure as eggs, he'll kill me.'

'You do realise, Sergeant, that you are implicating yourself in serious offences.'

'I'll put my hand up to being an accessory to blackmail, but not to murder.'

Inspector Lambert stood up to signal that this part of the process was over.

'Sergeant Sable will take your statement. Obviously, this is going to make working with Ron Dunnart impossible.'

'Sir, Ron Dunnart murdered a man; surely you're going to arrest him.'

Inspector Lambert looked at O'Dowd in genuine puzzlement.

'You are familiar with the Crimes Act, Sergeant?'

O'Dowd's silence suggested that he wasn't.

'You've made a serious allegation against another person. It doesn't matter that he's a fellow officer. You've made certain claims and those claims need to be tested. We'll speak to Ron Dunnart, but we won't be arresting him unless he refuses to cooperate, and even then, no charges will be laid on the basis of your accusation.'

O'Dowd stood up.

'He'll deny everything, sir.'

'Of course he will, Sergeant.'

'He'll kill me.'

'Then we'll have a strong case.'

The steel in his voice reminded Joe why Titus Lambert was the head of Homicide. That simple, dismissive sentence told O'Dowd precisely what Lambert thought of him and his accusation.

'Sergeant,' he said to Joe, 'when you've taken Sergeant O'Dowd's statement, would you take a constable with you and go to Ron Dunnart's house and bring him here. If he refuses, arrest him. He won't, however, refuse.'

'What am I supposed to do?' O'Dowd asked.

'After you've given your statement, I suggest you go home and explain to your wife that you may face suspension from duty and possibly dismissal. The nature of your character won't surprise her, I imagine. Its consequences may. At least have the decency to forewarn her.'

O'Dowd was numb. Somehow this had all gone pear-shaped. He'd lost control of it somewhere. Dunnart couldn't remain at liberty. Just a few hours ago he taken some pleasure in the thought that Joe Sable was about to be pilloried by his fellow officers for accusing Kevin Maher of murdering a man who deserved to be murdered. Now here he was, a mirror image of Sable's impending ostracisation. Only it was worse. Maher was a man unknown to most of the men at Russell Street. Ron Dunnart was their mate, and even if he wasn't their mate, he was owed too many favours to be cut loose in a show of loyalty to O'Dowd.

O'Dowd gave his careful statement to Joe. He changed nothing from what he'd told Lambert, although the weakness of his claim was very apparent in the second telling. Somehow, all the true stuff didn't prop it up as effectively as he'd hoped. It was his word against Dunnart's.

'We're in the same boat, you and I,' he said to Joe.

'You should go home,' Joe said.

O'Dowd walked out into the late afternoon. The architectural ponderousness of the Magistrates' Court opposite the police headquarters weighed his spirits down. Life would never be the same. He hadn't known until this moment that he would find the idea of being disgraced intolerable. He stood on the footpath and put his face in his hands. They smelled of the ink he'd used to sign his statement. A sound came out of him that startled a couple of passers-by.

'Are you all right, mate?' one of them asked.

O'Dowd didn't hear him. He remained standing there with his face in his hands and people moved around him, unwilling to involve themselves in whatever grief it was that was shaking this man's frame.

Ron Dunnart opened his front door and took a moment to accommodate the presence on his doorstep of Joe Sable and a gormless-looking constable. He didn't invite them in. There could only be one reason for them turning up out of the blue. Fucking Bob O'Dowd.

'What do you want?'

'I want you to get your hat and come with us to Russell Street. Inspector Lambert has a few questions he'd like to ask you.'

Dunnart, who was in shirtsleeves, raised his arm and leaned against the doorjamb. Despite the heat, the only smell that came off him was of clean linen.

'And why would I do that? My wife has prepared a decent dinner.'

'I'm sure we'll have you back in time for dinner.' Joe paused, before adding, 'Sir.'

Dunnart snorted. He looked at Joe and the loathing he felt for him contorted his face. Lambert had sent this junior officer and the non-entity beside him to humiliate him. There was some satisfaction in knowing that the fading bruises on Joe's face would soon be freshened up by someone at Russell Street who didn't appreciate snouts. It was inevitable. There were several men who'd be happy to follow Dunnart's suggestion that giving Sable a going over would upset Sable and Lambert and no one else. It could be done under cover of darkness. Sable wouldn't know what or who had hit him. Kevin Maher would need a good alibi when it happened, but that would be easy to arrange. All these thoughts flashed through Dunnart's mind as he contained his own urge to punch Sable.

'I don't need a fucking hat, and I'm not going to give a little cunt like you the pleasure of arresting me, so let's get this bullshit over with.'

He stepped outside and pulled the door shut after him. He didn't bother to tell his wife that he was leaving the house. He'd be back before she'd even noticed his absence. The only person who needed to worry about the consequences of this interview was Bob O'Dowd.

WITH NOTHING BETTER to do and not wanting to return to his room at King's Hotel, Guy Kirkham stood outside the Magistrates'

Court in Russell Street and looked across to police headquarters. He couldn't quite imagine Joe as a detective. He'd always seen Joe as an aesthete. Not a foppish aesthete — not at all. Still, peering at corpses was a long way from poring over a bad reproduction of a Gentile da Fabriano painting, or arguing that Piero della Francesca was *the* greatest of the Italian masters. He wished that he could talk to him before Monday.

It was only a day and two nights, but Guy dreaded the nights and believed that a drink with Joe would anchor him in some way, remind him that it was still possible to have conversations about things that mattered only to them. Guy didn't want to talk about New Guinea. He wanted to try yet again to convince Joe that James Tissot was a genius and not a frivolous painter of skirts.

In thinking about Joe, it was almost as if he'd conjured him into being, because a car pulled up at police headquarters and one of the three men who got out was Joe. They hurried into the building before Guy had a chance to call out. He was content to wait until Joe came out again, and he didn't risk walking in search of a newspaper to keep him occupied. He would lean in the shadow of the court and mull over the plot of his novel.

THE INTERVIEW WITH Ron Dunnart had gone exactly as Inspector Lambert had expected it to go. Dunnart hadn't spent most of his career blackmailing people to allow a man like O'Dowd to trip him up. He denied everything and claimed that O'Dowd had come to him with the idea of squeezing Peter Lillee. They'd found that address book at the scene of the murders of Mr McNamara and Mr Menadue (he'd been careful to use this respectful form of address). Naturally the names in the book would need to be visited as part of the investigation. That was routine, and that was why they'd gone to Lillee's house. Maybe it was a mistake to lie to the housekeeper about the purpose of the visit, but 'I didn't want to alarm or upset her'. O'Dowd had torn the page with Lillee's name on it out of the address book and shown it proudly to Dunnart, who'd been furious, and when he'd heard O'Dowd's scheme, he'd rejected it out of hand.

'I thought it was a ridiculous idea, and I thought O'Dowd was foolish to approach me. I barely knew him. We'd worked on a couple of cases together. I thought O'Dowd was a mediocre, lazy detective, with no initiative. He was a Mason, too, of course, so that was another reason to steer clear of him. He actually knew I didn't like him. This blackmail idea was his stupid way of showing initiative. He thought I'd be impressed, which just goes to show how fucking stupid he really is.'

And on the night of Lillee's death? Well Mrs Dunnart would support his claim that he'd come home from work and that he didn't leave the house until the following morning. No, he had no idea why O'Dowd would make these allegations against him. Why would anyone accuse an innocent man of murder? It was bizarre and upsetting. O'Dowd must have lost his mind, or maybe it was payback for refusing to join him in his scheme to blackmail Lillee.

Dunnart had betrayed no nervousness as he'd defended himself. It was an assured performance, full of the elegant ducking and weaving of the practised liar. There'd been no hesitations, no backtracking to cover mistakes. To anyone who didn't know him, it would have been convincing. Inspector Lambert hadn't believed a word of it, but as he had no reason to detain him, he'd been obliged to let him go. He'd even allowed the constable who'd driven him here to drive him home. When Dunnart had left Inspector Lambert's office, Lambert leaned back in his chair and put his hands behind his head.

'Why do men like that become policemen?' he asked Joe.

'Maybe they think it's the safest way to break the law and get away with it.'

'Do you think he killed Peter Lillee, Sergeant?'

'No, sir, I don't. I don't think he'd allow a situation to get so out of control.'

Inspector Lambert tapped his fountain pen on his front teeth, a habit he'd recently adopted. It put Joe's own teeth on edge.

'You're expected back in Kew, I imagine.'

'Yes, sir.'

'I know you're keeping Helen Lord up to date, which you shouldn't be doing. However, I'd like you to keep doing it.'

Joe said nothing, but felt a wave a relief. As he got up to leave, Inspector Lambert said, 'Tom wondered if you could come to South Melbourne for lunch tomorrow. The weather looks promising so maybe you could talk him into wandering down to the beach. It would do him good.'

'That would be fine, sir. I do feel a bit underfoot at Kew.'

'I'm sure they don't mean to make you feel that way.'

'Oh, no, just the opposite. But I hate to think they're worrying about me on top of everything else.'

'You think too much, Joe.'

Lambert's use of Joe's name was the signal that the day's work was over.

GUY ALMOST MISSED Joe. He'd kneeled to tie a shoelace just as Joe emerged into Russell Street. When he looked up, he saw a figure walking south in the direction of Flinders Street. The walk was familiar, although he'd never associated Joe with such fine tailoring, and he didn't remember him ever wearing a hat. He hurried after him, unsure that this man was in fact Joe Sable. He followed him for two blocks.

At the intersection of Russell and Collins Street, Joe stopped and turned around. He'd been aware that someone had been following him and his fists were clenched in expectation of meeting George Starling.

'Guy?'

Guy laughed because the expression on Joe's face had moved swiftly from hostility to pleasure.

'You looked like you were going to attack me.'

'If you'd been the person I thought you were going to be, I would have attacked you. What the hell are you doing here, Guy?'

'Christ, it's good to see you, Joe.'

Guy looked down at his feet and tried to loosen the tightening in his chest, which he knew was the prelude to sobs. He failed, and Joe stepped up to him, put his arm around his shoulder, and said, 'Let's get a drink, mate.'

Guy nodded and managed to control the shuddering that threatened to overwhelm him.

'It's nearly six o'clock. Nothing will be open,' Guy said, and his voice was steady. He offered neither an apology nor an explanation for his sudden rush of emotion.

'I've got a room at King's, and more importantly, I've got a bottle of whiskey there that I borrowed from my father, and when I say borrowed, I really mean stole.' Joe laughed. Guy grinned. 'He won't miss it and my need was greater.'

From the foyer of King's Hotel, Joe telephoned Ros Lord to tell her that he wouldn't be there for dinner. He asked to speak to Helen and explained that he'd met his old friend Guy Kirkham and that he should be back in Kew by 10.00, when he'd tell her the details of the interviews. He detected in her curt responses that she thought the investigation into her uncle's death ought to come before everything else. As Guy was within earshot, he was unable to say that he was troubled by Guy's appearance, and that their meeting was more than just catching up.

Once inside Guy's room they assessed each other, and each found in the other evidence of recent horrors. Guy's face was unmarked, but it displayed the strains he'd endured — there was a hollowness around his eyes and he looked exhausted. Joe's face, with its fading cuts and bruises, was more obviously damaged. Guy made no comment. He found a glass and a teacup and poured two whiskeys. Guy sat on the edge of the bed, and Joe sat in the only chair, facing him.

'It's good to see you, Joe.'

'What's happened, Guy?'

Because Joe Sable was the person Guy Kirkham trusted above all others, he said, 'There was a young man named Harry Compton. He was twenty years old. I killed him, Joe, and I don't know how to live with that.'

9

HARDY TRUSCOTT'S HOUSE in Warrnambool sat on top of an escarpment that overlooked the Hopkins River. A great wall of stone fell from close to his back door to the river below. In a perverse act of defiance of nature, Truscott had built his house so that the sedate view from his front door was his only view. An uncomfortable, narrow staircase at the back door, leading to the privy, limited the pleasure to be taken in the spectacular aspect across the river. He'd built the house when he was a much younger man and had been squeamish about heights and reluctant to experience daily the crushing sense of insignificance the escarpment imposed. If he were building the house now, he'd reverse its orientation and celebrate the view as being worthy of Odin's majesty.

Truscott's front yard was wide and deep, but the proximity of neighbours made it unsuitable for the performance of Odinist rituals, many of which involved fire and chanting. His backyard was small and made smaller by the privy. It ran down, unfenced, to the lip of the escarpment. He'd managed to stage a few rituals here, for himself alone, and just once for two men who'd come down from Melbourne, and who'd been disappointed to discover that Truscott had no interest in the ritual being performed naked. They'd gone through the motions unenthusiastically and hadn't hung around afterwards.

Truscott had been peeved that Maria Pluschow had denied him sex in favour of the much younger George Starling. Somehow, Truscott couldn't quite divorce George from his late, loathsome father, but by that evening's end he'd felt real satisfaction at having won over, by the force of his rhetoric, this fierce and fiercely committed young man. That kind of raw, essential energy was precisely what his church needed. There was something frightening and elemental about George Starling, and Hardy Truscott believed that he could marshal that force into the service of Odin. He'd glimpsed glorious possibilities in the writings of Rud Mills, and here was one of those possibilities, sprung into being, right on his doorstep.

Maria Pluschow had accepted an invitation to Truscott's house on Saturday night. They would eat, discuss politics, and he would begin to formally instruct Starling in the ways of the Anglecyn Church. He'd built a wooden frame for a bonfire in the small backyard. Within the frame he'd pushed kindling and pages from the bible, and because it gave him real pleasure, pages from St Thomas Aquinas's *Summa Theologica*. The fact that he'd torn these from an edition of that work that had been expensive to buy pleased him particularly.

Truscott was only interested in food when someone else prepared it. He ate blandly when he cooked for himself. He was a natural austerity cook, not out of patriotism, but simply because he'd never eaten large amounts of butter, beef, lamb, or sugar. For Maria and George, he'd thrown together a vegetable stew with carrots, cabbage, chokos, potatoes, onions, and parsnips. He'd gone to the trouble earlier in the day of boiling potato skins in water to provide the soup with a starchy stock. A handful of barley and an insufficient amount of salt completed the soup. The best that could be said about it was that it was nourishing and inoffensive, but that was fine. The visitors weren't there for the food. They were there to experience the exquisite spiritual elation that the worship of

Odin ensured. The combination of fire and prayer would secure George Starling as a convert. Truscott was confident of this.

Maria drove, and George sat low in the passenger seat. There wasn't much danger of anyone recognising him, or even of seeing him. Why take an unnecessary risk, though, by sitting tall? Maria had been displeased by his gradual lack of communicativeness as Saturday had progressed. She'd sat with him as he'd sunbathed, and she'd prayed. He'd remained silent, which she'd interpreted as contemplative. She'd changed her mind about this after he'd come inside. When he'd looked at her there'd been something sour in his face, and he'd refused to get dressed. He'd moved through her house in a way she'd found primal and unsettling, as if he were claiming his territory and marking it, like some dangerous mammal rubbing its musk on surfaces. She wasn't intimidated by this, she was amazed by it, and she recognised, too, that there was an element of the erotic in it. Nevertheless, she wasn't altogether happy.

She'd laid out one of her husband's suits for him, and he put it on without comment. It was slightly too big for him. This didn't bother him. It was preferable to possibly soiling one of his own suits if Truscott insisted on dancing around a fire.

On a side table in the front room, Truscott laid out his collection of works by Rud Mills. *The Odinist Religion: overcoming Judeo Christianity*; *The First Guide Book to the Anglegyn Church of Odin: containing some of the chief rites of the Church and some hymns for the use of the Church*; *And Fear Shall Be in the Way*; *Hael, Odin!*; and his two precious copies of *The National Socialist: a paper devoted to the British race and British culture*. Mills had only published two issues of this paper, in 1936. Truscott had acquired them at one of the Odinist Society meetings he used to attend in Melbourne. There'd never been more than half a dozen people at these meetings, but Mills himself convened them, and that was all that mattered. Truscott had long since lost touch with these fellow Odinists.

When Starling and Maria arrived, Truscott gave them a goblet of home-brewed mead, which tasted herbal and unpleasant. Maria drained the goblet. Starling sipped the liquid, put it down, and declared it undrinkable. Truscott ignored this ungracious act. Starling was, after all, an as yet unformed member of the Church. He allowed Starling to pick up and flick through each of the A.R. Mills books, giving him a brief commentary as he did so. Starling managed to maintain the fiction of his interest, but his mind wasn't on Odinism; it was on how ridiculous this small, ugly man was, and on how ludicrous it was that he would consider himself an exemplar of the benefits of racial purity. Starling believed in racial purity. He didn't believe that Truscott was evidence of it.

Truscott began to instruct Starling as they ate. The soup was edible, which was the only reason Starling stayed at the table. Maria looked at him nervously throughout the meal, trying to judge from his face how Truscott's words were being received. Starling was impassive, his face enlivened only by the livid scar. Truscott spoke of how German Christians had wrestled with the fact of Christ's Jewishness and how some thinkers who espoused Ariosophy — Truscott helpfully explained that this was the mystical truth of the divinity of the Aryan race — how these thinkers had come up with the idea of the Aryan Christ. Christ wasn't a Jew after all, but a true Aryan whose race had been denied by St Paul, who had propagated the lie of his Jewishness. However attractive this idea might be, Truscott said, it was false. Christ was a Jew all right, and Christianity was a Jew religion that worshipped a Jew as its god. Throughout Truscott's speech, Starling remained silent and ate. Having swallowed his last mouthful of soup, he said, 'Germany is losing the war.' He wasn't sure if he believed this, because the press was controlled by Jews, which meant all reporting was suspect. He said it because he wanted to hear Truscott's response.

'Herr Hitler is a great man,' Truscott said, 'and he is, I believe, inhabited by a great Aryan spirit, a great mythological being. However, Herr Hitler has made a mistake in rejecting Herr Himmler's call for Odinism to be the state religion. He has instead made Hitlerism the state religion. This, George, *this* goes to the heart of what we believe. Nordic ideals are not carried in the vehicle of politics. For Hitler, it's all politics, and yes, you can see it unravelling. Odinism is about you, George, and me, and Maria. Salvation and, ultimately, domination lies within each of us. The spirit of the ancient, northern gods cannot be contained by parliaments, or Reichstags. It can't be stopped by bullets or votes. It will sweep us up, one by one, until order is restored and the purity of the Aryan race resumes its rightful place, and then lies about equality and democracy will be exposed as tawdry and weak. This is the glory that awaits us, George. You, me, and Maria, here in this room, are more powerful than a battalion of tanks.'

Truscott reached across the table and took hold of Starling's hand. With his other hand he reached towards Maria who stretched out her hand and took his. Starling wanted to crush Truscott's fingers into shards of broken bone. He let his hand remain limp, certain that if he closed it even slightly the temptation to exert force would be too great to resist. Truscott accepted Starling's unresponsive hand as acquiescence, surrender. He squeezed Maria's hand to signal this. When she raised her eyes to Starling's face, she didn't see surrender. She saw the emotionless eyes of a crocodile.

Starling was staring at Truscott, and Maria thought he might be calculating Truscott's height and weight, the way a lion might do before it brought down a wildebeest. There was no way to warn Truscott, and a part of her didn't want to. A part of her wanted to see what George Starling was capable of doing. She felt no fear for herself. She was confident that Starling would never raise a finger against her. She'd made love to him and she'd felt his brutishness give way to fleeting tenderness. No, not tenderness exactly, but something other than violence. She'd seen him cry and believed that this was a privilege that offered her protection from the worst of him. Besides, if he ever struck her, she'd insist that he leave. Maria Pluschow wouldn't tolerate being hit. Her husband had slapped her once. Just once. She'd hit the hand that had slapped her, with a mallet, and had broken three of its fingers. Mr Pluschow never hit her again.

After dinner, Truscott took his guests into his backyard. He handed each of them a piece of paper on which he'd written prayers from *The First Guide Book to the Anglecyn Church of Odin*. He lit the pyre he'd built and stood back from it. He spoke a prayer, then asked Maria to do the same. Starling read his prayer tonelessly, and Maria thought that perhaps it was going to be all right, that George would put up with the evening and later complain about how boring it had been. His acceptance of the new faith might just take longer than she'd hoped.

Truscott explained that once the flames had died down it was important that they each jump across the diminishing fire, intoning certain phrases as they did so. They watched in silence as the pyre burned low.

Maria, mesmerised by the dying flames, didn't see Starling place his hand on the back of Truscott's neck. Truscott leaned his head back to accept the embrace. It was over in a matter of moments.

With astonishing ferocity and strength, Starling forced Truscott to his knees and drove his face into the glowing coals. He held it there, his knee pressed against Truscott's back. With a deft movement, he pulled Truscott's right arm back and out of its socket. Then, gripping the useless limb, Starling dragged Truscott across the yard to the lip of the escarpment. Maria caught a glimpse of Truscott's blistered, ruined face, before Starling simply pushed him over the edge. Truscott hadn't uttered a sound.

Maria, conscious only of the crackling of the fire near her, spoke the words that saved her life.

'The soup wasn't that bad, George.'

MARIA DIDN'T ASK why. She and Starling drove back to her house in silence. Once there, she matter-of-factly said, 'They'll find Truscott's body and they'll come here.'

'I know they will. I won't be here.'

'You'll need more clothes. Casual clothes.'

Together they chose an assortment of Mr Pluschow's shirts, trousers, socks, and underwear, and packed them alongside Starling's suits. In a separate, smaller bag, Maria packed her late husband's shaving equipment, a brush, and a comb.

'Did your husband have a gun?'

'He had a Luger, from the first war, yes. He used it to shoot rabbits and cats.'

Maria found the gun and put it, along with its remaining six rounds of ammunition, into the small bag. Starling retrieved it and felt its heft in his hand. Blondi, who'd been lying in the living room, came into the bedroom as Starling was holding the gun up to the light. The dog barked twice. Starling levelled the gun in Blondi's direction, and perhaps because the downward swing of his arm resembled the signal to sit, she sat obediently on her haunches. Starling sighted the pistol so that a bullet would hit the dog in the middle of its forehead. Maria, looking in the wardrobe, had her back to him. She turned in time to see him pull the trigger.

Click.

'Seems to be in good working order,' Starling said and called Blondi to him. She came and accepted the desultory pat he gave her. Maria, feeling giddy with relief, said, 'Where will you go?'

'Melbourne. I've got unfinished business there. The gun will be handy. Thank you.'

10

GUY KIRKHAM WAS drunk. Not falling down drunk, but sufficiently drunk to stagger when he stood up to use the lavatory down the hall. While he was away, Joe, also drunk, wondered if he should telephone Helen. He'd told her he'd be back at Lillee's house at a reasonable hour, and it was now close to midnight. It was too late to disturb the household. It was also too late to get to the house in Kew. He didn't have a car, he'd missed the last train, and there'd be no taxis about at this hour. The discourtesy irked him, but there was nothing he could do about it until the following day.

He'd spoken freely with Guy about the investigations he'd been involved in, and he'd withheld nothing. Telling Guy about his and Tom Mackenzie's torture at the hands of Ptolemy Jones had been easy. It had always been easy to talk to Guy. When Guy came back from the toilet, Joe told him that he'd have to stay the night with him in the hotel room.

'I've been sleeping with a lot of men recently,' Guy said.

'Oh?'

'I just meant sharing a tent. The army doesn't go in for separate quarters.'

'So, platonically then.'

'Yes, Joe.' Guy paused for deliberate effect. 'Mostly.'

'That can get you into trouble, Guy.'

'It isn't fucking a man that's got me into trouble, Joe. It's killing one.'

'You said you fall asleep suddenly. That hasn't happened so far this evening.'

'You know something, Joe? I have to piss sitting down now because once I fell asleep when I was standing, and I pissed everywhere. It's unpredictable. Like your heart. You just never know, do you?'

Joe finished his glass and stopped drinking the whiskey. He knew that at a certain point alcohol made him sick. Guy continued to drink while they talked, until finally he fell back on the bed in a stupor. Joe took Guy's shoes off and arranged him into a comfortable position on his side. It was 3.00 a.m.

Joe took his own shoes off, and his jacket, and lay on the bed beside Guy. There was one dim light on in the room, and Joe couldn't be bothered getting up again to turn it off. He'd had enough whiskey to cause his head to spin mildly.

Guy was breathing deeply, and then his breaths began to be interspersed with small, whimpering sounds. Joe shook his shoulder, but Guy didn't wake. The whimpering quietened, and then ceased. Joe leaned across to look at Guy's face, and was disconcerted to find that his closed eyes were streaming with tears. He lay back on his side of the bed and wondered if there was any good in the world. Buried deep in the daily newspapers, certain place names had begun to appear. Dachau, Auschwitz-Birkenau, and Bergen-Belsen. Joe spoke them quietly and thought, *No, goodness had fled from the world*. As if to prove that this was so, Guy uttered a single cry of terror.

WHEN JOE WOKE the next morning his throat was sore — he must have slept with his mouth open — the muscles across his shoulders ached, and the whiskey hangover was beginning to establish itself. Guy wasn't on the bed beside him. He must have gone to the toilet.

Joe stood up and assessed the damage the whiskey had done. His clothes looked slept in, which was hardly surprising, and he felt seedy. He hated sleeping in his clothes. It exacerbated the general seediness. He needed a bath and a shave. He looked at his watch. It was 7.00 a.m. Guy, who'd drunk a good deal more whiskey than Joe, must be feeling very hungover.

Joe looked round the room. Where were Guy's things? He'd noticed the night before that Guy had put a few belongings — his shaving kit, a book, his watch — on a small table, and his suitcase had been against the wall. None of these items remained in the room. Guy had left.

Joe attempted to straighten the creases in his shirt and trousers, put his coat on, and quickly ducked into the bathroom, where he glanced at his dishevelled head, cupped water into his dry, sour mouth, went to the toilet, and then made his way downstairs to the foyer of the hotel. There was no one there. He went out into Russell Street, where he found Guy standing on the footpath, his suitcase beside him, and his hands in his pockets. Joe stood beside him.

'Do you feel as bad as you look?' Joe asked.

Guy managed a weak smile. 'I was hoping to be gone before you woke up.'

'Gone where?'

'Anywhere. Just gone.'

'But you've paid for two nights.'

'I don't think I can manage a second night in that room.'

'If you're hoping to catch a taxi, forget it. It's Sunday morning.'

'You know what I was hoping for, Joe? I was hoping that if I stood here long enough, the earth would open up and swallow me.'

'I'm staying in a very big house, Guy. There's plenty of room.'

Joe said this without thinking. Peter Lillee's funeral would be in a few days. Would Ros and Helen want a stranger intruding on their grief? They'd welcome him, he had no doubt of that, but would they wonder at Joe's impertinence?

'Wait here a minute,' he said to Guy. Then he turned and went back into to the hotel foyer and telephoned the Lillee house. Ros Lord answered. She didn't ask why Joe hadn't returned the previous night. She didn't consider this any of her business. When Joe broached the subject of Guy's needing a place to stay, Ros was enthusiastic. She said that the house needed people in it and that she was sure that any friend of Joe's would be a decent young man. There was no question for Joe about Guy's decency, but he was uncertain about bringing Guy's night terrors into the quiet of the house in Kew.

Once he'd hung up the telephone, Joe hurried back into the street, afraid that Guy might have taken off, but he found him waiting there.

'Mrs Lord is very happy to put you up, and believe me, it's a big house. You won't be in anyone's way.'

Guy picked up his suitcase.

'This feels like sanctuary, Joe. I never thought I'd need sanctuary. God help me, Joe, I do.'

THE CONCIERGE AT The Victoria Hotel was trying not to show his revulsion at the sight of the wound on George Starling's cheek. The Victoria was a busy hotel, one of the busiest in Melbourne, and the concierge had seen several returned men with faces altered by an injury sustained in battle. He'd seen men with an ear missing, or an eye missing, or with dreadful, unsightly burns. It was bad form to show that you found the injuries disgusting or shocking. He'd perfected the art of the neutral expression, so when he looked at Starling's face, he gave nothing away.

'We have a room with a bath, Mr Collins,' he said. 'You must be a lucky man. We've had a cancellation.'

Starling had settled on Collins as a pseudonym at the last minute. He paid in cash and took the key.

Once in his room, Starling put his suitcase on the bed and opened it. To lighten the suitcase, he'd left a shirt and a pair of Mr Pluschow's shoes in the pannier of his motorcycle, which he'd parked in a remote corner of the cemetery in Carlton. On the tram ride into town, he'd noticed the looks on people's faces as they observed him, and he was certain that they weren't actually seeing his features, just the scar.

Among the items he'd laid out on the bed were the Luger and Joe Sable's scrapbook, with its dozens of newspaper clippings delivering the news that the Jews in Europe were being dealt with. A few hours earlier, Starling had pulled over and tested the Luger by firing a bullet through the scrapbook. The hole was clean, with cordite marks on each page. The gun had sat well in his hands. Maybe this was the way to dispose of Joe Sable. A headshot from nowhere might be as satisfying in its way as a slow kill. He picked the Luger up, held it under his nose, and breathed in its metallic gunpowder-and-oil smell.

He knew where Joe Sable worked, but today was Sunday, so he wouldn't be there. He wouldn't be at his flat in Princes Hill, either. He knew that because he was the one who'd burned it down. There was another house where he'd seen Joe Sable visit. It was up in Brunswick. He'd seen that other prick there, too — Tom Mackenzie.

He'd caught Mackenzie in the backyard dunny, and he'd given him a fright. Christ, he'd screamed like a fucking pansy. He should have killed Mackenzie that night, but he hadn't known how many were in the house. It had been too risky, and he hadn't come prepared. He'd retreated into the night and nursed his regret about not knocking Mackenzie to the ground and stomping on him.

Starling decided to return to the Brunswick house. Maybe Sable was staying there temporarily. He'd wait until nightfall to visit the house. To help pass the time, he read each of the articles in the scrapbook he'd stolen from Sable's flat. He wasn't a daily reader of newspapers, but he did pick them up irregularly, and he'd never noticed articles like these. They were from *The Argus* and *The Age*, so he ought to have seen them. None of them was from the front page, so perhaps they'd been buried among the blizzard of competing news. That was a pity, because if he'd missed them, it was probably true that most other people had missed them, too.

Starling had no desire to search out members of the group that Ptolemy Jones had gathered together. He hadn't liked any of them, and without Jones to lead them, what was the point? He didn't want to discuss National Socialism with them. He didn't want to discuss National Socialism with anyone. Political theory bored him. Action was what made a difference; action was what mattered. Thinking and theory created men like Hardy Truscott. They were a waste of space. He was happy to act alone. There was more heroism in that than in all of Truscott's Odinist rubbish. He didn't believe in any god. If God existed and had seen fit to deliver him into the hands of a man like his father, then God was an arsehole.

JOE AND GUY arrived at Peter Lillee's house in Kew just before 10.00 a.m. Joe couldn't judge from Helen's reaction to Guy whether she was genuinely happy to have him there, or whether she was being polite. Ros Lord was more effusive. She took them both upstairs and gave Guy a choice of two rooms.

'Peter always liked to have the guest rooms ready, even though no one ever used them.'

Guy, who had grown up in a large house, wasn't confounded by the extravagance of the Kew residence. He chose the first room he'd been shown and put his suitcase on the bed.

'I'll make us some tea,' Ros said. 'It's a lovely morning. We'll have it in the garden.'

As they were going down the stairs, the telephone rang. Helen answered it. Joe assumed it was for her, perhaps her friend, Clara. He and Guy went out into the garden, and Ros went into the kitchen to prepare the tea.

'They seem like nice people,' Guy said. 'It's damned decent of them to take me in like this.'

'I admire them both,' Joe said.

'Helen especially?'

If someone other than Guy had asked this question, it might have been impolite. Neither of them was aware that Helen had come out into the garden in time to hear the question, and to hear Joe's answer.

'Helen can be bloody touchy, but I don't blame her. She's smarter than anyone in Homicide. She's certainly smarter than I am, as she's pointed out more than once. I think she might be even smarter than Lambert. I'm intimidated by her. And you know, having shared this house with her, I'm getting to like her more and more.'

Helen hung back until the conversation had moved on. She sequestered Joe's comment for later deconstruction.

'It's Tom Mackenzie on the telephone,' she called from the back step, and then walked towards the two men. Joe stood up, remembering suddenly that he'd agreed to have lunch with Tom.

'He sounds good,' Helen said. 'We had a brief chat. I've never actually spoken to him before, which is odd, isn't it? Given everything that's happened.'

'He'd have liked the chance to talk to you. I've told him about you, of course. He knows what happened in Port Fairy.'

Helen narrowed her eyes slightly, and Joe thought he'd made a blunder. Would Helen think he had no business talking about her to Tom Mackenzie?

'I'd like to meet him,' she said, and smiled, which made Joe feel better. While Joe went inside to talk to Tom, Helen sat opposite Guy. She observed him closely, looking, as she always did when first meeting someone, for small tells that might provide clues to character, or simply to personal idiosyncrasies. She saw signs of nervousness and exhaustion. He was a good-looking man, she thought, but his eyes betrayed a night of heavy drinking, and the skin on his unshaven face was beginning to show signs of unhealthy living. Something had happened to him, and whatever it was, the memory of it plagued him.

'You've known Joe for quite a while,' she said.

'We met at university. We shared an interest in the impractical discipline of art.' He smiled. 'It was the interest we shared. We don't share the same tastes. I think of Joe as a mediaevalist. I'm a bit more up to date.'

'You might be interested in my late uncle's collection.'

'I did notice the Sargent knock-off.'

'I know Joe thinks I'm a nitwit when it comes to art. I've never taken an interest in it.'

'It's very good of you and your mother to put me up at such short notice, especially considering ...'

'Mum is very fond of Joe, so any friend of his is welcome.'

Guy refrained from asking if there was a discrepancy between Mrs Lord's fondness for Joe and Helen's fondness for him. Helen noticed this and appreciated the discretion, conscious that it was deliberate. A clumsier person would have asked without thinking, given the way she'd phrased her comment. Despite his hangover,

Guy Kirkham was astute — much more astute than Joe would have been in the same situation.

'I drank too much whiskey last night.'

'Whiskey is hard to get these days.'

'I stole it from my father.'

Guy raised his teacup to his lips, and Helen looked away, thinking that he might be embarrassed by the obvious tremor in his hand.

'It's not permanent, I hope,' he said, nodding at his hand. 'It comes and goes. You must think I'm a bit of a mess. The thing is, I am a bit of a mess.'

Helen had never before sat with a man who seemed so unguarded, so uninterested in shielding from view the rawness of his emotions. She didn't find it weak or pathetic. Her impulse — an impulse not often aroused in her — was to hold him. Instead, she reached across the table and put her palm over his still faintly trembling hand.

'You really are welcome here, Guy.'

He nodded and was about to say something, when Joe returned to the garden. Helen left her hand where it was. To do anything else would have created the ridiculous impression that she'd removed it guiltily.

'Tom Mackenzie has invited me to lunch. He said you'd be welcome to come along, Guy. It's almost warm enough to go for a swim at South Melbourne Beach.'

'I don't have any trunks.'

'I'm sure Uncle Peter has spare swimming trunks — and they won't have been worn. He always bought several pairs of everything.'

Neither Joe nor Guy had any real intention of swimming, but they followed Helen to Peter Lillee's bedroom to collect a pair of trunks each, just in case. There was a drawer that held only swimming trunks, and they chose two pairs of woollen blue

Jantzen trunks with white belts. As Helen had promised, they were in unopened cellophane packets and had clearly never been worn.

It was Helen who suggested that they use Peter's car. Getting to South Melbourne on a Sunday using public transport would take hours. Ros was in furious agreement, so Joe found himself behind the wheel of the most expensive car he'd ever sat in.

'That's a nasty scratch on the passenger side,' Guy said. 'Looks fresh, too — no rust. What happened?'

'We don't know. The car was locked up in the garage the night Peter died. He walked to the river.'

'Where were the car keys?'

'You should join the force, Guy. The keys were in the house, and the car was definitely locked. Someone from Homicide went over the car. There's a brief report on it, but it doesn't seem to have played any part in Peter's death.'

'Maybe some envious bastard gouged the car out of spite.'

'That's probably what happened. There's been a bit of that happening around town. People think anyone who drives a flash car must be rorting the petrol rationing.'

Tom Mackenzie was at home alone when Joe and Guy arrived. Titus and Maude had gone to their house in Brunswick to do some gardening and washing. Introductions were brief.

'I know what happened to you, mate,' Guy said. 'Joe told me. Hope you don't mind.'

'Not at all. It saves me explaining it. Joe mentioned on the phone that you had a bad time in New Guinea. I hope *you* don't mind.'

Guy put his arm around Joe's shoulder. 'Quid pro quo,' he said. 'Three wounded soldiers. What a sorry sight we are.'

'I think I look the sorriest,' Tom said. 'Not that it's a competition.'

'My scars are all up here,' Guy said, and tapped his temple. 'If you could see inside here, you'd run screaming into the street.'

Lunch was sandwiches, and talk among them was easy. Because George Starling was uppermost in Tom's mind, he wanted Joe to tell him everything he knew. It was clear to Tom that Joe told Guy everything, so he had no qualms about raising the matter of tracking Starling down. Joe wished he hadn't, especially as Guy became enthusiastic about joining them. That was out of the question, but Joe decided to wait before explaining why. It would have put a dampener on the lunch.

'Is it warm enough for a swim?' Guy asked. 'I suddenly feel like one.'

'Not warm enough for me,' Tom said. 'And I'm not supposed to get these splints wet. Besides, I don't think I'm ready to take my shirt off in a public place.'

They agreed that a walk along the Kerferd Road Pier would be ideal. Guy changed into the swimming trunks he'd borrowed and pulled his clothes on over them. Tom gave him a towel.

'I'll decide whether it's too cold or not when we get there,' Guy said.

They walked the short distance from Tom's house to Middle Park Beach. There was a good chop on Port Phillip Bay, which drove small waves onto the beach. There were a few people in the water and a few more on the sand. The wind was just strong enough to flick the sand about and cause people to turn their faces this way and that to avoid it. At the far end of the pier, half a dozen men were fishing.

Tom, Guy, and Joe walked the length of the pier. No one had caught any fish. Tom stood on the edge and looked down into the water.

'I could never have joined the navy. The ocean terrifies me. It's ruthless.'

'It holds you up,' Guy said. 'Unlike the air.'

'It doesn't want to hold you up. It wants to drag you under. It's a vast, liquid maw.'

Joe laughed. 'It's really just Port Phillip Bay.'

Guy took a step back from Tom and Joe and undressed so quickly that each of them was surprised when he pushed between them and stood on the edge of the pier. He said nothing and vanished, feet first, into the water.

It was this that made Joe's heart begin an erratic, nausea-inducing pattern of beating. Even though he knew it would pass, whenever it happened his response was to become highly anxious, which only made him feel worse. He sat down on the rough planks of the pier, fearful that he might topple into the bay, and put his head between his knees.

Tom, caught between Guy's disappearance and Joe's collapse — for that was what it looked like — hesitated. Then Joe got on all fours and began vomiting copiously over the edge of the pier, and Tom swiftly kneeled beside him and put his hand between his shoulder blades. He noted peripherally the looks of distaste on the faces of the fishermen. He didn't speak but hoped that the pressure of his hand might provide some reassurance.

Joe pulled back from the edge again and sat with his knees up and his arms resting on them. He breathed deeply. He was sweating, and his face was white, so white that his beard shadow looked like a large charcoal smudge.

'Guy,' he said. 'Where's Guy?'

Tom had no sense of how much time had passed.

'He's swimming,' he said.

'Where? Can you see him?'

It hadn't occurred to Tom to worry about Guy until he heard the tension in Joe's voice.

'Just this morning Guy said that he wanted the earth to open up and swallow him.'

'Oh, Christ,' Tom said. He scanned the water on one side of the pier, and then the other. There was no sign of Guy Kirkham.

'Did anybody see the bloke who jumped in?' Tom called.

'Saw him go in. Haven't seen him since,' one of the men replied. All six of them put their rods aside and came over to Joe and Tom.

'Have you blokes been drinking?' one of them asked.

'No mate, we haven't.'

Having seen Joe be extravagantly sick, they were unconvinced, but they began to scour the water for Guy.

'Can your mate swim?'

'Yes,' Joe said. 'He's a strong swimmer.'

Joe, still shaken, managed to stand up. No one knew quite what to do. A man had gone into the sea, and he'd failed to surface. The waters were rough, so it was possible he was hidden behind rising and falling waves at some distance from the pier. There was no point anyone diving in after him, so the only hope was to return to the beach and get help. None of the fishermen knew whether or not there was a lifeboat nearby, or even if there were lifeguards on duty. Surely there were. It was Sunday. *No*, thought Joe. *Summer is over. There'd be no reason to patrol the beach this late in the year.*

Three of the fishermen stayed where they were, watching the waves. The other three hurried with Tom and Joe back to the beach. They were halfway along the pier, when a man began climbing one of the ladders that were attached at intervals along its length. It was the furthest ladder, still some distance from the hurrying men, but Joe recognised Guy's silhouette as he hauled himself up and stood facing them, one hand on his hip, the other dragging his hair back from his forehead.

'That's him,' Joe said.

'You mean we left our fucking lines for no reason.'

'Listen, mate,' Tom said. 'He's just come back from the war, which you've spent dropping a fucking fishing line into Port Phillip Bay. We didn't know ...'

'All right, all right,' said the oldest of the three fishermen. 'Just get him out of here. The other blokes are going to be pissed off.'

'Thank you for your help,' Joe said.

The man he spoke to noticed for the first time the strapping around Tom's fingers, and his still swollen face, and he noticed too that Joe's face had evidence of recent injuries. *All three of these blokes must be on some kind of sick leave*, he thought.

'I'll get your mate's clothes,' he said and ushered his two companions back to their abandoned rods. Guy began walking towards them, and he thought something must have happened. The behaviour of the three strangers was odd. He got to Joe and Tom quickly, well before the fisherman had returned with his clothes.

'What's happened?' he said. If Joe hadn't been ill, this question might have been humorous.

'You just disappeared, Guy. We thought you'd drowned.' Joe said this with deliberate matter-of-factness. He didn't want Guy to see the mixture of relief and fury that was running through him. Tom wasn't willing to be so careful.

'Why did you do that? Why did you just drop into the water and not resurface where anyone could see you?'

Guy seemed genuinely puzzled.

'I was swimming under the pier. That's all. I was just swimming.'

'Joe thought — we both thought you'd ...'

'Tried to kill myself?' The chill of the water had cleared Guy's head and instead of exhibiting shock, or outrage, he laughed.

'I'm wearing another man's swimming trunks. I wouldn't kill myself wearing someone else's pants, and I wouldn't do it here in front of everyone. What if some busybody rescued me?'

The fisherman returned with Guy's clothes, and finding him laughing, threw them at his feet.

'Let's go home,' Tom said.

The tenor of the day had been altered by Guy's swim and by Joe's physical distress. Guy apologised on the way back to Tom's place when he realised that his temporary disappearance had thrown everyone, and especially Joe, into a panic. They agreed to meet again for dinner later in the week, and Joe and Guy drove back to Kew.

'I am really sorry, Joe. I feel sick that my stupidity made your heart go haywire.'

'It's fine, Guy. It was stupid of me to jump to the wrong conclusion.'

Joe had to brake suddenly to avoid hitting a dog, and Guy put his hand on the dashboard to steady himself. As he did so, he noticed that a gold fountain pen had been propelled from under his seat to settle near his left foot. He leaned down and picked it up.

'This is a bloody expensive pen,' he said.

'It must be Peter's. Whoever went over this car did a poor job. I'll give it to Ros Lord.'

'It's got an inscription on it. To misquote Wilde, is it un-gentlemanly to read a private fountain pen?'

'It's probably a gift from his fiancée, Lillian Johnson.'

Guy turned the fountain pen over in his hand. He read, '"To Ronald, from your loving parents 12/12/1923". That's all it says. Whoever Ronald is, he's held onto it for twenty-one years. It must mean a great deal to him. He must have dropped it. Who do you reckon Ronald is? A friend of Peter Lillee's?'

Joe reached across and took the pen from Guy. He put it in his jacket pocket.

'No. Not a friend. It might belong to the man who murdered Peter.'

GEORGE STARLING COLLECTED his motorcycle from the Melbourne Cemetery at 9.00 p.m. on Sunday night. He rode past the ruins of Rosh Pinah, just for the pleasure it gave him, and then on to Bishop Street in Brunswick. He parked the motorcycle at the southern end of the street and walked towards the house he'd recently visited. The blackout restrictions had been relaxed and several of the houses boldly showed lights. Number 17 was in darkness. He went back to the bike and wheeled it into the laneway behind the houses.

It was a clear, bright night and he found the back gate of the house easily. Standing on the seat of the bike he was able to see over the gate into the yard. There were no lights on and no sign of any activity. It was too early for people to have gone to bed, so Starling thought it a safe assumption that no one was home. Unlike on his first visit, the gate was locked. Before climbing over it, he took Joe's scrapbook from the pannier and tucked it inside his shirt, next to his skin.

He checked the outside toilet. It was unoccupied. He cautiously approached the kitchen window. There were no blackouts up, and, peering through the glass, he could see that it was tidy. If anyone had eaten there that evening, the mess had been cleaned away. He moved round to the side of the house and looked into the living room. It was too dark to see anything clearly. He listened intently for any sound that might indicate that the house was occupied. Nothing. He decided to break in.

He had no skills as a burglar, so he simply kicked the back door so that the lock shattered and it flew open. The noise this made wasn't as loud as he'd expected. Nevertheless, he waited a few moments to see if the crash brought anyone running. It didn't. He entered the house.

He'd come here for a purpose and the purpose wasn't to explore or to take anything. He went into the living room, and on the table there he propped open Joe's scrapbook, disfigured now with a bullet hole. He had no desire to linger, but before leaving he unbuttoned his flies and sprayed the room with his urine, like a tomcat marking his territory.

11

When Joe arrived at work on Monday morning, the hostility towards him was pointed. Officers with whom he'd had a cordial nodding relationship silently mouthed obscenities at him before turning their backs. His desk didn't at first appear to have been interfered with, but when he lifted a folder the word 'scum' had been scratched into its surface.

David Reilly, who arrived soon after Joe, saw the graffito and said that he couldn't understand the mentality of some people. Helen Lord would have suggested, if she'd heard this, that this was because Reilly wasn't very bright. Joe thought Reilly was all right. Helen's antipathy towards him sprang from Reilly's inability to accept, at least initially, that a woman could do the job of a Homicide detective. If there was one thing about Inspector Lambert that had always frustrated her, it was his inexplicable trust in Sergeant David Reilly. The best that could be said of Reilly was that he was a plodder, with a tendency towards incompetence. That was Helen's view. It wasn't Lambert's. He might agree that Reilly wasn't intuitive or particularly sharp, and he could be petulant, but he was reliable and, most importantly, he was honest and despised dishonesty or corruption in other officers. For Lambert, that was Reilly's most valuable asset. There weren't many officers Lambert trusted unequivocally. Reilly was one of them.

'I wish I'd been in that room with you, so I could back up your story. You know, not everyone believes Kevin Maher, Joe.'

Any further discussion was truncated by Inspector Lambert's arrival. He'd barely sat down when his telephone rang. Almost simultaneously, an envelope was delivered with Peter Lillee's autopsy and toxicology results in it. Joe entered Lambert's office while he was still on the telephone and put the envelope on his desk. Lambert signalled that Joe should stay.

'Are you sure you don't want anyone from here to come down to Warrnambool, Greg?' Inspector Lambert asked into the phone. Joe's muscles tensed. Warrnambool. That could only mean one thing, surely. George Starling. Lambert listened and took notes and, after some pleasantries, hung up.

'That was Inspector Halloran in Warrnambool. You may recall that he and I interviewed a man named Hardy Truscott. He was a National Socialist sympathiser, but with some fairly esoteric ideas about Nordic gods. He's dead, and it's pretty clear from his injuries that he was murdered.'

'Starling?'

'Well, maybe, but why would Starling murder a fellow Nazi? It's not really his style, is it?'

'I don't think of Starling as having a style, sir.'

'True. That was a poor choice of words on my part. If it *is* Starling, at least we know he's in Warrnambool, which gives you some breathing space. Inspector Halloran is going to keep me fully informed. The body was only found a couple of hours ago.'

'Before you read the autopsy report, sir, I think you should see this.'

He put the fountain pen on the desk in front of Lambert.

'A friend of mine, Guy Kirkham, found this on the floor of Peter Lillee's car. I had to brake suddenly, and it rolled out from under the passenger seat.'

Lambert picked up the pen and read the inscription. He called to David Reilly through the open door, and Reilly came into Lambert's office.

'Could you please bring me Detective Sergeant Ron Dunnart's personal file?'

Reilly left the room, and Lambert opened the envelope. He read the contents quickly, searching out the key details.

'This poses more questions than it answers,' he said. 'What seems certain from the colour of Lillee's blood is that he was poisoned.'

'Cyanide?'

'No. The toxicologist doesn't speculate except to say that the death wasn't natural causes. The purplish colour in the blood is consistent with some sort of toxin having been introduced into Peter Lillee's system. Whether it was self-administered or administered by another person is impossible to say. All of which points to the coroner delivering an open finding, which won't provide Ros and Helen Lord with much comfort.'

David Reilly returned with Dunnart's file. Lambert handed Reilly the pen and asked him to read the inscription. For a moment, Joe felt peeved. He'd found the pen, so why had Lambert handed it to David Reilly?

'"To Ronald, from your loving parents 12/12/1923".'

Lambert ran his finger down Ron Dunnart's file.

'Detective Sergeant Ronald Dunnart was born on the twelfth of December 1902, which makes him forty-two this year.'

'So in 1923 he'd just turned twenty-one. This is a twenty-first birthday gift.'

'I think it's safe to say that the fountain pen belongs to Detective Dunnart.'

'The question is,' Reilly said, 'what was it doing in Peter Lillee's car?'

Lambert turned to Joe.

'Sergeant Reilly has been working closely with Sergeant Dunnart on the murders of Sturt Menadue and Steven McNamara.'

'Which is where Ron found Peter Lillee's name: in Menadue's address book,' said Joe.

'Precisely,' said Reilly. 'Inspector Lambert suspected that Ron Dunnart was crooked, so he put me on Dunnart's team, to keep an eye on him. Of course, he knew that that's why I was there, and I was expecting him to make life difficult for me. He did the opposite and has conducted, and continues to conduct, the investigation with professionalism and, I have to admit, with expertise. I've been with him when he's interviewed acquaintances of the murdered men, and he's always been respectful. Now, I know he would probably have behaved differently if I hadn't been there, and he may well have pressed some of the men for money. But so far, he's done everything by the book.'

'He'd picked his target already, hadn't he?' said Joe. 'Peter Lillee. He must have thought that was enough for one case.'

'In your view, Sergeant,' asked Lambert, 'knowing what you know about Ron Dunnart and having worked up close with him, is he capable of murder?'

'He's not a nice bloke. He's arrogant and overbearing. He intimidates junior officers, and he engages in blackmail. I have no doubt about that. But murder? He's a good detective. He knows he'd get caught. So, no sir, I don't believe Ron Dunnart killed Peter Lillee.'

If Helen Lord was right about David Reilly, Joe thought, his opinion wasn't worth much. But if Lambert was right about him, he ought to be listened to.

'Dunnart's pen surely puts Dunnart in the car with Peter Lillee,' Joe said.

Lambert nodded.

'Sergeant Dunnart has lied to us about blackmailing Mr Lillee. He may well have sat in his car with him, but where and when, who knows? Well, Dunnart knows, and we need to find that out. However, that is a long way from proving that he killed him, and our biggest hurdle is the "how". How did he do it? And how did he dump the body and leave no trace?'

'Sergeant Reilly has said that he's an excellent detective. Perhaps he's also an accomplished killer.'

'No,' Reilly said. 'I simply do not believe that Ron Dunnart killed Peter Lillee.'

Why? Joe wondered. *Why are you so sure?*

SERGEANT BOB O'DOWD didn't show up for work on Monday. When Lambert was talking to Joe Sable and David Reilly, he was still in bed. He wasn't asleep. He was paralysed with anxiety. He'd told his wife a version of what he'd told Lambert, and had told her, too, that there was every chance that he'd lose his job. If he lost his job, they'd lose the house. O'Dowd had never been good with money and they lived from pay to pay.

Vera O'Dowd didn't despise her husband, but the thought that he would shame her in this way, that he'd be exposed as a nasty blackmailer, was too much for her. She'd punished him often with silence, but had never left him. She'd listened to his confession with what felt to her like a breaking heart. She was angry, because although she'd always thought him dull, she'd never thought of him as a wicked man. He was unexciting, but reliable, and she'd loved him. She may not have called it love, but as her feelings for him curdled, she'd realised that such a falling away was a falling away from love. Just twenty-four hours ago she would have applied ointments to his psoriasis, and she would have done it with tenderness and with no hint of revulsion. Now, the thought of touching him made her feel queasy, and the thought of sexual contact with him turned her stomach. She'd packed her bags and moved to her sister's house in Montmorency, a suburb a long way from their house in Fitzroy.

Bob O'Dowd didn't want to get out of bed. If he got out of bed, the day would have to progress. His bladder defeated him. He thought about returning to bed, but the stale air in the room, which he hadn't noticed until he'd left it, made him change his mind. His left ankle was itching badly. He went into the bathroom, took off his pyjamas, and was shocked at what had happened to his body overnight.

The psoriasis on his ankle was red and angry, and it had spread beyond its usual boundaries. A rash had appeared on his chest and shoulders, and a red and scaly mark had broken out on his face. The more closely he looked at himself the more flare-ups he noticed. The skin around his ankle was broken and bleeding. He must have scratched it during the night. He began to itch simultaneously in different areas. Having satisfied one itch, he had to pursue another and another, and the more he scratched the more insistent the itches became.

He lit the chip heater at the end of the bath, and when he'd filled the tub with hot water, he lay down in it. The shock of the hot water eased the itching, and as he lay in it, noticing a few patches of mould on the ceiling, he wondered how his life had come to this. When would Dunnart come for him? He listened intently, diagnosing each small sound the house made, fearful that an unfamiliar one might signal Dunnart's arrival.

The sharp rap at the front door made him sit bolt upright. Water spilled onto the floor. He began to shiver with both cold and fear. He waited. Whoever was at the door knocked again, and more insistently. O'Dowd figured that Dunnart wouldn't announce his arrival, so he stepped out of the bath, wrapped a towel around his waist and moved cautiously towards the front door.

'Who is it?' he called.

'Telegram.'

O'Dowd was relieved and opened the door a crack, just wide enough to take the telegram and prevent the telegram boy from seeing his torso. He began to itch again. He went to the front room and sat, still damp from the bath, in the damask chair that Vera O'Dowd had inherited from her mother. It was more comfortable on his bare skin than the leather armchair. He turned the envelope over in his hands and opened it.

'Where will you hide? Because you'll need to'

There was no name, but no name was necessary. A strong itch in his armpit demanded his attention. O'Dowd had never in his life before felt desperation. It must have been desperation that made him think that he needed to beat Dunnart to the punch. Dunnart knew where he lived, but he knew where Dunnart lived, and he had an advantage. Dunnart wouldn't be expecting him.

When Inspector Lambert entered the Melbourne Club, he felt a mixture of revulsion and envy. Wealth and privilege had never impressed him. There was something about the Melbourne Club, though, that was seductive. There was an immediate sense, in its deliberate lack of ostentation, that this was a place where power was exercised with quiet certainty and with wily discretion.

Lambert had heard of Sir Marcus Ashgrove and knew that this would be a difficult interview. He'd spoken to him briefly on the telephone, and Sir Marcus had seen no reason at all why he needed to speak to a policeman about Peter Lillee's death. It was unfortunate, but what had it got to do with him? Lambert had been frank and had mentioned the Wombat Forest goldmine. He could feel Ashgrove's indignation rushing down the line towards him.

'I would be happy to visit you at home, Sir Marcus.'

'Lady Ashgrove would not be happy to have a policeman in the house. The club would be the best place to get this over with.'

Inspector Lambert didn't have to wait long in the foyer of the Melbourne Club. The porter had been told to expect him and as soon as he'd arrived had telephoned for one of the staff to take him to Sir Marcus. The porter, in his sixties, was deferential without being obsequious. As he followed the gentleman upstairs, Lambert thought that it would have been a mistake to have asked Joe Sable to interview Sir Marcus Ashgrove. His youth would have worked against him in this place, although he might have appreciated what was hanging on the walls.

Sir Marcus had chosen a small, private sitting room on the third floor. When Lambert entered the room, Sir Marcus was seated, reading *The Age* newspaper. He didn't stand up to greet Lambert, but merely indicated that he should sit down.

'At least you didn't send some acne'd constable, Inspector. I suppose I ought to be flattered.'

'I'm not here to flatter you, Sir Marcus.'

'I hope you're not going to take up much of my time.'

'That feeling is mutual.'

As if Sir Marcus couldn't conceive that someone else's time might be valuable, he said, 'What's that supposed to mean?'

'We're both busy men, Sir Marcus.'

If Lambert had been observing one of his men conducting this interview, he would have been annoyed at that officer's having allowed the interview to get off to a hostile start. He was glad no one was observing him. His instant dislike of Sir Marcus had got the better of him. It was unprofessional and a mistake someone like Helen Lord would never make. He wanted her back in Homicide, though he had, as yet, no clear idea how to accomplish this.

Sir Marcus folded the newspaper.

'Well, get on with it.'

'What was your relationship with Peter Lillee?'

'Cordial. He had a lot of talent. I got him into this club.'

'Is that of some significance?'

'Of course it's bloody significant. You have to be somebody to be a member of this club.'

'You were at odds with him, though, weren't you?'

Whatever else Sir Marcus was, he wasn't stupid, and he knew that this policeman would have talked to various people before turning up here at the Melbourne Club.

'I wasn't just at odds with him. I was so disappointed in his actions that I was prepared to have him blackballed.'

'Why?'

'Lillee was on the Capital Issues Advisory Committee, and he was actively blocking an investment opportunity into which several members of this club, including me, had sunk considerable funds. He was in a position to advocate for the investment and to protect us against losses. He refused. This was disloyal and, I believe, self-interested. Don't talk to me about the bloody war. My son is in a bloody prisoner-of-war camp. Lillee wasn't blocking us out of some sort of patriotism. He had something up his sleeve. I don't know what it was, but he was ambitious. The thought that he would sit back and watch fellow members possibly go bankrupt made me sick. So, yes, I wanted him blackballed.'

He paused. Lambert waited.

'Wanting him blackballed is not the same thing as wanting him dead, Inspector.'

'But he is dead, Sir Marcus.'

'His death doesn't benefit me. The committee has made its decision, and it doesn't benefit anyone else here, either. Quite the reverse.'

'Oh?'

'As I said, he was talented when it came to money. Lots of men would go to him for advice.'

'But you were going to blackball him.'

'Money trumps everything, Inspector. I could have got him kicked out of the club, but chaps would still have gone to him, and each of them would have told him, of course, that he had been opposed to the blackballing. Peter Lillee's exit from this club wouldn't mean the end of his career. It would just have given me satisfaction. Invitations to things might have dropped off, but Lillee rarely went to such events anyway. And if I'm being perfectly honest, I'm not sure the blackballing would have been successful. He was too well-liked, and he was too bloody rich.'

'You don't seem very curious about how he died.'

'I've heard rumours, but it's none of my business.'

'What sort of rumours?'

'The same sort you've heard, I imagine. The grubbiest is that he was murdered by some bloke he met down by the river. I've heard of men getting up to that sort of thing. I'd like to think Lillee wasn't one of them, but if he was, well, there it is, and that's what happens. I was also told that he might have taken his own life, but I don't believe that for a second. Not at all the type.'

Inspector Lambert came away from his interview with Sir Marcus Ashgrove believing that Ashgrove wasn't implicated in Lillee's death, but also believing that there was nothing admirable about him. He supposed it was unfair to think it, but he thought that whatever Sir Marcus had achieved in his life it would have been at the expense of someone else. Nevertheless, as he stepped out into Collins Street and looked back at the front door of the Melbourne Club, he couldn't entirely extinguish a small part of him that felt it might be grand to belong to such a place. He knew that when he told Maude about it later, he could rely on her to snuff out that little pilot light of envy.

MAUDE LAMBERT HAD stopped worrying about her brother's recovery, up to a point. His physical wounds were healing well, and he was in the hands of a good psychiatrist. She couldn't imagine herself ever discussing her private fears with a stranger, especially one who took notes. She had Titus, of course. She still had one worry about Tom that she'd never expressed to Titus. Tom was over thirty, and he was unmarried. It bothered Maude that her concern about this might indicate that she was a deeply conventional woman — an accusation she would have been unhappy to hear from somebody else. She knew Tom liked women. He'd had several girlfriends over the years and any one of them would have made a decent wife — well, except for the actress, who Maude had thought vain and empty-headed, and to whom Tom had actually become engaged. Still, Tom's female companions were the least of his worries at the moment.

Maude thought that it was time for Tom to retrieve his privacy. If she and Titus moved back to their house in Brunswick it would be a sign to Tom that life was returning to normal. There were still the nightmares, but Maude was sure these were becoming less intense. It was Monday. Her plan was to return permanently to their house on Friday, which she realised, suddenly, was Good Friday.

She didn't like leaving the house unattended. Houses became stuffy so quickly, so she'd gone back often to open windows and to water plants. It was 2.00 p.m. when she put the key into the lock of the front door. As she pushed it into the barrel, she experienced an odd sensation of dread that passed from the key into her body. Maude Lambert didn't believe in ghosts or any occult phenomena. People who did believe such things were gullible fools who deserved to be relieved of their money by charlatans. Nevertheless, this feeling engulfed her, and she withdrew the key. This was absurd. It was just some sort of panic attack. She'd read about these in material associated with some of Titus's cases. She took a couple of breaths and reinserted the key. This time there was nothing. She turned it and opened the door.

The smell of urine wasn't overwhelming, but it was strong, and Maude's first thought was that there must be a problem with the plumbing. The smell became stronger as she walked down the corridor towards the living room. She could see through the far door of the living room that the back door had been smashed open. Her immediate fear was that whoever had done this might still be in the house. She froze on the spot and listened. She ought to have gone out into the street, just in case, but she saw the open scrapbook on the table and was drawn to it.

She could see that there was a spray of what she assumed was piss across the table, and that some of it had dried, which indicated to her that the intruder had defiled the house several hours earlier. She knew better than to touch anything, but the nature of the clippings in the open pages meant that surely this could belong to only one person. Sergeant Joe Sable. The bullet hole and the act of befoulment meant that that, too, could be attributed to only one person. George Starling.

Fighting anger and nausea, Maude hurried into Bishop Street and knocked on the door of the house opposite. Mrs Read, whose husband was somewhere in the Pacific, had a telephone. Maude's knocking woke the youngest of her three children. Maude telephoned Titus and waited with Mrs Read, and her crying child, for him to arrive.

CLARA DAWSON AND Helen Lord stood at the place where Peter Lillee's body had been found. All evidence of the tragedy and of the police investigation had been removed. Joe had told Helen approximately where the place was, and she had confirmed it using one of the photographs he'd taken from Inspector Lambert's desk.

'It's been well and truly trampled now, but when Uncle Peter was found, his were the only footprints — his and the footprints of the man who found him.'

'What do you know about him. He's not a suspect?'

'No. He's been questioned, but there's nothing to link him to Uncle Peter.'

'So there's no evidence of any kind of sexual contact?'

'Like what?'

Clara took Helen's hand.

'I know you're a policewoman, but if my frankness offends, I'm sorry.'

'Don't be silly, Clar. Sparing my sensibilities is the last thing I want.'

'All right. If Mr Lillee was down here to meet someone — a man, say — for sexual purposes, there may be evidence of it. As there are only two sets of footprints, the man who found him might well have been the man he was meeting. Or if he wasn't meeting him by arrangement, perhaps this is the spot where men know they'll meet other men late at night.'

'That was raised, apparently. Joe's been very good about passing on the more lurid speculations.'

'You'll need to see the autopsy report to see if there's any evidence of semen.'

'That might be difficult.'

'Mr Lillee's clothes will have been gone over for fluid stains, and the doctor doing the autopsy will be looking for foreign hair, especially pubic hair on your uncle's body.'

'Christ. So much for dignity.'

They walked around the scene, comparing the two photographs with what was in front of them.

'The shot from the water is interesting,' Clara said. 'I suppose you noticed the dead fish.'

'Cyanide?'

'Possibly. You know what, Helen, I think we need to pay a visit to the local council office.'

'You're wasted as a doctor, Clar. You should be a bloody detective.'

'I prefer my bodies to be breathing.'

INSPECTOR LAMBERT'S INTERVIEW with Sir Marcus Ashgrove had left him in a bad mood. Which is how Ron Dunnart found him when Lambert called him into his office. He'd also called Sergeant Reilly in. He didn't want this to be an unwitnessed discussion. Dunnart was wary, but gave no indication of nervousness. Lambert didn't beat about the bush.

'Your investigation into the murders of the two homosexual men has been exemplary.'

Dunnart looked at Reilly. It was an involuntary glance which Lambert noticed and which he took to confirm that Dunnart knew perfectly well that he was being watched.

'I hope all my investigations are exemplary, sir.'

'You knew you were being watched on this, though, didn't you? So many tempting targets to touch.'

Dunnart leaned back in his chair.

'I think you'll find that's more Bob O'Dowd's thing, sir.'

'You've had a bit of time to think about this, Ron. Is there any part of your version of events that you want to change?'

Dunnart was genuinely puzzled by this question.

'Bob O'Dowd's accusations against me are grotesque, sir. What you call my "version" is the truth.'

'Without any evidence, I'm afraid the word "version" will have to do.'

He let the word 'evidence' settle.

'If you're trying to rattle me, it won't work. There is no evidence. There is no possibility of evidence, because I am telling you the truth.'

Inspector Lambert put the gold fountain pen on the desk in front of him. He said nothing.

'That's mine,' Dunnart said.

'I know it's yours, Ron. What I want to know is, what was it doing in Peter Lillee's car?'

Without missing a beat, Dunnart said, 'I have no fucking idea, but if I was a betting man, I'd bet that Bob O'Dowd put it there. I thought I'd lost it.'

'Sergeant O'Dowd's fingerprints aren't on it.'

'Of course they're not. He's not a very good detective, but he's not that bad.'

'That's all for the moment, Ron. Thank you.'

Dunnart was taken aback. This was clearly a strategy. He knew that much. What was Lambert up to? He stood up and left the office without so much as a glance at Reilly. Outside in the corridor he stopped, took out a handkerchief, and mopped his brow, which had only now begun to sweat.

'Fuck, fuck, fuck, fuck.'

DUNNART HAD JUST left the office when Maude was put through to her husband. When he'd replaced the receiver, he said to Reilly, 'Where's Sergeant Sable?'

'He's out interviewing a couple of Peter Lillee's business

associates. He should be back by 3.00.'

'Leave a note on his desk telling him to wait here until I return.'

'Yes, sir.'

'I want you to come with me to my house in Brunswick, Sergeant. I think George Starling has paid us a visit.'

Joe returned to Russell Street at 2.30 p.m. He read the note, and rather than sit at his desk, he decided to visit the gymnasium, and perhaps test the level of antipathy for him among his fellow officers. He took a locker key from the board near the entrance. When the gymnasium had first become available, there'd been no locks on the doors of the lockers. It had become clear within the first week that there were light-fingered policemen who helped themselves to wallets and watches. Locks were as essential inside police headquarters as they were outside it.

Joe didn't have shorts and a singlet to change into. He was only filling in time. He put his suit coat and tie, along with his watch and his wallet, into the locker, and put the key into his trouser pocket. He intended to do no more than sit on a bench and do a few dumbbell curls. There were two men near the lockers when he entered, and both of them turned away from him.

In the gymnasium there were a dozen men doing various exercises, and the smell of sweat was strong. Joe picked up two small dumbbells and sat on a bench near a wall, away from much of the activity. Gradually, the exercising officers noticed that he was there, and one by one they stopped what they were doing and stared at him. There was silence as men stopped skipping, punching, and grunting under weights. They simply stared at him. Joe, in turn, stared at each of them, one by one. Not all of them could meet his eye, but most of them did. Four of them walked across to where he was sitting. He knew them to nod to and to make small talk with, and none of them had ever made ugly remarks to him or treated him differently from any other officer. Clearly the veneer of politeness had been wafer-thin, and now these four men formed a phalanx in front of him.

Joe was conscious of the fact that now no one else could see him. A skipping rope dangled from one of the men's hands. It twitched in response to a slight movement of his wrist. Joe placed the dumbbells on the floor. The gymnasium was eerily quiet. The sound of a locker door slamming, which would normally have been lost amid the echoes of the high-roofed space, sounded like a gunshot.

'Am I about to have an accident?' Joe's voice was strong. None of the men spoke. First one, then each in rapid succession, leaned in towards him and deposited a gobbet of phlegm near Joe's feet. They were careful not to hit him. It was a warning, telling him the gymnasium was off-limits to him. It was clear from the expressions on their faces that this was just the opening salvo. They'd begin by spitting near him, but that wouldn't be where matters would end. The implication of a grim, ugly, and inevitable declension was obvious.

The men moved away from him, and everyone went back to what he'd been doing. Joe stood up and returned the dumbbells to their rack. Not a single man looked at him as he did so. He unlocked his locker, retrieved his belongings, hung the key back on the board, and left the gymnasium. Well, now he knew where he stood. He was a pariah, and he'd have to watch his back. He was in physical peril, of that he had no doubt. He was oddly exhilarated by this sense that he was an outsider. It didn't feel like banishment. It felt like liberation.

MAUDE HAD WEANED herself off sugar since the beginning of the war, and she'd learned, too, to drink her tea black, which is how her brother Tom presented it to her. Titus had dropped her in South Melbourne before heading back to Russell Street. She'd seen no reason to keep the news of what had happened from Tom.

'We were hoping to leave you in peace, Tom, but moving back to Brunswick will have to be postponed.'

'Starling really is a kind of monster, isn't he?

'No, Tom. He's not a monster. He's just a man. A nasty one, I grant you, but he's just a man, and he can be stopped.'

'So he actually urinated in your living room?'

'If he'd done it in one place it would have been revolting, but manageable. It's impossible to sponge him away.'

'What are you going to do?'

'Well, he's not going to drive us out of our house, but he has forced us to redecorate. Everything in the room is going: all the furniture, the carpet, and the curtains. And we're repainting, including the ceiling. That is, if we can get paint.'

'Surely he didn't piss on the ceiling.'

'I'm not taking any chances that any trace of him remains.'

'I really did see him that night, didn't I?'

'I never doubted you, Tom.'

'I doubted myself.'

'Nightmares don't have bladders that they empty in other people's living rooms.'

INSPECTOR LAMBERT CALLED Joe into his office and placed the damaged scrapbook in front of him.

'I presume this belongs to you, Sergeant. You can pick it up. It's been dusted for fingerprints.'

Joe didn't need to pick it up.

'Yes, sir, it's mine.'

'It's been damaged, and we both know who did the damage.'

'I thought it had been burned in the flat.'

'I read the articles, or most of them. I'm afraid I had to stop reading them, and I'm ashamed to say the extent of this hadn't registered with me.'

'It isn't registering with anybody, sir.'

Lambert felt unable to offer anything that might pass for solace. The accumulation of details in the articles in Joe's scrapbook defied belief. Titus hadn't been able to transmute the words into images. His imagination failed, because despite his knowledge of how bleak human behaviour could be, this seemed to belong outside the human realm. He'd seen bodies mangled, mutilated, and violated, but he was unable to multiply this by one thousand, ten thousand, one hundred thousand, one million. Who could imagine this and still be able to speak? The images that had refused to come to him hadn't failed to form for Joe Sable. Lambert was sure of that. Joe's loathing of George Starling and other trumped-up National Socialists and Hitlerites must be extreme. Why was it Joe who had had to see Kevin Maher shoot Watson Cooper? Lambert wondered if he would break under the strain of what Joe Sable was carrying.

'As you know, the body of a Nazi sympathiser and twenty-four-carat nutter was found in Warrnambool early on Sunday morning. We'd assumed that Starling might be implicated — and he still might be — but how did he get from there to here in time to piss in my living room on Sunday night, or early this morning?'

'He must have a vehicle.'

'And if he has a vehicle, he must have money to buy petrol on the black market.'

'He feels close, sir.'

'I hope that's not because some of his stink has stuck to me.'

'No, sir. I just feel it.'

'It is absolutely imperative, Sergeant, that as few people as possible know your current living arrangements.'

Lambert had said this before, and it didn't need to be repeated. It made Joe think that his presence in the Kew house put everyone there at risk.

'We have to lay a trap for him, sir. We can't just wait for him to make another move. We have to control this.'

'If you're offering yourself as bait, Sergeant, it's out of the question.'

'Why?'

Titus didn't want to say that Joe had done enough, that to ask any more of him would be inhuman. Joe would hear such an explanation not with gratitude, but with a terrible belief that Lambert thought him weak and incompetent, and no reassurance would change that. Titus knew Joe well enough to be sure of this.

'I'm not putting the lives of any of my officers at risk to catch George Starling. He'll come out into the open. He can't help himself.'

Joe thought this was a disappointing answer. The reality was that Starling was in Melbourne for one reason, and one reason only: to kill Joe. He was prey. Well, if Inspector Lambert was reluctant to make use of this fact, he and Tom Mackenzie would construct a trap of their own devising.

'I'd like you to get to Kew before dark, Joe. Helen Lord has a right to know that Starling is in Melbourne, and you have my permission to tell her. Vigilance is everything now.'

Joe stood up to leave.

'Do you want your scrapbook?'

'No, sir. George Starling has touched it.'

12

WHEN JOE LEFT police headquarters he waited on the pavement for a full minute before heading for Flinders Street Station. He stood close to the gutter and scanned the other side of Russell Street. There were a lot of people about. There was no stationary figure leaning against the wall of the Magistrates' Court, or sitting on its steps. He looked to the left and the right. He wanted Starling to be there. He wanted this to be over.

By the time Joe reached Peter Lillee's house — he had to stop thinking of it as Peter Lillee's house — he'd checked his surroundings dozens of times. There was no Starling, and as far as Joe could tell, no policeman who'd been deputised to beat him up. He was back in Kew well before dark and discovered Guy Kirkham trimming shrubs in the front garden.

'It's busy work,' he said. 'They have a gardener, but I couldn't sit around all day doing nothing. I got on the roof and cleaned the gutters, too. At least that needed to be done.'

'Six o'clock is sherry time in the house. Put your shirt on and join us.'

'I stink.'

'You've got time for a whore's bath.'

'Joe, no one has said anything, but did I have a nightmare last night?'

There was no point lying.

'Yes, you did. Not a bad one, but I heard you.'

'And so did Mrs Lord and Helen?'

'I presume so.'

Guy shook his head. 'I'm embarrassed.'

'No one else is, so don't worry about it.'

The six o'clock sherry wasn't really a fixed tradition, and it had only been observed when Peter Lillee was home. Tonight, Joe intended to ask Ros Lord if sherry could be served in the library. He had an idea and he needed the shot of courage that alcohol might provide in order to put it to Ros and Helen.

Joe found them both in the kitchen, preparing the evening meal. The radio was on. Helen was shelling peas, and Ros was trussing a chicken.

'Mrs Anderson, two doors down, gave us the bird,' Ros said. 'Her son had brought down two from Lilydale, and she said she didn't need two chickens and that it would spoil. What a shame we don't have anything to celebrate.'

'Uncle Peter loved chicken, but even for him it was an extravagance, so let's call it a commemoration. Clara Dawson is coming for dinner tonight. She'll be here any minute. We thought we'd have sherry in the library.'

'I haven't seen Clara for ages,' Ros said.

'She's never liked this house, although she likes the people in it.'

'She's rather marvellous, I think,' Ros said as she pushed the chicken into the oven. 'Smart as a whip. Will Guy join us, Joe?'

'Yes. He's gone upstairs to clean himself up.'

'He did the gutters for us. He clambered up on the roof, and my heart was in my mouth. In the end I couldn't watch. He was balanced on the tiles, so close to the edge. He said he wasn't afraid of heights.'

Joe had felt awkward when his assumptions about Guy's jumping off the pier had proved wrong. Now he wondered if he'd been right and Guy's jaunty assurance about his intentions had been a cover for a last-minute failure of nerve. Why would he engage in the reckless folly of climbing high onto a roof when he might slip into brief unconsciousness at any moment? Perhaps that was precisely why. It wouldn't be suicide, would it, if he passed out and fell?

'He used to be afraid of heights,' Joe said. 'He must have grown out of it.'

'He had a bad night last night.'

'I think he has a bad night every night.'

There was a knock on the front door.

'It's all set up in the library,' Ros said. 'It's so nice to have people here.'

Joe went through to the library with Ros while Helen attended to the door.

'I suppose this house is a bit of a mausoleum,' Ros said. 'It feels less like a home now that Peter is gone. He loved all his pictures, but without him here to talk about them or move them around, it does have the air of an art gallery.'

'I think this is an absolutely beautiful room, Mrs Lord. It feels homely to me.'

'Rooms need people as much as people need rooms, don't they?'

The door opened just as Ros said this, and as Clara crossed the carpet towards her, she offered, 'I always said, Mrs Lord, that if you were in a room, the wisest person was in attendance.'

Ros laughed.

'This is Joe Sable,' Helen said. She knew she could rely on Clara not to reveal or even hint at the feelings she'd expressed to her about Joe.

'Oh, you're the detective who Helen used to work with.'

Helen could see that conversation would be awkward unless Joe knew that Clara had been told certain things about the incident in Port Fairy.

'Clara knows about George Starling, and she knows that you're staying here, Joe, and why.'

'And you're a doctor,' Joe said.

'I am. Please don't show me a troublesome rash, unless it's so spectacularly hideous that I can turn it into an anecdote.'

Guy had entered the room without anyone noticing.

'What about a parasite that might be new to science,' he said. 'I'm just back from New Guinea. I warn you, though, you'll need a torch.'

Clara laughed, and so did everyone else.

'This is Guy Kirkham,' Joe said.

'Do you have a torch, Mrs Lord?'

'All right, all right. There is no parasite.'

'Oh, I think we're all a little bit disappointed,' Clara said.

They drank sherry and talked for over an hour. Joe thought that it had probably been a very long time since so much laughter had echoed through the house. The conversation flowed easily. Joe had never seen Helen so unguarded and witty, and Guy, who had anyway a natural capacity for charm, seemed more the Guy Kirkham who Joe had known before the war.

When Ros and Helen left the library to prepare the meal, Clara, Guy, and Joe, under the warming influence of sherry, began to discuss the pictures on the walls.

'They all meant something to Peter,' Joe said. 'I think he was guided by sentiment rather than value.'

'Really?' Clara said. 'I'm always sceptical when art collectors make that claim. Mr Lillee didn't get rich by being sentimental. Besides, there are some good pictures here. That's a Goya drawing for a start.'

Guy was impressed. 'Well spotted.'

'No. I'm cheating. Mr Lillee pointed it out to me a few years ago when I'd come round for tea.'

'It didn't cost him very much,' Joe said.

'He might have told you that to discourage you from stealing it,' Clara said.

Joe had no quick comeback. He wasn't skilled at banter. Guy was, but he was closely studying a Lloyd Rees drawing. Clara looked at Joe and tried to see what it was about him that had caused such a tangle of emotions in Helen. He was sufficiently good-looking, sufficiently amusing, sufficiently intelligent, and well turned out, though he could take no credit for the latter given that the clothes were Peter Lillee's. Everything about him was sufficient. There must be something she wasn't seeing. In Clara's experience, sufficiency in people never grew into something more; it only declined into something less.

Guy Kirkham, on the other hand, was a different kettle of fish. The problem with Guy, though, for all his wit and charm, was that there was something wrong with him. Clara saw that immediately. Even though he seemed relaxed, she noticed the tremor in his hands, which he tried to disguise by keeping them in his trouser pockets. There was something about his face, too. She couldn't quite put her finger on it. Perhaps it was a muscle jumping, or how he stopped smiling when he thought no one was looking. She was interested because she was drawn to him, and decided to observe him over dinner.

They were called into the dining room. Clara offered Guy her arm, which he took. This small gesture, from which he was excluded, made Joe realise that something had happened to him. Was it possible to fall in love with someone in just one hour? Joe tried to dismiss the sensation as ludicrous. It was difficult, however, to dismiss the sudden and appalling self-consciousness that sideswiped him. How was he going to get through dinner without Clara thinking him a clumsy simpleton? And now he was sweating.

No ONE AT the table knew anything about wine. Ros had pulled a bottle of red at random from Peter Lillee's cellar. There was no doubt that it would be a good wine, but its virtues were lost on the assembled palates.

'I suppose it's quite nice,' Clara said.

'Uncle Peter would be appalled by our ignorance.'

The chicken was a little dry, and Clara suggested that perhaps Mrs Anderson had slipped them a rooster. A second bottle of wine was opened, and as people became comfortable, the main reason for Clara's presence was revealed.

'Clara and I went down to the river this morning.'

Joe looked at Ros, trying to judge the effect these words had on her. She leaned forward with interest.

'Afterwards, we went to the council offices.'

'The council offices?' Mrs Lord said. 'Why?'

'Because Clara is a genius.'

'It was the dead fish,' Clara said. 'I believe the Americans have an expression, something about left field. I remembered that, as a child, we visited an aunt in Sydney, near the Lane Cove River. I remember days when the air stank of rotten eggs, and on the day before we left to come back to Melbourne, dead fish started surfacing and collecting near the banks. Apparently, this had happened before. Even at eleven years old, I knew that the rotten egg smell was hydrogen sulphide, but that's as much as I knew. My aunt said that she'd been writing to the council about the smell for years, but nothing was ever done. It made some people quite ill. I know now that hydrogen sulphide in dense concentrations can kill you.'

'I had no idea where this was leading when Clara outlined it to me,' said Helen, 'but we went to the council and asked if there'd been any recent complaints about a bad smell or fish kills. There had been. The council had sent someone to investigate, and the best he could offer was that the river was polluted because industries had been pouring waste into it for generations, and in that part of the river in Kew raw sewage was a problem.'

'I'm lost,' Joe said and immediately wished he'd waited for either Guy or Mrs Lord to make that admission. Clara looked at him, and Joe interpreted the look as a confirmation that she thought he was a dolt.

'I didn't know what it might mean either,' Clara said. 'I just had this vague idea that it might mean something, and to be honest, I'm still not one hundred per cent sure, but I have a theory that might be worth taking to the coroner, depending, of course, on the autopsy report.'

'Inspector Lambert received that this morning,' Joe said.

'You've waited until now to mention that?' Helen snapped.

Joe looked stricken.

'I'm sorry, Joe. That was unfair.'

He rallied. 'I haven't read the report, Helen, and if I had, I don't think discussing its contents over sherry would have felt right.'

There was an awkward silence, and Clara could tell that Helen was struggling to absorb this public chastening.

'Did Inspector Lambert mention anything at all, Joe?' Clara asked, and discreetly placed her hand on Helen's knee under the table. Joe, unaware of the effect his words had had, said, 'There was nothing conclusive. He mentioned something about Mr Lillee's blood being a purplish colour, which is consistent with some kind of poisoning.'

'My God, Helen. I think I might be right.'

'Are you saying you know how Peter died?' Ros asked.

'I think I do, Mrs Lord, but there are a few gaps in my theory, and a whole lot of things would have had to come together perfectly for it to work. I do believe, however, that it's possible.'

'You have our full attention,' Guy said and put down his wine glass to underline the point.

'I'll try to keep the chemistry to a minimum. River mud, especially in areas of high pollution, can hold large quantities of hydrogen sulphide. If the conditions are right, it can escape the mud in the form of hydrogen sulphide gas. We all know what that gas smells like, rotten eggs. It's disagreeable, but in high concentrations, it's also poisonous. In very high concentrations just breathing it in will stop the heart. It's also heavier than air. Now, this is where the conditions on the morning of Mr Lillee's death would have had to freakishly align. And this is critical: he would have had to have been lying down at the time of his death.'

'Uncle Peter could easily have lain down to look at the stars. I've seen him do that here, in the backyard. It was perfectly still that night.'

'Here's where it gets complicated. There must have been an eruption of sulphide gas somewhere not too far upstream of where Mr Lillee was lying.'

'Why upstream?' Guy asked.

'Because hydrogen sulphide gas will roll towards a point lower than where it emerges. I know this sounds absurd, but it could have rolled down to Mr Lillee, and he wouldn't have known what he was breathing in. The gas would shut down his sense of smell. He may have sat up and become disoriented, which explains why he was found on his stomach, but he would have died very, very quickly.'

'Has there ever been a recorded case of someone dying like this?' Joe asked.

'I don't know enough about it to answer that. I certainly know from what I read this afternoon that hydrogen sulphide gas has been implicated in some industrial accidents, and of course in fish kills. What we know for certain is that hydrogen sulphide poisoning causes blood to discolour to purple.'

'Why wasn't the autopsy explicit about that?'

'I imagine it would have been, and Inspector Lambert either didn't understand it, or hadn't read it closely when he gave you a précis.'

'I believe that Clara is right about this,' said Helen. 'This was death by misadventure. It was a freak accident. There is no lover, no thug, no assignation gone wrong, and Lillian Johnson and Ron Dunnart are in the clear.'

'And you say this gas would have killed Peter quickly?' Ros said.

'Yes, Mrs Lord. Mr Lillee wouldn't have suffered. He would have become unconscious, and his heart would have stopped. He'd have had no time to be afraid, no time to panic.'

'I suppose I should be comforted by that, but it was a lonely death.'

Helen reached across and put her hand on her mother's wrist.

'No, Mum. It was clean and painless. He was alone when he died, but he was never lonely.'

Ros tried to smile, but her eyes filled with tears, and she left the table and went into the kitchen. Helen followed her.

'It's all a bit much to take in isn't it?' Clara said.

'It's not what you told us that upset her,' Guy said. 'Her brother is dead. I'm sure Mrs Lord just gets hit sometimes by his absence. The dead can fuck you around much more than the living. Pardon my French.'

Joe could tell that Guy was slightly drunk. He wished he wasn't, because it made him unpredictable. He wouldn't suddenly overturn the table or become abusive, but unpredictability can manifest itself in all sorts of ways. To Joe's and to Clara's astonishment, Guy's eyes closed, and his head lolled forward. This wasn't the result of intoxication. After exchanging a glance, they watched in silence. Then Guy's eyes opened again, and he lifted his head.

'Oh, Christ,' he said. 'It happened, didn't it? I fell asleep. How long for?'

'About ten seconds,' Clara said.

'I'm so sorry. It's …' Guy struggled to finish the sentence.

'I know what it is.'

'Do you know how to fix it?'

The question wasn't belligerent.

'No, Guy, I'm sorry I don't.'

Helen came back into the dining room and saw that something had happened in her absence.

'Is everything all right?'

'Guy just fell asleep for a moment,' Clara said.

'It is late.'

'No, I'm not tired, Helen. I'm ill. I fall asleep suddenly, some-times for seconds, sometimes for minutes. It's called narcolepsy, which is a word I can barely bring myself to say. It happens anywhere and everywhere. I'm afraid I find it deeply humiliating.' This last he said firmly, as if it were a bland statement of fact. He didn't wish to provoke sympathy or, worse, pity. 'I won't be applying for a job in a munitions factory.'

Further discussion of his condition would have made Guy uncomfortable, so Joe thought it was time to drop his grenade into the conversation.

'George Starling is in Melbourne.'

At the conclusion of his story, Joe said, 'Mrs Lambert is having the room repainted and recarpeted.'

'Have you seen those flamethrowers in the newsreels?' Guy said. 'I'd use one of those on the room.'

Ros Lord hadn't emerged from the kitchen, and they could hear the sound of her washing up.

'We have to flush him out,' Joe said. 'We can't wait for him to find us.'

'And it is "us", isn't it? He has unfinished business with me as well as you,' said Helen.

'Precisely. He won't stop at me.'

'What does Lambert say?'

'Inspector Lambert doesn't have a plan. How do you find one man in a city this size?'

'You control how he finds you,' Helen said.

'I have an idea, and it's not guaranteed to work, and you and your mother might find it offensive.' Joe was peripherally aware that Clara was watching him with interest. Over the course of the dinner, he'd stopped feeling like a tongue-tied schoolboy, but he hadn't been able to shake the suspicion that she wasn't impressed by his intellect. Would she be appalled by what he was about to suggest? 'When is Mr Lillee's funeral?'

'It's on Thursday. We wanted it to be on Friday, but we forgot it's Good Friday. It was all sorted out this afternoon. I hate to admit it, but the Melbourne Club has been incredibly generous and helpful. They're managing everything. Someone telephoned Mum and offered to take care of all the ghastly organisation and preparation. It's at St Paul's Cathedral, which thumbs the nose at the Catholics. Mum and I had no idea how influential Uncle Peter was. The man at the Melbourne Club said that St Paul's would be full.'

'What if we could get Starling to show his face at the funeral?'

'Go on,' Helen said. 'But I don't want my uncle's funeral disrupted by that bastard.'

Joe thought quickly.

'St Paul's is too big for him to do anything. What about afterwards?'

'What do you suggest?'

'Starling doesn't know who Peter Lillee is, but he knows your name, my name, and Tom Mackenzie's name. If he knew that we were all going to be in one place at the same time, it might prove irresistible.'

'The newspapers,' Clara said. 'The funeral notice.'

Helen was now ahead of both Clara and Joe.

'Yes, but a notice that's not just in one newspaper, but in all of them, and on the front page. We'll buy the space in Wednesday's papers.'

Joe withdrew a notebook from his pocket, and Helen began to dictate.

'"The funeral of Mr Peter Lillee will be held at St Paul's Cathedral on Thursday, sixth of April. Beloved brother of Rosalind Lord, beloved uncle of Miss Helen Lord, and beloved friend to Mr Joseph Sable and Mr Thomas Mackenzie. A reception will be held afterwards at the Portico Room at Melbourne Town Hall. Invited guests only." Is that too contrived? Uncle Peter didn't know Tom Mackenzie.'

'Starling doesn't know that. A stranger reading it will just think it's a typical funeral notice.'

'But Starling isn't a stranger,' Guy said. 'I think you should leave Tom's name off. It does look contrived. Starling will twig.'

'I think Guy's right,' Clara said, 'and I don't think you should put "beloved" in front of Joe's name. Just "friend" would do.'

When they'd completed the notice, Helen said, 'We can't do this without Mum's agreement. She knows the bare minimum about George Starling.'

'You're kidding,' Clara said.

'We don't talk about those things.'

'Well you bloody well should. She's your mum, and, unlike my mother, she's lovely.'

'I know. We just have never talked about my work.'

'She was married to a policeman. Do you want me to talk to her?'

Helen was tempted to say yes, but said that she'd talk to Ros that night and let people know her decision in the morning.

'It's a bit hit and miss, isn't it?' Helen said

'It feels like we're doing something,' Joe said. 'If Mrs Lord agrees, I'll telephone Tom Mackenzie. He'll want to be involved.'

When Mrs Lord returned to the table, she was composed, although her eyes were red-rimmed from crying.

'I'm going up to bed. Your room is ready, Clara. I'm sure you'll be comfortable.'

'Thank you, Mrs Lord, I'm sure I will. I'll be going to bed soon, too. I have an early start.'

Helen stood up and followed her mother upstairs.

'That's going to be a difficult conversation,' Clara said.

'Do you think Mrs Lord will be shocked?' Joe asked.

'The only thing that will shock her is that Helen is talking to her about something that actually matters.'

'There's brandy in the library.'

'No, thanks. I really do have to get to bed. It's been a long day.'

'Guy and I will tidy up down here.'

'We will catch him, Joe,' Clara said.

Joe nodded and was unable to respond. She must have noticed how awkward he was. The thought made him feel worse, and he was relieved when she left the room.

In the library, he and Guy drank Peter Lillee's brandy from beautiful balloons. Guy said nothing about Joe having made a fool of himself in front of Clara, so perhaps he hadn't looked as silly as he'd felt. Joe told Guy about the incident in the gymnasium.

'You have to tell Lambert.'

Joe shook his head. 'He warned me this would happen, and he also warned me that there was nothing he could do.'

'What about the pen I found in the car?'

'I handed it over to Inspector Lambert. I haven't heard anything further. What are your plans, Guy?'

'It would be nice if I had any. I don't. I can't go home. I can't stay here. I need work, but who's going to employ me, Joe? Who wants someone who falls asleep on the job?'

'You don't have to leave here in a hurry, Guy,' Helen said from the doorway.

'What did Mrs Lord say?'

Helen came and sat with them.

'She listened and got more and more angry. Not at me, at Starling. My mother never swears, but she said it didn't matter what it cost, we had to stop that bastard. She may burst into tears when she sees you tomorrow, Joe. I told her everything. She already knew about the flat, of course.'

'Everything about me, or everything?'

'I told her what Starling did to me. She wants him dead.'

Helen didn't say that her mother had kissed her and said, 'No more secrets, Helen. I don't need protecting.'

Guy announced that he was going to bed.

'Tell me the truth, Helen, if I asked Clara to come to the pictures with me, would she say yes?'

'I have no idea, Guy. What's your batting average with women you ask to the pictures?'

'Not enough experience to work as a useful statistic. I'll ask her in the morning. Good night.'

Joe looked into his brandy glass rather than at his friend.

GEORGE STARLING WAS bored. There was only one way to find Joe Sable now that he was homeless. He would have to wait outside Russell Street and follow him. This was risky, but he could think of no other solution. If he hadn't burned down his flat, it would have been simple. Still, even though it complicated matters, he was glad he'd done it.

He couldn't face sitting in his room at The Victoria all day. He went down to the foyer, thinking that he might while away the day visiting the War Memorial, or even Wirth's Circus. He quite liked the circus. He admired the lion-tamer's ability to subdue a wild animal. There was, too, the pleasurable frisson that it might go horribly wrong.

The door to one of the two telephone booths in the foyer was open, and the directory caught Starling's eye. He entered the booth and found Joe Sable's name and address in the directory. This was no good to him, of course. The address given was now a pile of ashes. However, he had another name: Helen Lord. He ran his fingers down the Ls. There was no 'H. Lord'. In fact, there were no Lords listed at all.

There was one more name that he had. When he'd cleansed the world of those two fairies, he'd set fire to their sad, decadent club, and he'd returned to the alley off Little Bourke Street the next day, to see his handiwork. He'd followed two smug detectives afterwards, and had walked so close behind them that he'd overheard that one of them was named Reilly. Reilly had said something that had annoyed him. He couldn't remember exactly what it was, but he did remember thinking that Reilly would benefit from being given a fright. More importantly now, he might be persuaded to tell him where Joe Sable could be found. They worked together after all. But what was Reilly's first name? Starling telephoned Russell Street police headquarters.

'I have a message for Detective Reilly,' he said. 'I don't need to speak to him, I just need to make sure he gets it.'

'Go ahead, sir.'

'It needs to be the right Reilly.'

'There's only one Detective Reilly, sir. Detective David Reilly.'
Starling hung up.

There were three D. Reillys in the directory. Two of them lived in
the far western suburbs. A telephone call to each revealed, through
the women who answered, that one was Donald Reilly and the other
Daniel Reilly. That left D. Reilly in Northcote. He telephoned the
number. There was no answer. That was fine. He had nothing
better to do, so he decided to pay the address a visit, just on spec. It
might be a waste of time. David Reilly might not have a telephone.
Reilly would be at work, though, which might explain why no one
answered. He probably lived alone — if he was married, surely Mrs
Reilly would have picked up the phone. That was good. He'd break
in, make sure he had the right house, and come back later, when
Detective Reilly was at home.

Ron Dunnart suspected that Inspector Lambert was playing
a waiting game, watching to see the effect O'Dowd's accusation
was having on him. The fountain pen had rattled him, that was
true, but he'd thought on his feet. Lambert would need more than
a dropped fountain pen to stitch him up for murder. It looked
like Bob O'Dowd was staying away for a second day in a row.
This meant working more closely with David Reilly, Lambert's
spy. Although he couldn't stand Reilly — and this was a long-
standing detestation, predating Reilly's now open efforts to
prove him guilty of murder — although he couldn't stand him,
he would maintain a cool distance from him and share whatever
new information came in about the cases they were working on.
He'd be the consummate professional, despite the forces ranged
against him.

When Reilly came in, checking to see if O'Dowd had turned
up, Dunnart handed him some case notes and said, 'He's supposed

to be going through these. Looks like you'll have to do it. I'm going to the dunny. I may be some time.'

Dunnart took off his suit coat and hung it over the back of his chair. Reilly, who'd wondered about the gouge down the side of Lillee's car, looked at Dunnart's coat. He'd told Inspector Lambert that he didn't believe that Ron Dunnart was capable of murder. He still held this view, but he also had no doubt that he'd been attempting to blackmail Lillee, and proving that would be a feather in his cap.

Reilly put his hand into the left-side pocket of the coat. He pulled out a bunch of half a dozen keys, tied together with a thin, round leather thong. They were house keys, although one of them probably opened a shed, another a gate, and a third perhaps a strongbox. Not expecting to find anything, he examined each of them. The most used key, no doubt the front door key, was obvious from the wear on it. The least used of the keys, dull with age not wear, made Reilly's heart skip a beat. Caught in the grooves along its edge were small pieces of paint.

Reilly's fingers fumbled with the knot in the thong. Had Dunnart been serious when he'd said that he'd be gone for some time, or was this something he always said to be humorous? The knot hadn't been untied in years. Reilly found a paper knife and used the tip to force the knot apart. He heard Dunnart's voice. He'd stopped to talk to someone on his way back from the toilet. Reilly's fingers managed to free the knot and the key. He retied it in a hurry, and knew he hadn't got it right. He dropped the keys back into the pocket, picked up the case notes Dunnart had given him, and returned to his own desk in the office next door.

He remembered too late that he'd left the paper knife on Dunnart's desk. He took out an envelope, wrote 'Urgent' on it, and slipped the key inside. On a piece of notepaper, he wrote, 'The paint on this key, which belongs to Ron Dunnart, should be checked against the paint on Peter Lillee's car.' He slipped the note inside, next to the key. He then put the note on Inspector Lambert's desk.

When he came out of Lambert's office, Dunnart was waiting for him.

'You left this on my desk, Sherlock.'

That was all he said, which unnerved Reilly.

WHEN JOE STEPPED over the threshold of police headquarters, the passage to the office he shared with David Reilly was like running the gauntlet. No one spoke to him, and he caught several sotto voce obscenities directed at his back. The only person who did speak to him was the woman on the front desk, who asked him to pass on to Inspector Lambert that Sergeant O'Dowd had called in sick. *No surprise there*, Joe thought. Dunnart of course would be at work as usual. Staying at home would be an intolerable sign of weakness.

David Reilly wasn't at his desk. He had taken the notes Dunnart had given him and gone to another part of the building. He wanted to be as far away from Dunnart as possible. Inspector Lambert wasn't at his desk, either.

Joe took the opportunity to telephone Tom Mackenzie and brief him on the plan that had been agreed to the previous evening. He invited him to dinner at the Kew house that night. Helen had suggested it as he'd left for work that morning. It was to be a strategy meeting, and Tom needed to be a part of it.

GEORGE STARLING ALMOST changed his mind about visiting David Reilly's house. He'd go to the pictures instead. He liked the pictures, and there were one or two showing that he wouldn't mind seeing. There was *Suspicion*, a Hitchcock picture. He liked Joan Fontaine and he quite liked Cary Grant. No, he'd see it later that afternoon, after he'd made his visit.

He took the train to Northcote and walked from the station to Reilly's house. It was convenient of Reilly to live on Station Street. Starling hadn't bothered looking it up in the frayed *Morgan's Street Directory* that had sat beside the telephone at The Victoria Hotel. It was the 1927 edition, but Station Street in 1944 would doubtless be in the same place.

Reilly's house was a California bungalow. It was a good size, on a large block. *He didn't buy that on a detective's salary*, Starling thought. There must be a Mrs Reilly after all, who'd brought some money to the marriage. The front yard was neat. The lawn was manicured, and the box hedges that lined the driveway were well trimmed. He went up to the front door and knocked. He wasn't expecting anyone to answer. No one had answered his telephone call. He was surprised, therefore, when the door was opened by a woman.

Barbara Reilly's hand flew to her mouth when she saw George Starling's face. She immediately tried to adjust her look from horror to sympathy, assuming that this was a returned, disfigured soldier trying to sell her something — probably a rabbit. This thought had barely formed when Starling's hand reached for her throat and closed around it. He pushed her back into the house, kicking the door shut behind him on the way, and drove her towards the living room. In a matter of seconds, he'd shoved her into a chair where she sat, choking, too shocked and confused to yet be afraid.

'If you scream, I will push my thumbs into your throat. Do you understand?'

Barbara Reilly didn't understand, but she nodded.

'Your husband is David Reilly, the policeman?'

Again she nodded. Fear began to rise in her, and she couldn't take her eyes off this man's face, with its livid, unhealed wound.

'Where is your telephone?'

Barbara tried to speak, but the pressure of the man's hand had done something to her, and she could only produce a gurgle. She pointed to the hallway. He grabbed a handful of her hair, lifted her out of the chair, and pushed her towards the telephone.

'You can speak. I didn't do any damage. Say something.'

Barbara Reilly tried again, and this time words formed.

'Who are you? We don't have any money in the house.'

'Good.' Starling didn't like that she wasn't terrified of him. Never mind. There'd be time for that.

'I want you to telephone your husband at work, and I want you to say precisely what I tell you. Do you understand?'

She nodded.

'I want you to tell him that you're very ill and you want him to come home, now. Go on, say it.'

'I'm very ill, and you need to come home now.'

Her voice was croaky. Starling produced the Luger from his suit pocket.

'If you say anything more than that, or anything different from that, I'll shoot you. Understand?'

Barbara Reilly did understand. What she didn't understand was why she wasn't more afraid. The presence of this creature in her house, and the fact that he'd laid hands on her, filled her, instead, with indignation. The barrel of the gun at her temple focussed her mind. She telephoned police headquarters and waited to be put through. Out of the corner of her eye, she noticed that the hall clock said 11.00 a.m. What would this man do if David was out of the office? Starling heard Reilly say his name.

'Sergeant David Reilly.'

He tapped Barbara Reilly's temple with the end of the barrel.

'It's me, Barbara. I'm very ill, David. I need you to come home, now.'

Starling broke the connection.

'Well done.'

'How dare you come into my house.'

'Oh, shut up.'

He shoved her so that she fell heavily and hit her head. She didn't lose consciousness, but her disorientation suited Starling. He hauled her to her feet and half-walked, half-carried her to the living room. Before shoving her back into the chair, he tore off her dress and began taking off the slip she wore beneath it. He changed his mind. He didn't want to sit looking at her flabby nakedness while he waited for Reilly to arrive. He ripped the dress into lengths and tied her arms and legs so that she was immobilised. He put a gag in her mouth and tied it around her head tight enough to be uncomfortable but bearable. He then positioned the chair so that the spectacle of his trussed wife would be the first thing Reilly saw when he came down the hallway. Starling sat in a chair opposite Barbara Reilly and closed his eyes against the drool that had begun to flow around the cloth gag. She ought to have pissed herself by now. It was galling that she hadn't. Later. He'd save his energy for later.

DAVID REILLY HAD returned to his office just before 11.00 a.m. Joe Sable had already left, and Inspector Lambert hadn't yet made an appearance. He must have been at some meeting or other. The envelope with the key in it was still on his desk, unopened. When the telephone rang, he was toying distractedly with the paperknife.

'It's me, Barbara. I'm very ill, David. I need you to come home, now.'

Then silence. She'd hung up. He tried ringing back, but the phone must have been left off the hook. He couldn't get through.

Should he telephone one of the neighbours? Barbara, whose voice had sounded odd, had asked him to come home. She wouldn't do that without a good reason. He scribbled a note for Lambert and left. The situation demanded the extravagance of a taxi, and Reilly caught one as soon as he'd exited the building.

BARBARA REILLY'S HEAD cleared, and she stared at the man who sat opposite her. His eyes were closed. He was well dressed; his shoes were newly polished, and he was clean-shaven. But the way he sat gave him away as not belonging in the clothes he wore. Barbara recognised slovenly habits, and his sprawled legs and the casual way he scratched at his crotch told her he was no gentleman. Strangely, after a small rush of fear, she was free from it again. Perhaps she had concussion. She tried the knots, but couldn't budge them, so went back to examining her captor. The man opened his eyes and caught her staring. He smiled, or maybe just bared his teeth. Without warning, the terror that had been put somewhere safely inside her broke free and roared through her like a cyclone. She writhed and whimpered, and she emptied her bladder.

Starling quickly came across to her, sniffed theatrically, and said, 'Dirty bitch.' Then he sat down again.

Barbara heard Reilly put his key in the lock before Starling did. It was the look in her eyes that alerted him. He remained seated and balanced the Luger in his lap.

'Barbara?'

Reilly called a second time as he hurried down the hallway. 'Barbara?'

He caught sight of her, and it made no sense to him. Why was she sitting, tied up, in her slip? He rushed into the living room, and didn't see George Starling immediately. He'd pulled the gag from his wife's mouth before he noticed him.

'Put the gag back.'

Reilly saw the Luger, which was pointing at Barbara's face.

'Put the gag back,' Starling calmly repeated. Reilly did as he was told. His eyes hadn't quite adjusted to the dimness of the living room.

'Who the fuck are you?'

'I'm the man who killed those two perverts. There you go. Mystery solved. Now all you have to do is arrest me. That's the hard part.'

Reilly looked into his wife's terrified eyes. Why was this man here?

'You're not very talkative, are you?' Starling said. 'Why don't you tell your smelly wife that everything is going to be all right? It won't be the first time you've lied to her, I'll bet.'

Starling waited.

'Tell her!' he bellowed. Both David and Barbara jumped.

'Everything's going to be all right,' Reilly said quietly and placed his hand on his wife's arm.

'The little gesture was a nice touch,' Starling said. 'You're good at this. A lifetime of lies. Practice makes perfect.'

He waved the gun at Reilly.

'Sit in that chair over there. Just do it. All this will be over so much quicker, and I'll be out of your hair and on my way. If you do as you're told.'

Reilly sat in the indicated chair, and Starling stood up. He moved to stand beside Barbara Reilly.

'Now, we're all calm. All I want from you, Sergeant Reilly, is some information.'

Reilly nodded.

'Do you know a policeman named Joe Sable?'

Reilly went cold. This was George Starling. What was that scar? No one had ever mentioned a scar.

'Well?'

'Yes. I know Joe Sable. I work with him.'

'Do you know he's a Jew?'

'Yes, I know that.'

'That doesn't bother you?'

'No. Why should it?'

Starling looked as if he'd just smelled something disgusting.

'I want to know where he lives.'

'A flat in Princes Hill.'

Starling shook his head.

'OK. Let me make myself crystal clear. I don't have time to listen to bullshit. You and I both know that Sable's flat was destroyed. You know it because you work with him. I know it because I burned it down. Now, if you give me another smart answer, I'll fire a bullet into your wife's knee.'

He leaned down and placed the gun at the side of Barbara's right knee. Her eyes opened wide.

'And I think you know I will pull the trigger, and I think you know I'll enjoy doing it. So, let's try again. Where is Joe Sable living?'

With no time to think, Reilly said, 'Eighty-four Kerr Street, in Fitzroy.'

'Who lives there?'

'He's staying with a fellow officer named Bob O'Dowd.'

'Go and get the telephone directory.'

Reilly, his head spinning, walked unsteadily to the telephone and came back with the directory.

'Find that name and address. If it's not there, your wife will be in great pain.'

Reilly fumbled with the pages and prayed that O'Dowd was in the directory. He'd said his name in desperation. It was there. He showed the entry to Starling.

'Well, you gave him up without much of a struggle. Sit back down. What time does he finish work?'

'Five o'clock.'

'Do he and O'Dowd go home together?'

'No. Not usually. Bob O'Dowd likes a drink after work. Joe Sable doesn't. Why are you asking these questions?'

'Because I'm going to kill Joe Sable tonight.'

What would this man do when he discovered that he'd been lied to? He'd come back. Poor bloody O'Dowd. He was married, wasn't he? Christ. Would Starling put O'Dowd's wife through this, too?

'You're not a very brave man, are you, Sergeant Reilly?'

'My wife comes before Joe Sable.'

Starling turned to Barbara. 'Are you proud of your husband, betraying his friend like that?'

'Joe Sable isn't a friend,' Reilly said. 'Like you said, he's a Jew.'

Despite what he'd said earlier, just for a moment Reilly thought that this deliberately ugly remark had softened Starling. He took the Luger away from Barbara's knee, raised it, and fired at David Reilly's face. The bullet hit him in the mouth. Starling walked to him and fired a bullet into his forehead, just above the top of the nose.

Barbara Reilly's ears were ringing. Her eyesight was blurry, and she wasn't sure what had just happened. David had slumped in his chair. The man returned to her and held her chin between his thumb and forefinger.

'Now, what are we going to do with you?'

He let his hand slide down inside her slip and cup her breast. With his other hand he released the gag. The gun barrel, still hot, touched her cheek. He pinched her nipple, forced the barrel into her mouth, and pulled the trigger. The mess was astonishing.

He stood back. He'd go and see that picture with Cary Grant and Joan Fontaine. The 3.15 session. And afterwards, well, afterwards Joe Sable would wish he'd never been born.

He'd go back to his room in The Victoria first. He needed to collect his filleting knife.

RON DUNNART HAD been dismissive of David Reilly's snooping. There was nothing incriminating on his desk or in his drawers, so he had nothing to worry about. He couldn't think of a reason for the paperknife, unless Reilly thought he could force a drawer with it. He wouldn't have found any of them locked, anyway. He didn't like being under surveillance, and there was only one person to blame for that. Bob O'-fucking-Dowd.

The way to end this was to get O'Dowd to withdraw his accusation. O'Dowd's career in the police force was over. Nothing was more certain than that. So if he withdrew the accusation and said that he'd made it because he was pissed off with him, well, he wouldn't be charged with anything. He'd be dismissed, but he was facing dismissal as it was.

These were inchoate ideas that Dunnart was turning over, but the more he thought about it, the more he thought he could bring enough pressure to bear on O'Dowd to make him do it. He'd scare the shit out of him and beat him where the bruises wouldn't show. Dunnart wanted Lambert off his back and soon. This needed to be done tonight. Bob O'Dowd wouldn't like it one little bit when he opened his front door tonight to find Ron Dunnart standing there.

13

Inspector Lambert would have described his relationship with the Police Commissioner, James Cottrell, as respectful, but not intimate. He had no ambitions in this direction. In fact, if he were ever offered the job, he'd turn it down. Cottrell had never been a gifted detective. He was, however, a gifted administrator. Lambert thought he was a decent man and was confident that he was neither on the take nor in the pocket of politicians. He did his job well, if unremarkably. This sort of steady mediocrity was his defence against being held personally responsible by the newspapers when a spate of crimes occurred, or when a particular case which the journalists had adopted wasn't solved quickly enough. Cottrell seemed not to take any of their criticisms to heart. He gave boring answers to impertinent questions until journalists became reluctant to interview him. As a strategy, Inspector Lambert thought this was inspired.

James Cottrell was not in fact a boring man. Cottrell had no illusions about the failures of integrity in his force, but he was convinced that this was true for only a minority of his men. For the most part, Cottrell had great admiration for the men who chose to serve as police officers. He wasn't so admiring of the few women who'd become sworn officers. Surely policing was unequivocally and uncontroversially men's work? No sensible person could take a policewoman seriously. They'd never be promoted above constable, so at least they didn't pose a threat to a male officer's career, and someone had to deal with drunk women and prostitutes, and clean out the cells when they were sick in them.

Inspector Lambert had gone behind Cottrell's back in seconding Helen Lord into Homicide. Cottrell would never have given his permission, but once it had been done, he'd had enough trust in Lambert to tolerate the secondment. The incident in Port Fairy had confirmed for Cottrell all his reservations about women in the force. Helen Lord had had to go. Cottrell hadn't made a fuss about it. He'd simply let Lambert know that the experiment was over.

Now, on this Tuesday morning, Lambert had come to James Cottrell to discuss Kevin Maher, and Bob O'Dowd's statement about Ron Dunnart. Cottrell had been fully briefed about the Maher affair and had come to a conclusion about it. The O'Dowd/ Dunnart mess gave him a headache.

'We're going to have to let Kevin Maher get away with it, Titus. Frankly, that irks me. I believe young Joe Sable's account of what happened, but neither you nor I can do anything about that without evidence.'

'And there is no evidence. Two men in a room with no witnesses, but with the corpse of a cop killer.'

'Joe Sable comes out of this more damaged that Kevin Maher. That's why I believe him. He would have known that Maher couldn't be prosecuted. He would also have known how despised he'd become. And yet he made the accusation. Admirable? Foolish? I don't like martyrs, Titus. Why did he do it? If he'd just kept quiet, the result for Kevin Maher would have been exactly the same — the admiration of his peers.'

'But it wouldn't have been the same for Sergeant Sable, sir. It would have made him no different, in his own eyes, from Kevin Maher.'

'He's right, of course. I hope he understands when he learns that there'll be no official outcome. There'll be some people who might be wary of Maher in the future, but not many. This business with O'Dowd and Ron Dunnart. That's a right royal mess. Give me your gut reaction about what the hell is going on there.'

Lambert had had one brief meeting with Cottrell about this already, so he reiterated what he'd already outlined. Lambert didn't believe that Ron Dunnart had killed Peter Lillee. He did believe that he'd tried to blackmail him, and the fountain pen found in Lillee's car confirmed this. He didn't for a moment believe that O'Dowd had planted the pen. When would he have done this, and how?

'I think Bob O'Dowd genuinely believes that Dunnart murdered Lillee, and he confected an elaborate lie to protect himself from being found to be an accessory. Dunnart wouldn't admit to killing Lillee to O'Dowd. He thinks O'Dowd is small-part copper, large-part moron.'

'I don't like it, Titus. I want both of them out of Homicide.'

'O'Dowd has called in sick two days in a row. Dunnart is here. He'll brazen it out.'

'I don't want him in the building. I'm willing to offer them both paid leave until this is sorted out. If they refuse — and by that I mean if Ron Dunnart refuses — if they refuse, I'll suspend them from duty, which won't do either of their careers any favours.'

Inspector Lambert saw the sense in this, even though it meant his investigative resources would be depleted. Getting Helen Lord back would be useful, but out of the question. He didn't bother raising the possibility with Cottrell.

When Lambert returned to his office, he signalled to Joe, who was on the telephone, that he wanted to speak with him as soon as he was finished. When he sat down at his desk, he saw the note and envelope.

'Sergeant!'

Joe excused himself to the person on the other end of the line and hung up. He went into Lambert's office. Inspector Lambert held up the key.

'Sergeant Reilly has found this. I presume he took it from Ron Dunnart's bundle of keys. I don't know how. He'll tell us when he comes back. Mrs Reilly is ill, and he's gone home. His note says he'll be back as soon as he can.'

'Ron Dunnart is still here, sir. Should I get him?'

'No. I'm hoping he won't miss this key until we've got a match for the paint on it with Peter Lillee's car. I want you to drive to Kew now, get a sample of the paint from the car, and get back here. While you're gone, I'll get the key photographed and take it to forensics. If there is a match, Ron may have trouble explaining it. We might at least get an admission of blackmail from him.'

Joe took a deep breath.

'Before I go, sir, I have a theory about how Mr Lillee might have died. Well, it's not my theory. Helen Lord has a friend, a doctor named Clara Dawson. She came to dinner last night. It was the dead fish.'

'The dead fish in the photograph you removed from my desk.'

Joe blushed.

'And which you showed to Helen Lord.'

Joe was covered in confusion.

'I hope you don't think I hadn't noticed, Sergeant. We'll discuss that later. Go on.'

'It was the dead fish in the photograph, yes. Clara — Dr Dawson — and Helen went down to the river.'

'I would have expected nothing less from Constable Lord.'

'Dr Dawson noticed that the place where Mr Lillee's body was found had features that made her theory plausible.'

Joe laid out, in as much detail as he could remember, Clara's belief that Peter Lillee had died from hydrogen sulphide poisoning.

'She acknowledges that the conditions would have had to be exactly right. She's going to write it all up and offer to give evidence at the coronial inquest.'

Joe, already shamefaced about the photographs, came close to not mentioning the autopsy report. He couldn't, however, fail to do so.

'You mentioned, sir, that Mr Lillee's blood was purple. I told Dr Dawson that, and she said it was consistent with hydrogen sulphide poisoning. She is a doctor, sir. I didn't think that was too much of a breach.'

This wasn't the time to dress Joe down for sharing aspects of an investigation with a stranger. Given that he'd invited Joe to keep Helen Lord informed it would also have been inconsistent.

'I'd like to organise a meeting with Jamieson, who did the autopsy, and Dr Dawson. They may already know each other, of course. For now, though, Sergeant, the paint.'

Ron Dunnart put on his suit coat, preparatory to leaving the building. It wasn't the end of his working day, but he needed a drink, and the bar at The Hotel Windsor was close by. He instinctively patted his pocket to make sure his keys were still there, and immediately noticed that they didn't make quite the same sound. He took them out of the pocket. The knot was wrong, and one key was missing. Fucking Reilly. Why would he take one of his keys?

The reason hit him like a truck. Lillee's car. He'd underestimated Reilly. He cursed himself, first for dragging the key down the side of the car — it had given him pleasure at the time, but at what cost? — and secondly for not checking his key closely. That was a dumb, amateur error. He began to calculate the consequences for him if there was paint on the key. Of course, there must be paint on the key or why else would Reilly have taken it? He couldn't convincingly blame O'Dowd for damage to the car. He'd have to own up to it. He needed time to figure this out.

He figured he had twenty-four hours. Lambert wouldn't act until he had a positive match from forensics. It would be enough to prove that he'd been with Lillee at some stage. It was too circumstantial to link him definitively with Lillee's death. He was facing suspension from duty, at the very least. On his way down the stairs, Dunnart passed two detectives who he didn't much like.

'You look flustered, Ron,' one of them said.

'Working with Reilly will do that to you,' Dunnart said and moved quickly past them.

'David Reilly's all right, isn't he?' said one of these men.

'Course he is. Ron on the other hand ...'

GEORGE STARLING CAUGHT the 3.15 session of *Suspicion* at the Australia picture theatre. He dismissed the newsreels as propaganda. He liked the movie. Cary Grant was a fine actor, and Joan Fontaine could put her slippers under his bed any time. He went straight from the theatre to the address in Fitzroy. He was carrying his suitcase with a change of clothes in it. Though he had managed to keep them clean in the killing of the Reillys, he was expecting the clothes he was wearing — Mr Pluschow's clothes — to be soiled by Joe Sable's blood and viscera. He'd dispose of them afterwards.

It was almost 6.00 p.m. when Starling stood at the gate to Bob O'Dowd's house. It was a modest, semidetached Victorian terrace — the kind of place you'd expect a copper to be able to afford. It was well maintained, but it wasn't flash. He hoped Sable would answer the door, but it didn't really matter if O'Dowd answered. The Luger, which he held by his side, would guarantee him entry, and he'd take it from there.

As Starling raised a hand to knock, a thrill ran through him of such intensity that he shuddered. He knocked.

Bob O'Dowd was sitting in the living room when he heard the knock. He was wearing shorts and nothing else because his psoriasis had begun to gallop over his body and the itching was both painful and irresistible. Cloth exacerbated it, so he sat bare-chested. He'd barely moved for hours, except to tear at his inflamed skin. The knock startled him. Would Ron Dunnart knock? Of course he would, but the knock had been quite gentle, and Dunnart would hammer on the door. O'Dowd decided to ignore it. Maybe it was a telegram boy. Telegrams were usually bad news, so if it was a telegram boy he could just bugger off. There it was again, a little louder this time, but not impatient. Christ! All bloody right, he'd answer the fucking door.

Starling was just thinking about how he'd break into the house when he heard someone approaching down the hall. He raised the Luger. The door opened to reveal a man in his late forties in shorts, and with a torso covered in angry sores and flaking skin.

Bob O'Dowd was looking at the man's face, at the scar that ran from his eye to his mouth. It took him a moment to notice the gun.

Starling said nothing, but pushed the barrel of the gun so hard into O'Dowd's belly that he propelled him back into the house. He closed the door behind them and put his suitcase on the floor.

'Is he here?'

O'Dowd, still uncertain of what was happening, said, 'Who?'

'Sable.'

'Sable?'

Starling caught the tone of genuine surprise, but mistook the nature of that surprise.

'He thought he'd be safe here. A Jew haven.'

'I haven't got a clue what you're talking about, mate. Has Ron Dunnart sent you to do his dirty work?'

The question meant nothing to Starling.

'When is Sable due home?'

'Joe Sable?'

The question enraged Starling. He shot O'Dowd in the foot. It took a moment for O'Dowd's body to register the shock. He looked at his shattered foot, his ears ringing, and the pain cascaded through him. Starling was out of patience. He hustled O'Dowd, now hobbling and still unable to make sense of what was happening, towards the bathroom. Once there, he toppled him into the bathtub. O'Dowd, now shivery with shock, made no effort to resist. Starling sat on the edge of the bath.

'What time is Joe Sable due back here?'

Starling's voice sounded far away to O'Dowd, as if it were coming from the end of a tunnel. He made an incoherent sound.

'You will answer me.' Starling stood up and with calm deliberation he undressed, took the filleting knife from the pocket of his discarded coat, and climbed into the bath with O'Dowd. He sat astride him and placed the blade against O'Dowd's lips.

'Last chance. When is Joe Sable expected to arrive here?'

He lifted the knife so that O'Dowd could speak. O'Dowd made a small sound. No words would come. The question was meaningless.

George Starling began his work. He thought of it as a rehearsal for Joe Sable.

AFTERWARDS, WHEN HE'D wet some towels in the laundry to sponge off the blood, and when he'd dried himself, he returned to the bathroom to get dressed. He looked at the body in the tub and could barely credit that it had once been a man. Starling had thought, after the first few passes of the blade, that O'Dowd would break. He hadn't seemed to grasp the meaning of the question, and it occurred to Starling, well before O'Dowd had died, that David Reilly had lied to him. This realisation hadn't hurried him along. On the contrary, in his fury, he'd slowed down the work the blade was doing.

When he was dressed, he searched the house and found no evidence that a second male was staying there. There was a spare bedroom, but it was obvious that it wasn't being used and that it hadn't been used for a while. Before he left the house, he checked the bathroom one more time, just to reassure himself that the evening hadn't been entirely wasted. There was a bonus, too, because he hadn't had to dispose of the clothes he'd arrived in. He could walk back into the city from Fitzroy and get something to eat along the way.

RON DUNNART HADN'T returned to his desk. He'd intended to, but once he was outside he couldn't face it, and he'd gone home. He'd told his wife he had a migraine and wanted to be left alone. They'd had dinner together, and Ron had feigned the after-effects of the headache while they ate. He'd said he had to return to work to catch up on what he'd left undone that afternoon. He'd taken the car, which rarely was driven these days.

'It needs a bit of a run,' he'd said.

When he arrived at Bob O'Dowd's house at 7.30 p.m., he found the place in darkness, but the front door ajar. This seemed wrong. A voice behind him said, 'If you're looking for Mrs O'Dowd, she's taken off.'

Dunnart turned. A woman in her sixties stood at the gate. There was still enough light in the fading day for Dunnart to see that she was stout, and without a hat.

'It was Mr O'Dowd I was looking for.'

'Oh, he's still there. They must have had a row. I'm not a busybody, so I don't know the details. Good evening to you.'

She walked away.

Dunnart pushed the door open. He hadn't arrived with a clear strategy, and the dark house so disconcerted him that he wasn't sure what his first words would be.

'Why are you sitting in the dark, Bob?'

It seemed a ridiculous question. He turned on the hall light, expecting this to rouse O'Dowd if he'd fallen asleep in a chair somewhere. There was no movement, no sound. As he moved down through the house, Dunnart flicked on the light in the master bedroom, the spare room, the living room, and the kitchen. The open front door might have signalled a burglary, but the house didn't seem to have been disturbed.

Maybe O'Dowd was in the dunny. Dunnart remembered that O'Dowd had boasted once that they'd brought the dunny indoors at vast expense. It was next to the bathroom. Both rooms were also off the front hallway, but he hadn't checked them on his way to the living room. Well, you don't just throw open a bathroom door, do you? Or a toilet door. The last thing he wanted to see was O'Dowd squatting on the dunny. There was frosted glass at the top of the bathroom door. The toilet door was solid. He knocked on it.

'You in there, Bob?'

He waited. Nothing. He opened the door and turned on the light. Mrs O'Dowd kept the lavatory spotless. He didn't like the square of carpet at the foot of the toilet. That would soak up droplets of Bob O'Dowd's piss. The thought disgusted him.

There was no light on in the bathroom, but Dunnart was nothing if not a thorough detective, and besides, where else could O'Dowd be? He was careless and lazy, so he was quite capable of not closing the front door properly, and he was probably one of those people who take long baths and fall asleep in the tub. If this is what had happened, Dunnart would have him at a disadvantage. No one likes to be caught naked.

Dunnart opened the bathroom door and was assailed by an abattoir smell. He snapped on the light.

He was unable to assimilate what he saw. There was a shape, no, there were shapes, because gobbets of stuff sat on the floor and hung over the edge of the bath. Everywhere, blood glistened: wet, oily, dark, bright, dripping, viscous, pooling. There was pink skin and, catching the light, the stark white of bone.

Was this a body? Just one body? Dunnart's eyes followed the strange, butchered shape from its feet to its head. There was no face. Was this even a man? There were no genitals.

Dunnart had seen a hundred corpses. He'd never seen anything like this, and he felt his stomach rebelling. He hurried to the dunny, kneeled, and vomited in the toilet, indifferent now to the piece of carpet. He was so violently ill that he passed out briefly. When he came to and got to his feet, he leaned against the toilet wall. It needed one more flush, so he waited, dazed, for the cistern to fill.

He went back into the bathroom. He had to know if the thing in the tub was Bob O'Dowd. O'Dowd had a badly drawn anchor tattooed on his left forearm. Dunnart approached the bath, unavoidably stepping in blood as he did so. He wasn't thinking clearly. All his senses were overwhelmed the closer he came to the corpse. There was the forearm. The right one had been butterflied open. The left had been overlooked. It was covered in blood. Dunnart leaned in and wiped the blood away with his fingers. The tattoo was there. This was Bob O'Dowd, and given the freshness of the liquids that oozed from him he'd been alive a very short time ago.

When Dunnart stepped away from the bathtub he could see that his trousers were stained, as were his shirt sleeves. He needed to wash the blood from his fingers, so he found the laundry with its wet, bloodied towels, and put his hand under the tap. The cold water sharpened his mind. He'd walked blood from the bathroom to the laundry. When he checked the carpet and flooring, he saw that the murderer had been more careful than he'd been. His were the only footprints. This detail chilled Dunnart. What kind of person could do what he'd done to another human being and remain so calculating as to leave no marks? Apart from the towels. Had he intended to remove the towels? Had Dunnart disturbed him? Was he still in the house?

Dunnart, whose shoes still left traces of blood wherever he walked, quickly checked the back door. It was locked from the inside. Every room was empty.

Dunnart stood in O'Dowd's living room and looked at the state of his clothes. He sat down and tried to calm the chaos of thought and emotion that was unmanning him. Who would want Bob O'Dowd dead? This was always the first question. Titus Lambert would ask it, and the name at the top of his list would be his, Ron Dunnart. Could he leave and wait for some other poor bastard, or O'Dowd's wife, to find the body? No. His prints were now all over the house. He'd touched every door handle, placed his hand against walls and walked blood everywhere. Even his serpentine mind couldn't come up with a convincing reason for visiting the man who'd accused him of murder. He'd never known despair, but as he looked at his bloodied shoes, trousers, and shirt front, despair was what crept up on him.

Someone he'd spoken to about O'Dowd must have done this. Someone must have thought that this is what he'd meant when he'd said that O'Dowd needed to be taught a lesson. Had he actually said this to anyone? He couldn't remember. His mind was breaking into fragments. The smell from the bathroom had attached itself to his clothes. He had to make a decision.

O'Dowd had a telephone. He'd seen it in the hallway. He'd telephone Russell Street, but he wouldn't wait here in the house. No. Why bother telephoning? He'd made a decision to run, and he needed a head start. But why should he run? No one could pin Lillee's murder on him, and if he'd really sliced and diced O'Dowd, he'd be a lot bloodier than he was. He'd done nothing. If he ran, they'd find him. He didn't have enough fuel in his car to run far. No. He'd stay. He'd telephone and stay. He'd sit here and wait.

He went to the telephone, and when his call was answered, he gave his name and the details of Bob O'Dowd's murder. When he put the receiver down, his mind played one last trick on him. It suddenly seemed sensible to him that he should drive home and change his clothes. He wouldn't burn them. He'd put them in a bag and hand them to Homicide. He couldn't bear the thought of wearing them much longer. He'd put on his other suit and come straight back to Fitzroy. If he was quick, he might even beat the police who'd been assigned to attend. Lambert would be one of them. This would interrupt the inspector's evening. That was something, at least.

He knew that leaving the house was wrong, that it would do him damage. The urge to get back to his own house was so strong, it overrode common sense. He left the front door ajar, walked to his car, got in, and started the engine. He felt numb. His life could now be divided into the time before he pushed open the front door of O'Dowd's house and time after he left it ajar for his colleagues to enter. It was strange. As he turned the car into Nicholson Street and headed north, he wondered if his

wife loved him enough to stay with him through what was about
to hit them.

TWO HOURS BEFORE Ron Dunnart entered O'Dowd's house,
Inspector Titus Lambert stood with Martin Serong in David
Reilly's living room. Serong had finished photographing the
bodies. Lambert hadn't asked Joe Sable to go with him to Reilly's
house after the telephone call from a hysterical neighbour had
come through. Joe had been about to leave for the day, and
Lambert had overruled his insistence on joining him.

'I'm taking Jackson and Hart, Sergeant. I want you to go home.
I'll phone you there later. It won't be good news. It seems pretty
clear that Sergeant Reilly and his wife have been murdered.'

'I worked with him, sir. I want to be there.'

'I don't want you there. Jackson and Hart are good detectives.'

'Why am I being excluded, sir?'

'You're not being excluded, and you're not being protected.'
Joe was about to speak. Lambert stopped him. 'Even if you don't
understand my reasons, Sergeant, I am giving you an instruction,
and I expect you to obey it. I want you to go home to Kew and
wait for my telephone call.'

Inspector Lambert left the office without saying anything
further. Joe's frustration was unbounded, but he no choice other
than to head home. David Reilly dead? This seemed outlandish
and unlikely. It would turn out to be a mistake of some kind.
David Reilly and Peter Lillee? Was there some connection? Ron
Dunnart, Joe thought. That was a connection.

'LET'S GO OUTSIDE,' Lambert said.

He and Martin Serong stood in the Reillys' neat front yard

while the various attendants on the dead went about their work, determining roughly cause and time of death, and finding evidence. The doctor had already established that Mrs Reilly had not been sexually interfered with and that death for each of them had probably been quick. There was no evidence of torture. The murderer had lavished no more than a single bullet on Mrs Reilly, and two on David Reilly.

'Do you agree it was quick, Martin?'

'Yes. They may have died quickly, but Mrs Reilly was tied up, which suggests she had a long wait for the bullet.'

'And she would have been terrified. Who died first?'

'I think David did, Titus. I think the killer was standing close to Mrs Reilly and fired at David from across the room, then killed Mrs Reilly. There's psychological sadism here, even if there's no physical evidence of it.'

'Sergeant Ron Dunnart left Russell Street early this afternoon. I checked on his movements before coming here. He didn't return. Two men passed him on the stairs. They said he seemed agitated and that he made a disparaging remark about David Reilly.'

'That's a long way from a double execution, Titus. I've worked with Ron Dunnart. I don't like him particularly, but what would make him do this?'

'Can someone just snap and go berserk?'

'There's nothing berserk about this crime scene, Titus. It's controlled. It may look messy in there, but that's just blood. Whoever did this approached it with discipline. There's nothing frenzied about it.'

Titus had come to the same conclusion. It was good to hear Martin Serong confirm it. No one was better at reading a crime scene than Serong.

When the coroner had finished his work, the bodies were removed to the city morgue, and the work of knocking on neighbours' doors began. Detectives Jackson and Hart had been dispatched to Dunnart's house in Coburg. They were to bring him to Russell Street. He was a plausible person of interest, although Titus couldn't accept that Dunnart's suspect morality could mutate so suddenly into psychopathy. He tried to picture Ron Dunnart putting a gun into Mrs Reilly's mouth. It was impossible.

Lambert returned to Russell Street to wait for Dunnart's arrival. He telephoned Maude to tell her that he wouldn't be home for several more hours. He told her why. She hadn't known David Reilly, but she knew that Titus had valued him and that he must be taking this hard. She said she'd wait up for him. He then rang Joe Sable and confirmed that both David Reilly and his wife were dead, and that they'd been murdered. Each of them had been shot.

'I understand Tom is there for dinner.'

'Yes, sir.'

'Ron Dunnart is being brought in.'

There was silence for a moment.

'I can come into Russell Street, sir.'

'Out of the question. First thing tomorrow. You may of course pass on this appalling news to Helen Lord. I know she didn't like David Reilly, but she'd want to know. He was a colleague after all.'

'Helen will be shocked.'

'All right. Thank you, Joe.'

'Sir, could Ron Dunnart have discovered that David Reilly took his key?'

'Speculation at this stage is pointless, Joe. Good night.'

BETTE DUNNART HAD learned over the course of her marriage not to ask questions about her husband's work. It wasn't usual for detectives, or policemen, to visit Ron at home. It did happen from time to time, and then Bette knew to make herself scarce. She'd told the two detectives who now sat in her front room that Ron was rarely so late home, but that he'd gone into Russell Street to complete some work. She didn't ask why they were there. Ron would have been unhappy if she'd done that. She offered to make them a cup of tea, which they declined. They hadn't been there very long when they heard a car pull up outside. Bette Dunnart, who'd left Detectives Jackson and Hart on their own, heard the car also and shouted from the kitchen, 'That'll be Ron, now.'

John Jackson and Abraham Hart, neither of whom had worked closely with Ron Dunnart, but each of whom had some respect for him, stood up and prepared themselves for an awkward encounter. Mrs Dunnart opened the front door. She was unable to see the state of Ron's clothes when she said, 'There are two gentlemen here to see you.'

Then Ron moved into a pool of light on the front porch, and Bette's mouth fell open. Dunnart was annoyed that he had to deal with his wife on top of everything else, so he pushed past her without saying anything. How had they beaten him to his house? The telephone at Russell Street had been answered by a constable who'd said that uniformed men would get to O'Dowd's house as quickly as possible, but that there were no homicide detectives in the building at present. That had suited Dunnart. Now, somehow, there were policemen in his front room. He entered the room and was taken aback to find Jackson and Hart. They, in their turn, were taken aback by Dunnart's bloodied clothes.

'I didn't kill him. I found him, but I didn't kill him.'

'What do you mean you found him?' Jackson said. 'He was found by a neighbour late this afternoon.'

'What? I've only just left him. He's been dead for an hour at the most.'

'Who are you talking about, Ron?' Hart asked.

'I telephoned Russell Street. They know. Bob O'Dowd.'

'O'Dowd. Jesus Christ. We're here to pick you up about David Reilly and his wife.'

Abraham Hart would say later that the look of shock on Dunnart's face at the mention of Reilly's name was so remarkable, so ungovernable, that he knew Dunnart was hearing the news of Reilly's death for the first time.

Everything in Dunnart's world had now shifted into unrecognisable disorder. A self-defence mechanism rendered him almost monosyllabic and numbly cooperative.

'I need to change my clothes.'

'I'll come with you,' Hart said. 'We need to collect everything you're wearing. Everything. Shoes, socks, underwear — the lot.'

Dunnart nodded and took Hart with him into the master bedroom. Bette Dunnart, who'd overheard the exchange in the front room, came to Detective Jackson and said, 'I don't understand what's happening here.'

'I'm sorry, Mrs Dunnart, I'm not at liberty to say, but Ron is coming with us to Russell Street. He may be gone for several hours.'

'But he will be coming back.'

John Jackson, having seen Dunnart, wasn't sure about that, but said, 'Yes, Mrs Dunnart. I imagine he'll be back much later this evening.' *Bob O'Dowd*, he thought. *Bob O'Dowd is dead.* What the fuck was going on?

It HAD SEEMED until now to Tom Mackenzie and Helen Lord that they'd known each other for some time. This was an illusion of course, created by their separate involvement in the same crimes. Helen had never thought of him as Titus Lambert's brother-in-law, which he was. His resemblance to Maude Lambert was strong. The evidence of what had been done to him was still so apparent that she found herself unexpectedly moved by it. Everyone sitting at the dinner table was suffering the consequences of personal trauma. *Is this*, Helen thought, *how life was supposed to be — a continuous and exhausting endurance test?*

The In Memoriam notice was due to appear on Wednesday and Thursday, on the front page of *The Argus*, *The Age*, and *The Sun News-Pictorial*. They agreed that this was very uncertain. It was Guy Kirkham who asked the pertinent question that no one had thought to ask.

'What do we actually do if George Starling turns up?'

'We arrest him,' Joe said.

'Only you and Helen can do that, and I imagine Helen will be a bit busy.'

'And he's not going to come quietly, is he?' added Tom.

'Inspector Lambert won't be happy that we've done this,' said Joe. 'But it's done now, and maybe he'll see that it's our best chance of trapping Starling.'

'He'll resent the fact that we've forced his hand,' Helen said, 'but he'll organise a police presence, I'm sure. He'd never forgive himself if he didn't. The question is whether he'll ever forgive *us*.'

'It will all have to be done quickly. We've got a good sketch of Starling, an accurate one, which can be passed around. We may not need that many policemen — maybe half a dozen? In mufti.'

They talked about strategies and about the Pyjama Girl inquest, which was still occupying a great deal of newspaper space. Guy was telling them about the film he'd been to see that afternoon, *The Leopard Man* at the Lyceum, when Inspector Lambert telephoned. When Joe returned to the table with the news of David and Barbara Reilly's deaths, it took a full minute for anyone to speak. It was Helen who broke the silence.

'Who would do that? Who would do such a thing?'

Ron Dunnart sat in the interview room for three hours before Inspector Lambert spoke to him. Lambert was exhausted, and there was something in his eyes that Dunnart had never seen before — a look of having been stunned.

It was 1.00 a.m., and Lambert had left O'Dowd's house in Fitzroy in the hands of the coroner and three detectives whose abilities he trusted. Martin Serong had left at the same time as Lambert, and Serong had been shaken by what he'd photographed in the bathroom. Serong had seen the worst that people were capable of, or he'd thought he had.

'The person who did this,' he'd said to Titus, 'is only nominally human. He took his time and every slice of his blade gave him pleasure.'

'He's human, all right. I sometimes think, Martin, that this is who we truly are. We're a terrible and terrifying species.'

As he sat now in the stuffy room with Ron Dunnart, Titus wondered if this man could really be among the worst of his kind. If Peter Lillee was included, could he have murdered four people in a matter of days and sit here looking, or trying to look, defiant? He wasn't being entirely successful.

From Dunnart's point of view, his defiance was based on the fact that he hadn't murdered Bob O'Dowd or the Reillys, and he was confident that Lambert would know this.

'Is this a formal interview?' he asked.

'Two of my detectives and a woman have been savagely killed today, Ron. I'm not in the mood for games. If you want a lawyer, just ask.'

'No. I'll answer your questions. I have nothing to hide.'

Lambert established Dunnart's version of his arrival at O'Dowd's house and his discovery of the body. Dunnart denied any knowledge of the scene in Reilly's house.

'You were aware that he took a key from your pocket?'

Dunnart decided to lie about this. He wanted there to be no connection between him and Reilly's death.

'No. I have all my keys.' He withdrew the keys and put them on the table. 'They're all there, all six of them.' He made a show of pointing at them and counting.

'There's one missing,' he said and performed being perplexed. He picked up the keys and looked at them closely. 'The key to the back shed is missing. Why would Reilly take the key to my back shed? What did he think he'd find in there?'

Lambert, whose senses had been brutally assaulted that day, didn't detect that Dunnart was lying. His responses seemed genuine and Lambert was convinced by them.

'Why do you think Sergeant Reilly went to the trouble of taking one of your keys, Ron?'

'I presume he thought I was hiding something to do with Lillee's death, in my shed.'

'Let me tell you something, Ron. I don't think you killed Peter Lillee, and how would he know that that missing key was the key to your shed? I'll ask you again, why do you think David Reilly took that particular key from your bundle of keys?'

Lambert already knew the answer to that question. This crashed in on Dunnart and simultaneously he realised that he had no convincing alibi for that afternoon. As a copper, he'd never considered alibis given by wives as convincing. Inspector Lambert watched as Ron Dunnart seemed to collapse inwardly. His breathing altered, and his face drained of colour. His eyes, usually signalling arrogance and certainty, now had an unfamiliar pleading look in them.

'Reilly was a better detective than I thought. There was paint on the key.'

'Where did the paint come from, Ron?'

'It came from the side of Peter Lillee's car, where I scratched it.'

'And when did this happen?'

'On the night that he died. He came out of his fiancée's flat, although I didn't know that at the time, and I was waiting for him. I got into his car.'

'Why?'

'You know why. I was trying to get money out of him.'

'Where were you this afternoon?'

'I went home. My wife will confirm that, but I suppose you'd expect her to.'

'Tell me what you think this looks like, Ron. David Reilly takes a key that will prove you were with Peter Lillee on the night that he died. David Reilly and his wife are murdered. You have a weak alibi. Later, the man who accused you of murdering Peter Lillee is found dead. By you. There are no witnesses. You have blood all over you. Why? When I looked into that bathroom I wanted to turn and run. I certainly didn't want to get close enough to soil my clothes.'

'I didn't kill David Reilly, Titus, or his wife. I don't even know how they died. No one has told me. I didn't want to go near Bob O'Dowd's body. When I first saw it, I threw up in the toilet. I think I passed out. But I had to know who was in the bathtub. Bob had a tattoo of an anchor on his arm. There was so much blood I couldn't see it, so I wiped some away and saw the anchor. I knew of course how this would look and what you'd think. Who had a motive? I suppose I did. I telephoned here. I could have left without telephoning, but it would have been pointless. I'd been seen going into the house by one of the neighbours. I should have waited but I couldn't bear being in the house, and I couldn't bear the smell that was coming off my clothes. I went home to change. I was going to put all my clothes in a bag and hand them over, but you won't believe that. How could you believe that? If I'd killed him, my clothes would have been soaked in blood. They're not.'

'The towels in the laundry suggest the killer wiped himself down, which suggests that he took his clothes off to commit the murder, cleaned himself up and put his clothes back on.'

'The person who butchered Bob O'Dowd is a fucking monster. I may be many unpleasant things, but I'm not a monster.'

Inspector Lambert didn't believe in monsters. He also didn't believe that he was looking at the man who'd murdered three people in a single day. Dunnart had motive, possibly, and opportunity. What he didn't have was the bleak wasteland of spirit that such acts required. He had enough circumstantial evidence to put Ron Dunnart under arrest. Instead, he sent him home and told him that he was suspended from duty. He wasn't to come near Russell Street until further notice, and he wasn't to communicate with any fellow police officers.

'Don't disobey that instruction, Ron. I'll find out if you do, and I *will* arrest you. You need to tell your wife that your policing career is over.'

'I'll hand in my resignation.'

'No. I won't accept it. You will be dishonourably discharged, and you may even go to prison.'

They both knew prison was unlikely. The Commissioner liked to discard bad apples discreetly. Corrupt police officers eroded public trust. Dismiss them certainly, but keep it out of the papers.

Titus DIDN'T GET back to the house in South Melbourne until close to 4.00 a.m. Tom Mackenzie was asleep, having returned from dinner in Kew at midnight. Maude was still up. When Titus entered the house, she met him in the hallway. He held her without speaking, and she felt his body give way to tremors that ran through him. They grew until he was unable to control the sobs that wracked him in a way that terrified her. She'd seen her husband cry, but not like this. She held tightly to him until she realised that she was holding him up. His weight pulled them down to their knees. She cupped his face in her hands and with her fluttering fingers tried to still the small muscles that leaped and quivered there.

'Tell me, Titus, tell me what's happened.'

When he was able to, he told her everything.

Everything.

14

GEORGE STARLING CAME down to the foyer of The Victoria Hotel early on Wednesday morning. There was an alcove with two armchairs in it and a newspaper rack. He took a copy of *The Argus* and *The Age*. He was hopeful that Reilly's murder might have been reported. O'Dowd's had happened too late to make Wednesday's paper. It would surely make Thursday's. The news from Europe was lies. The Russians were claiming that the German army had lost close to 210,000 men in a matter of weeks. This was clearly Communist propaganda. There was nothing of interest on the front page, until his eye was snagged by a black-bordered rectangle near the bottom right. He noticed, too, the same box on the front page of *The Argus*, which was lying across his knee. Someone important must have died. He read it with growing excitement.

> The funeral of Mr Peter Lillee will be held this Thursday 6 April at 11.00 a.m. at St Paul's Cathedral and afterwards in the Portico Room at Melbourne Town Hall. Beloved brother of Mrs Rosalind Lord, beloved uncle of Miss Helen Lord, and friend to Mr Joseph Sable. Rest now from your labours.

Hardy Truscott would have claimed that this was the hand of Odin, controlling his fate and shifting elements in the universe in his favour. Joe Sable and Helen Lord were being delivered to him on a platter. He lost interest in whether Reilly's death had been reported. He left The Victoria Hotel, dapper in his best suit and pale-grey fedora, and walked to St Paul's Cathedral. He'd never been inside it. He'd never had any reason to do more than walk past its unavoidable heft.

As soon as he entered the cathedral's interior, he decided that this wasn't the place to mete out punishment to Joe Sable and Helen Lord. It was too big. Peter Lillee, whoever he was, must have been a wealthy man to score a funeral in this place. He didn't venture much beyond the last rows of pews. The lushness of the polychrome stonework and dazzling floor tiles reminded him that the people who worshipped here were complacent in their privilege and ripe for the cold, hard shock of National Socialism.

The Town Hall sat just a block north of the cathedral, in Swanston Street. Starling had never been inside this building either. The front doors were closed, but he walked further along the front of the building and found an open work area. This was where deliveries must be made. He entered, his hat pulled low. Two workers, who assumed from his clothes that he must be someone, nodded a polite 'Good morning', and Starling pushed open a door.

He found himself in a corridor and walked along it, unchallenged by a woman who was hurrying somewhere. Another woman, trailing behind, said 'oh' when she saw Starling's face. He asked her where the Portico Room was, and, embarrassed by her reaction to this poor man's scar, she gave him directions. Starling thanked her and within minutes had found the door two floors up to the Portico Room. He opened it.

There was no one in the room, which was surprisingly modest in its dimensions. Even so, it would be busy with people on the day of the reception. He'd have to surrender his long-cherished wish to get Joe Sable alone. What mattered was that Sable died. A slow and exquisitely judged and painful death was the ideal, but war demanded sacrifice, and dispatching Sable in a crowded, noisy place would have to do. Starling didn't think he'd have any trouble getting into the post-funeral reception. He wouldn't come through the front door. He'd come through the service entrance.

There was a public lavatory outside the Town Hall, on the Collins Street side. Starling stood at the urinal, relieving himself, and imagined finding Joe Sable in the crowd, standing behind him as he spoke to someone, preferably Helen Lord, and reaching around his shoulders and drawing his filleting knife deeply and swiftly across his throat. Sable wouldn't know what happened. No one would know what had happened for the few seconds it took for the wound to gape as the jugular pumped blood into the room. Perhaps before melting into the crowd he'd shoot Helen Lord, in the middle of her forehead, her eyes wide with shock at Joe Sable's gushing throat. As Starling replayed this action in his head, he settled on it as the best possible plan. It was almost elegant in its simplicity.

INSPECTOR LAMBERT WAS at Russell Street by 8.00 a.m. He'd had two hours' sleep. Vera O'Dowd had been located, and she'd agreed to meet Inspector Lambert at the City Morgue at 9.00 a.m. Titus considered his presence there a courtesy he couldn't refuse. He'd seen Bob O'Dowd's corpse. Vera O'Dowd wouldn't be asked to look at his face. There'd be no point. All its features had been sliced away. She'd make the identification, as Dunnart had done, from the tattoo on his arm.

When Joe Sable arrived at 8.30 a.m., Titus briefed him immediately, almost mechanically, on Bob O'Dowd's death and on his interview with Ron Dunnart. He added details he hadn't told Joe the previous day about Barbara and David Reilly's murders.

'I don't have a report for you to read. There hasn't been time. Martin Serong hasn't even developed his photographs yet.'

Joe heard what was being said, but its grotesque excess kept its full meaning at bay. Reilly and O'Dowd dead? And Ron Dunnart sent home? Had Inspector Lambert had some sort of breakdown?

'Sir, surely Sergeant Dunnart is a suspect?'

Lambert shook his head.

'If you'd seen Bob O'Dowd's body and what had been done to it, you'd know Ron Dunnart didn't do it.'

'Why didn't you ring me last night, sir, when you were told about Bob O'Dowd?'

'It was very late, Sergeant. There were other officers available. I need at least one of my men to have had a decent night's sleep. Can you imagine what the newspapers are going to do with this? Four policemen killed in a matter of days. The Premier is going to want this cleaned up as quickly as possible. He's going to want an arrest immediately, and so is the Commissioner.'

'This is going to have a terrible effect on everyone here.'

'Yes, it is. The Commissioner is going to address all the officers who are in the building at ten o'clock. It's possible that among them is the man who killed Reilly and O'Dowd. And Mrs Reilly.' Titus was aware that Barbara Reilly had already become an addendum. This was fatigue. He wouldn't normally have been guilty of such thinking. Still, if he thought like this, other officers would do the same. He'd need to ensure during this investigation that Barbara Reilly's death wasn't spoken of in ways that suggested it was of less importance than David Reilly's death. She must always be Barbara Reilly and not David Reilly's wife. 'We're in uncharted waters, Sergeant.'

'Were they killed by the same person?'

'I hope so. Christ, I hope so. On the surface, at least, it doesn't look like it. The Reillys died quickly and cleanly. O'Dowd's death was ghastly beyond measure.'

'The only link between them, sir, is Ron Dunnart.'

'Do you think I should arrest him?'

'It would send a shock wave through here, but it might satisfy the press.'

'I'm assuming, hoping, you're playing devil's advocate, and that that is not really what you believe.'

This hadn't been Joe's intention and now he was confused. He sensibly fell silent.

'I'm not going to arrest Ron Dunnart just to appease the press. I want to make this very clear to you, Sergeant. I do not believe that Sergeant Dunnart is a psychopath. He disliked, even loathed, both of the dead men, but he did not kill them.'

Inspector Lambert asked Joe to speak with Martin Serong, John Jackson, and Abraham Hart. They would brief him fully. He left a few minutes later for the City Morgue. Joe sat, still, not quite able to understand what had happened. Questions were racing around in his head, and the one that disturbed him most was about Inspector Lambert. Why was he protecting Ron Dunnart?

VERA O'DOWD CAME to the morgue with her sister. Inspector Lambert introduced himself at the morgue's entrance. She answered dully, her face impassive. She had a cast-iron alibi, but could she have paid someone to murder her husband? Even the thought felt like a calumny, and Titus wondered if such thoughts were doing irreparable damage to his mind. Murder focussed the mind on everything that was base in human nature.

The smell of the morgue, sharp carbolic acid and something cloying and foul, clutched as it always did at Titus's stomach. For Vera O'Dowd and her sister, who said nothing, the smell must have been overwhelming. Bob O'Dowd's body lay on a gurney in a small room, which had been attached, almost as an afterthought, to the large autopsy room. Dr Jamieson, a man whose compassion, like Martin Serong's, somehow survived the grim rhythms of his working life, stood by the body. He'd seen grief in all its manifestations, and Vera O'Dowd's shut-down quality didn't surprise him.

'Mrs O'Dowd, I know how difficult this is, but would you help me identify this man?'

Titus thought this a gentle question, and Vera O'Dowd nodded in response.

'Do you recognise this tattoo?' As he said this, he lifted the sheet carefully, so that only that part of O'Dowd's arm was visible. Vera looked at it and nodded.

'I always hated that tattoo. May I see my husband's face?'

'No, Mrs O'Dowd. I'm sorry, but his face was very badly damaged.'

Vera, whose last words to her husband had been unpleasant, wanted somehow to make amends, and, in an irrational rush, she pulled the sheet from Bob O'Dowd's body. The revealed creature had been washed and sluiced, and the damage done by Starling's filleting knife was stark and appalling. Vera's sister ran from the room, and Vera, in a strange reaction, sank to the floor and sat there, her head dropped forward, and her breaths coming in shallow gasps. Titus and Dr Jamieson lifted her to her feet and helped her to the reception area. Her sister was there, shaking from head to foot and weeping. The two women didn't fall into each other's arms. They sat side by side in chairs near the door, a lifetime of distance between them unbridgeable even by what they'd both just seen.

'We will find the person responsible for this,' Titus said, and his words sounded hollow to his ears.

JOE TELEPHONED HELEN to tell her about Bob O'Dowd and to express his doubts about Inspector Lambert's judgement.

'He knows Ron Dunnart, Joe. He's worked with him.'

'Does he know him, though? Could anyone ever really know the darkest things we're capable of?'

'We both know someone who might be capable of this.'

'The viciousness is familiar, but there's absolutely no connection. We know he's here, but he can't be guilty of every vile thing that happens. The world is full to overflowing with George Starlings.'

WHILE THE VICTORIA police force was coming to grips with what had happened in Melbourne — and news had travelled as far as the remote police station at Pyramid Hill — George Starling was at the pictures, watching first *Random Harvest* and then *The Desperadoes*. The pictures filled in his day and calmed him down. He planned to watch a third picture that night or perhaps see whatever was on at the Comedy Theatre. He'd have an early night. Tomorrow, Easter Thursday, he had work to do.

He intended to get up early, find a barber, have a clean, close shave, and find his way into the Town Hall several hours before the Peter Lillee funeral party was due to arrive. An event like that would be invitation-only. The newspaper notice was a statement of fact, like the vice-regal notices, and was certainly not an open invitation to the public. Riffraff might make it into St Paul's to gawk, but they'd be denied entry to the Town Hall. Starling would find a place to wait, unseen, and then appear among the assembled guests, and in his finely tailored pockets would be a Luger and a filleting knife.

ON THE MORNING of Peter Lillee's funeral, Joe came in to Russell Street early. He intended to go from there to St Paul's Cathedral. Inspector Lambert was already at his desk. A copy of *The Age* was in front of him. He called Joe into his office.

'When did this notice first appear?'

'Yesterday, sir.'

'Yesterday. I didn't see the papers yesterday, and neither did Maude. At least this explains why no paper appeared at the house. I presume Tom knew this was being printed and made sure Maude didn't see it. Whose idea was this?'

'It was mine, sir.'

'And just what do you plan to do if Starling shows up? That, I presume, is the point of this ostentatious notice?'

'I plan to arrest him?'

'Do you expect him to come quietly?'

'No, sir, I do not. I will be armed, and I won't be alone.'

Inspector Lambert leaned forward and with fierce precision he said, 'This is ill-conceived and ill-thought-out. No doubt Constable Lord and her mother agreed with you. That disappoints me, but I don't expect them to be thinking clearly at this time. You have invited a brutal, ruthless man to disrupt the funeral of a good and decent man. You will have no control over what happens — none whatsoever. You can't predict how Starling, if he sees that notice, will behave. You have endangered the life of every person who attends the funeral or who goes to the wake.'

Joe tried to summon self-righteousness to defend himself against this tirade. He failed, and every one of Lambert's blows landed. Why hadn't any of them thought of this?

'This may come as a shock to you, Sergeant, but however much pressure you feel you're under, you're not alone in that. Two of my officers are dead, and now, instead of concentrating our efforts on that, I'm going to have to send God knows how many men to Peter Lillee's funeral.'

'I'm not asking for any back up.'

'It isn't back up. It's insurance against your foolish plan creating chaos. You've forced me into putting the lives of these men in danger and at the very least, if Starling doesn't turn up — and let's hope he doesn't — into wasting hours of their time with standing around. Only you and Constable Lord know what Starling looks like. Did that occur to you?'

'Tom knows, too.'

Lambert was beginning to lose his patience.

'I don't think I'm getting through to you, Sergeant. You seem to be labouring under the delusion that the world revolves around you.'

A white flash of anger jolted Joe into hot speech.

'The man who burned down my flat, the man who has come here to kill me, is within reach because I've brought him within reach. You seem to be labouring under the delusion, sir, that this shouldn't matter to me. It does. Self-defence is not the same as self-regard. I'm sorry if that distinction had escaped you.'

Joe had never before displayed such insubordination, and it both appalled and thrilled him. He took a breath. 'Whatever happens today, I'll tender my resignation.'

Inspector Lambert leaned back in his chair and folded his arms.

'One thing you can be sure of, Sergeant, is that I will accept it.'

As Joe walked to St Paul's Cathedral, he felt elated. This would be his last day in Homicide, his last day as a detective. He was strangely energised by this. He hadn't intended to resign, but when the moment had come, it had seemed right, even if it had been done in anger. There had been something of the inevitable about it. His position had never felt secure to him.

He reached the cathedral at 10.00 a.m. The casket was in place before the altar. The doors weren't to be opened until 10.30, and Joe and Tom were to stand on either side of them, watching for Starling as people filed in. None of the side doors were to be opened, so if someone entered, he had to do it from the main entrance.

The Melbourne Club had pulled serious strings to secure the cathedral on Easter Thursday. It must have been a great inconvenience and a disruptive interference in the setting up for the Good Friday program of worship, and for the Holy Thursday services. Someone at the Melbourne Club had enough sway to have done this.

The club had promised Ros Lord that she would have to do nothing, and that promise had been kept to an extravagant degree. Staff from the club had defied wartime austerity and had found enough flowers to subdue the smell of furniture polish and floor wax. A condolence book had been organised, club members had volunteered as ushers, and eulogies had been settled. There were to be four of these — two by Melbourne Club members, and two by artists, one a woman, whose names Ros vaguely remembered Peter having mentioned.

Helen, Ros, Clara, and Guy arrived not long after Joe, followed by Tom. Ros moved about the cathedral thanking each person she met for his part in shouldering the burden of the funeral arrangements.

When the doors opened, Joe and Tom took up their positions. Helen greeted each person as he or she approached the aisle. Within twenty minutes the cathedral was full and people were spilling onto the Flinders Street footpath. There was no sign of George Starling. The only people Joe recognised were several policemen in suits. Inspector Lambert wasn't among them.

The service went smoothly. Each of the eulogies was anodyne — even those delivered by the artists — which disappointed Ros. The impression left by them was that Peter Lillee kept all of his friends slightly at bay and sequestered them one from another.

At the end of the service, six pallbearers, none of whom Ros or Helen knew, carried the coffin to the waiting hearse. It was taken to the Fawkner Crematorium, accompanied by two Melbourne Club members. Ros and Helen had elected not to attend the cremation. They moved with the crowd to the Town Hall.

Joe realised, as he and Tom stood at the Collins Street entrance to the Town Hall, that it was unlikely that Starling would make an appearance here. Only eighty people had been invited to the wake, and when the last of them had been crossed off the list, the doors were closed.

Tom and Joe followed the Town Hall employee, whose job it had been to check guests' names against a list, up well-worn marble steps to a corridor and into the Portico Room. Joe had expected a much grander space. It was surprisingly small and rather bare. Fortunately, the doors to the portico were open, and most people had chosen to move out onto the balcony. The Melbourne Club hadn't been stingy with the food or the drink — and it was the club that was picking up the bill for both the funeral and the wake.

'We're not going to catch him here,' Joe said, and had to raise his voice to be heard.

'Maybe afterwards,' Tom said. 'He's probably hanging around outside waiting for this to be finished.'

'I can't see any police here.' Joe was looking about him.

'I didn't mention this to Titus, and I kept yesterday's papers out of the way.'

'He saw today's paper, and he's so angry that he wants to fire me. He feels manipulated into using police to shore up what he considers a selfish personal whim of mine.'

'But he hasn't used them. You said there are none here.'

'There were plenty at the cathedral, though, and they'll be somewhere in the Town Hall — checking lavatories, that sort of thing.'

Guy came towards them, holding three beers. 'There's no way he can get in here,' he said. 'A beer won't go astray.'

Helen and Clara joined them, each holding a glass of wine.

'I had no idea Uncle Peter knew so many people. They've all been very kind, but I get the impression no one knew him very well. They all seem to have met him at functions or sat with him on committees. And we invited Lillian Johnson, but she sent an apology. I don't blame her. This would have been awful for her.'

'It makes me think I need to meet more people,' Clara said. 'If I died they could hold my wake in a telephone booth, and there'd still be room for latecomers.'

'I'd come,' Guy said.

'That's very nice, Guy. Maybe I should go to the pictures with you, after all. I'd hate our first date to be post-mortem.'

If anyone but Clara had said this it would have sounded crass and tactless. It made Helen smile.

'Thank God you're here, Clar. You always know the wrong thing to say.'

'It's my special gift.'

'It doesn't seem like he's going to show up,' Helen said. 'If he read the notice, he's probably waiting until afterwards. I'm going to try to relax and help Mum get through this.'

Ros Lord was talking to her neighbour in Kew, Mrs Davies, one of the few people she actually knew.

'It's a very nice turnout,' Mrs Davies said. 'Mr Lillee would have been chuffed at the number of people who came to the church. And isn't it lovely here? And such elegant finger food.'

Ros was happy to listen to her neighbour's banalities. They protected her from forced conversations with, and repeated condolences from, strangers. Nevertheless, Helen and Clara rescued her and left Mrs Davies to sample the food laid out on a sideboard. They took her out onto the balcony. It was crowded, but the Portico Room had become a bit stuffy, despite the doors to the balcony being open. Joe and Guy helped themselves to a sandwich each, and went out onto the balcony. The view of the Manchester Unity Building across the street was magnificent. Tom had said that he'd join them, but that he had to go to the dunny first. He walked out into the corridor and turned left. The lavatories were nearby.

GEORGE STARLING HAD had no trouble getting into the Town Hall early. He'd simply repeated what he'd done the previous day. He'd used the tradesmen's entrance, and no one had stopped him.

Starling discovered that there were any number of empty offices on the upper levels of the Town Hall to wait in. Easter Thursday was obviously not a working day for most of the staff. He chose an office, on the same floor as the Portico Room, and sat in a comfortable chair. Whoever worked in here was very tidy. The desk was so neat that it must have been especially put into order in expectation of a few days' break. Starling wouldn't be discovered in this office. All that was required of him now was to lock the door and be patient.

It was the sudden jarring of a lift that woke Starling from a doze. He opened the door slightly and watched as the first people to arrive at the wake made their way into the Portico Room. Soon the corridor was noisy with voices. Starling shut the door. He would wait until everything was in full swing. Adrenalin began to seep into his system. He loved this feeling. He took out his gun and his knife. The knife's edge was still razor-sharp, despite the work it had recently done. Soon, Joe Sable would feel its edge, and it would be the last thing he'd ever feel.

INSPECTOR LAMBERT'S ANGER had not abated. He knew it was unfair to blame Sergeant Sable alone for the misguided attempt to entrap George Starling. Helen Lord and his own brother-in-law, Tom Mackenzie, were equally implicated. However, his anger needed a focus, and so it rested on the person who ought to have argued against such a plan, but who instead claimed authorship of it: Joe Sable.

Lambert had been at the cathedral, but had stayed out of sight, and now he stood in the corridor outside the Portico Room. Everyone who'd been invited was on the other side of the doors, so at least people were safe for the duration of the wake. A sweep of the offices had revealed nothing. It would only be afterwards that Constable Peterson admitted that, annoyed at being called into work on his day off, he hadn't bothered to check behind any doors that were locked. Lambert unfolded a copy of the sketch made of George Starling's face and studied it. Both Joe and Helen had assured him that it was an excellent likeness. It wasn't an ugly face, but it was striking and vicious. If Starling was in front of him, surely he'd recognise him.

His back was turned when Starling came out of the office he'd been waiting in. Starling saw the man near the door, examining a piece of paper and then putting it into his pocket. He walked towards him, his grey fedora in his hand. Lambert turned when

Starling was just a few steps from him.

'Excuse me,' Starling said, and smiled. 'Were you a friend of Peter Lillee's?'

Lambert failed to see that the man before him was George Starling. Instead, he saw an elegantly dressed and well-spoken young man, whose face bore the disfiguring evidence of war.

'No. I didn't know Mr Lillee personally.'

'He was a friend to me when I needed one,' Starling said, and Titus believed him and was moved by his words. He offered his condolences and opened the door to the Portico Room for him. Starling nodded his thanks and passed inside.

'Titus?' Lambert looked up from reclosing the door to find Tom Mackenzie approaching him on his way back from the toilet. 'What are you doing here?'

'I hope I'm wasting my time,' said Lambert.

'You saw the notice.'

'No thanks to you. I don't want to talk about this now, Tom. You should go back to the others.'

Tom didn't react to the implied rebuke. He wasn't an underling to Titus, and yes, he'd be very happy to talk about it later.

'There's no point standing out here, Titus. You might as well come in and have something to eat and drink.'

Titus hadn't intended on doing this, but Tom was right. It would be interesting to see who these people were who considered themselves the inner circle of Peter Lillee's wide circle of friends and acquaintances. Tom held open the door, and Titus preceded him into the room.

Ros Lord caught sight of Titus immediately and gave him a small wave. Titus took this as an invitation to speak to her. Across the room, out on the portico, Tom saw Joe and Helen talking to Clara and Guy. Joe and Helen had their backs to him. Guy was leaning against one of the columns that held up the portico roof. Was it Ionic, Corinthian or Doric? Guy was looking at Clara, who was speaking. Tom decided to get another beer and go out to them. That was when Starling's silhouette interposed itself between him and his friends.

Tom knew who it was, instantly. He didn't need to see his face. There was something familiar in the way he stood, poised in the doorway to the balcony. He saw Starling reach into his pockets and withdraw two objects. The sun caught the blade of a knife in his left hand and the sheen of a gun in his right. Starling dropped his hands to his sides. No one else had noticed the weapons, and Starling began to shorten the distance between himself and Joe Sable.

Starling's heart was pounding. This was it. He'd waited for this moment, and he saw no need to hurry it. He was just a few feet away now, and still no one had guessed his intention. He was close enough to reach out and touch Joe. Here, surrounded by people, he chose the efficiency of the gun over the knife. Killing Joe from behind, however, wasn't enough. He wanted to see his look of terror.

He raised the gun, and, with his arm outstretched, he tapped the barrel on the back of Joe's head.

It was the expression on Guy's face, rather than the hard steel, that puzzled Joe. It was at first quizzical, then stricken, and in the split second it took for that transition to occur, conversation died on the balcony. It was as if everyone had noticed the man with the gun at once. He was rigid, statuesque, perfectly still, and something emanated from him that seemed to stun onlookers. Helen was simultaneously aware of both the silence and the faint hum of conversation from inside the Portico Room. What was happening?

Starling took two steps back and said, 'Turn around, Jew.' As he spoke, with the instincts of a predator, he glanced either side and behind him. He didn't see Tom, hidden in the shadows. Joe turned and faced George Starling. The disfiguring scar barely registered with Joe. He looked directly into his eyes. He wasn't afraid. He was calm. There was a strange, inexplicable intimacy that moved from one man to the other. For each of them this felt like a consummation.

'This might be the happiest moment of my life,' Starling said.

'What a miserable life that is,' Joe said.

'Funny man. You'll be dead in a minute. Just one more dead Jew, like all the others in Europe. I read your scrapbook. Now *that* was funny.'

The voices in the Portico Room had, by now, been stilled, as people had become aware of what was happening on the balcony. Inspector Lambert reached Tom Mackenzie's side.

'I let him in,' he said. 'I let him in.' His voice sounded flat and defeated, as if he knew that Joe Sable was about to die, and that it was he, Titus Lambert, who'd allowed it to happen.

Starling was reluctant to truncate his pleasure. He ought to have simply pulled the trigger, he knew that, but he'd waited so long, and he felt so in control here that he wanted to linger. Helen Lord still had her back to him, and he wanted to see the fear in her face, too.

'Turn around, you ugly bitch.'

Helen, who'd already experienced terror at the hands of this man, now felt oddly composed, or was it a kind of numbness? She turned. Starling sighted the Luger between her eyes. He held up the filleting knife in his left hand.

'This is for you,' he said. 'No quick death for you.' Starling knew that he wouldn't get to use the knife, but saying the words was delicious.

Clara sensed that Guy was about to move, and she put her hand on his arm to stop him. Starling saw the movement, and his eyes caught Clara's. She remembered what Helen had said about him, that he was ordinary. Only he wasn't ordinary. There was a fierceness in his gaze that chilled her, and the scar, which she knew from its raw edges was fresh, made him monstrous. His was not a face, or nature, that aroused pity.

When Starling's eyes fell briefly on Guy, Guy experienced revulsion and contempt in equal measure. He wasn't afraid of this creature, but Clara's touch reined in his urge to act. Starling would pull that trigger at the slightest provocation.

The next few moments were recalled afterwards as a confusion of sound and movement. The roar of Tom Mackenzie's voice distracted Starling, and he made the mistake of lowering the gun and turning his head.

'Drop, Joe! Drop down!'

Joe saw Tom rushing towards them, holding a chair like a crazed lion-tamer. Joe fell to his knees as the chair connected with Starling's torso. Joe felt the clumsy tangle of Starling's legs against his side. The momentum pushed Starling into Joe's crouching form, and Starling fell heavily, his nose hitting the edge of the balustrade so forcefully that Clara heard the crunch as the cartilage collapsed.

Starling, dazed, was aware that people were moving. Uncertain what to do, he climbed onto the balustrade, where he could see over the crowd. He was dizzy, and he waved the Luger about loosely. He fired off a reckless shot. This, at least, had the effect of stopping people in their tracks. The undirected bullet hit a roosting pigeon in the eaves, which fell at a woman's feet and fluttered wildly, but briefly.

The noise of the Luger cleared Starling's head. Blood poured from his nose. He could taste it. He thought he could smell the salty air of Murnane's Bay. There was Sable, crouching and staring up at him. He raised the gun and pointed it at Joe's face. No lingering now. He pulled the trigger.

There was no explosion, just the click of an empty chamber.

It took a moment for this to register with Starling. All six bullets had been spent. Why was Sable still staring at him? Focussed on this, he didn't see Guy Kirkham move towards him, but he felt his hands close around his ankles. He looked down. Who was this man? He still had his knife, which he swung in an arc, expecting it to slice across the stranger's throat. Guy stepped back out of its reach. As he did so, he yanked Starling's ankles, which were at waist-height, towards him.

Without flailing or crying out, Starling fell backwards, into the open air beyond the balustrade. For a split-second, he fell soundlessly. Then he landed below in a fortunate space that had opened up among the pedestrians on Swanston Street. Starling's body hit the concrete awkwardly. If he'd been lucky, he might have survived the fall. He hadn't been lucky. His head crashed into the pavement, and his neck snapped.

Later, when the pandemonium had died down, and the balcony and Portico Room had been vacated, a cleaner would find George Starling's grey fedora, apparently forgotten by one of the guests. It was quality. He'd leave it with the porter at the Melbourne Club. A hat like that must surely belong to a member.

15

One Week Later. Saturday 15 April 1944

CLARA DAWSON'S EVIDENCE, supported by Dr Jamieson, who'd performed the autopsy on Peter Lillee, convinced the coroner to hand down a finding of death by misadventure. 'In the absence of any plausible suspects in this case, however extraordinary it may seem, accidental death by hydrogen sulphide poisoning remains the most likely probability,' he said.

Ros Lord had suggested that lunch on the day following the inquest would be a good idea. It would be an opportunity to honour Peter Lillee privately after the fiasco of the official wake. It was a small gathering. Clara Dawson, Helen Lord, Tom Mackenzie, Guy Kirkham, Joe Sable, and Ros Lord. Inspector Lambert and his wife, Maude, had been invited, but they'd declined. As it happened, Maude had decided at the last minute that she'd come, and when she arrived with Tom, Joe was hopeful that this might signal the possibility that his relationship with Inspector Lambert might be reparable.

They'd spoken only once, briefly, since Joe's tendered resignation had been accepted. On that occasion, Lambert had said very little. He'd certainly made no effort to dissuade Joe from his decision. Two days after his resignation Inspector Lambert had telephoned Joe, as a courtesy, to tell him that Ron Dunnart wasn't implicated in the murders of the Reillys or Bob O'Dowd. The Reillys had been shot with George Starling's Luger, and there was enough blood trapped in the crevices of his filleting knife and, bizarrely, under his toenails, to link him also to Bob O'Dowd. Lambert could only speculate how Starling knew either Reilly or O'Dowd, but the evidence was irrefutable that he'd been present at both crime scenes.

In Starling's room at The Victoria Hotel, the key to which had been in his pocket, the police had found among his clothes a coat with the name 'John Pluschow' stitched into its lining. Inspector Halloran in Warrnambool had been informed, and Maria Pluschow was to be questioned. It was possible that this might help solve the murder of Hardy Truscott, although Inspector Lambert wasn't optimistic about this.

The police had also found close to five thousand pounds in cash, and the key to a motorcycle, which was yet to be located. He'd imparted all this information concisely and in a tone that closed off conversation. Joe thanked him and asked if Ron Dunnart would be returning to Homicide.

'Sergeant Dunnart is to be discharged. This unit is now very seriously undermanned. Kevin Maher has applied to join Homicide.'

Joe felt sick.

'I won't take him, of course, although one of the unfortunate consequences of your resignation has been that people, some people, believe that it gives credence to Maher's version of what happened in Watson Cooper's house. I need hardly tell you that it hasn't changed my view of that incident. I believed you then, and I believe you now. I think you would have made a fine detective, Joe. Your poor judgement has more to do with your age and inexperience than with your ability. I'm partly responsible for that.'

'Promoting me was poor judgement on your part. Is that what you're saying?'

'Yes. That was a mistake. I'm sorry, but that's the truth, and I'm sorry that that decision exposed you to such horrors.'

There was a strange absence of emotion in Lambert's voice, as if he was trying to keep his words to a minimum. Joe didn't know how to respond, and Inspector Lambert's coolness and brutal assessment of Joe's time in Homicide made him uncomfortable and eager to get off the phone.

'I'm sorry I let you down, sir,' he said, and before Lambert could respond, he hung up.

Joe had mulled over this conversation for days. He'd told everyone the details about George Starling, but he'd kept back the humiliating news that Inspector Lambert considered him proof of what happens when you make an error of judgement. This was such a blow to his ego that he couldn't even discuss it with Guy Kirkham.

Now Maude Lambert was here for lunch. It was she who broke the ice. As she shook his hand in greeting, she said, 'The Homicide department will miss you, Joe. Titus will miss you. You may not think so, but he will. You'll come to dinner soon, won't you?'

'Of course,' Joe said, although the prospect of dinner with Inspector Lambert seemed unlikely. Over the days since his resignation he'd come to terms with what he took to be a simple fact — that Inspector Lambert would prefer not to set eyes on him again. He was a junior officer who hadn't lived up to his promise. He was an error of judgement.

Helen Lord had always been wary of Maude Lambert. When Inspector Lambert had first seconded her to the newly formed Homicide department, she'd had lunch with Mrs Lambert, and she'd felt that she was being auditioned, or vetted, and that if Mrs Lambert disliked her she'd be returned to her previous position. Helen couldn't deny Maude's intelligence, or her astuteness. Still, the idea that Maude had been granted the right to judge her had struck her as an impertinence and presumptuous. The Maude Lambert who came to lunch seemed to her to be a very different person. She was warm and amusing, and the almost twenty years that separated her from most of the people at the table were of no consequence.

Helen had suspected, from watching and listening to Joe, that there was more to his resignation than he was letting on. Maude's presence confirmed this, and the way she reached out at one moment and closed her hand over the back of Joe's hand, made Helen's wariness of her evaporate.

At the end of the meal, they stood and raised their glasses to the portrait of Peter Lillee that dominated the dining room. Once they'd sat down again, Helen said, 'I have news. I'm resigning from the police force.'

'Oh, Helen, no,' Maude said.

'I am, Mrs Lambert.'

'But you're one of the best brains they've ever had.'

'Thank you. I agree.'

Clara laughed.

'The Victoria Police for the most part — there is one honourable exception — isn't interested in a brain when it is inside a woman's head. I don't have to suffer those fools any longer, thanks to Uncle Peter. If I have to suffer them in the future, it will be on my terms.'

Ros Lord rose from the table and came back with a sheaf of paper. She handed one sheet to each person. They each read the letterhead.

Helen Lord and Associates
Private Inquiry Agents
Suite 4, 45 Albert Street
East Melbourne

It took a moment for this to sink in.

'I've rented a suite, and within a week, I'll be fully registered, thanks in no small part to Inspector Lambert, who has used his influence to remove any official barriers. I presume you knew that I'd asked for his help, Mrs Lambert?'

'Well. Yes, I did, and I told him I'd divorce him if he hesitated for a moment. He didn't.'

'This is a new start, and I can afford to do this the way I want to do it.'

'It says, "Helen Lord and Associates",' Guy said.

'I don't have any yet.' She paused. 'But I'm hiring, if anyone at this table is interested.'

The End

Acknowledgements

First and foremost, thank you to Helen Murnane, the wisest of readers. I also want to thank the community of my fellow writers, especially Jock Serong, Tony Thompson, Angela Savage, Sulari Gentill, and Greg Pyers. Thanks to Henry Rosenbloom, who cares deeply about books, and to everyone at Scribe, all of whom share his passion. And finally, thanks to my editor, Anna Thwaites, who hates being called brilliant, but she is, and that's all there is to it.

'Gott's new book is as close
to perfect as a mystery can be.'
Sunday Age

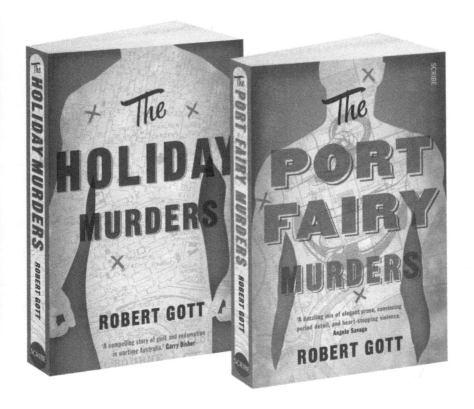

'Dickensian or even Jamesian in its breadth ... a very "literary"
crime series that works so well on many different levels.'
Saturday Age

While you're waiting for the next book about Joe Sable and Helen Lord, try Robert Gott's comic series, the William Power books, starting with *Good Murder*...

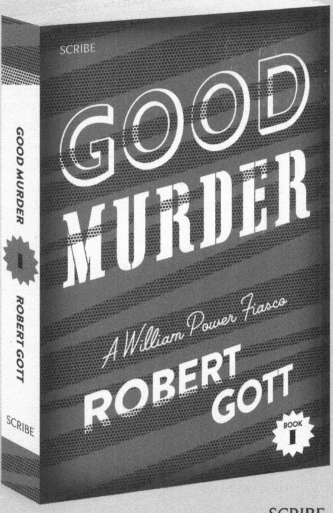

Chapter One

MAKING AN ENTRANCE

THE WATER TOWER in Maryborough sat on the corner of Adelaide and Anne Streets. It held one million gallons of water and, for two weeks in August 1942, it also held the body of a 24-year-old woman named Polly Drummond. Afterwards it was impossible not to be appalled by the realisation that each time we drank a cup of tea we were imbibing Polly Drummond, and that each time we took a bath we were splashing ourselves with Polly Drummond. As she slowly dissolved up there, bloating and exuding the corrupt gases and liquids of the dead, we in the town strained her through our teeth, gargled her, washed our hair with her, and imbedded her in the very clothes we wore.

I was among the gawkers who gathered at the bottom of the tower when word was passed around that her body had been found. My interest was not entirely voyeuristic. I was, after all, the main suspect in her murder.

She had been discovered by two city council workers who had climbed the 52 feet to the top of the tower to fix a faulty indicator. They knew immediately who it was floating face down in that reservoir. The *Maryborough Chronicle* had been publishing almost daily accounts of the search for the missing woman. In a small town like Maryborough, everyone knew Polly Drummond, and everyone had a theory about what had happened to her. Many of those theories featured me.

Getting Polly out of the tower and down to the ground was no easy task. I can understand the reluctance of those helping to simply sling the body across the shoulder and climb down. Eventually, using a block and tackle, Polly's body was clumsily lowered to terra firma. This took more than two hours, and by this time most onlookers had given up and gone home. I hung well back, in the grounds of the Christian Brothers school opposite. There was no one from Polly's family to accompany the body to the morgue. Her brother, who I knew slightly, had himself died two days previously, and her mother was barking mad. I did not believe my presence would arouse anything more than further suspicion. Under cover of the gathering darkness I walked back to the hotel where my company and I were staying.

There was a war on, don't forget, and I was doing my bit. That's why we were up there, in Maryborough. The William Power Players were boosting morale all over rural Queensland by bringing Shakespeare to the barbarians. We had played Gympie before coming to Maryborough. It had not gone well, to be perfectly honest. We had underestimated their readiness for a daring tilt at *Troilus and Cressida*. It was an artistic triumph for those with eyes to see and a heart to feel, but Gympie was a bit light on in those departments. It didn't help that the crowd had been agitated by the news that there had been heavy losses in the Solomon Islands and that the Germans were advancing rapidly on Stalingrad. The progress of the war often had a detrimental effect upon how our performances were received. Only a handful of people turned up for the second night's performance. Gympie is a small pond, and I had overestimated the population of pond life that might wish to drag itself out of the slime for one evening. We decided to move on to Maryborough and mount a challenging new take on *Titus Andronicus*.

The 'we' I mention was my troupe, my company, the Power Players. There were eight of us: my leading lady Annie Hudson (not a great talent, but very easy on the eye); Kevin Skakel (clubfoot, unfit for active duty); Bill Henty (blind in one eye, unfit for active duty); Arthur Rank (one arm, and one testicle as a matter of fact, unfit for active duty); Walter Sunder (65 years old, unfit for active duty); Adrian Baden (queer, unfit for active duty); and Tibald Canty (morbidly obese, unfit for active duty). I happened to be slightly flat footed, although not in any obvious way. In fact, I didn't even know it until I enlisted and had the medical. I wouldn't have been accepted anyway. Entertainers, particularly first-class ones, were considered a reserved profession. What we offered was more than a bag of flesh to stop a bullet.

Despite Annie Hudson's frequent suggestion that, in view of its personnel, playing a scene with the Power Players was like working in a field hospital, we were a professional outfit. Everybody had been connected in some way with the business before the war. Theatre was in our blood, no matter how small or large our parts had been. Tibald Canty, to choose just one of the troupe — the largest one, as it happens — had had quite a successful career in radio, although his real love was the kitchen, and he had trained under some of the best chefs in Europe. Unfortunately he couldn't appear as his character when it was mooted to put his radio show on the stage. Listeners thought he was a 25-year-old dentist, lean and smouldering, with coal-black hair and crisp blue eyes. The sight of a 40-year-old obese man with thinning, dirty yellow hair was considered too disillusioning, even in the early days of the war. He was replaced on stage, and afterwards his replacement slipped into his radio part, too. That freed him up to join my company.

In 1942, I was in my prime. I was a serious actor. Whether I was a great actor is for others to judge. I have learned, though, to take the judgements of others with a grain of salt. I have presence. I can hold the stage. I can drag an audience to its feet with the lift of an eyebrow. I have elegant eyebrows, shaped by nature, not by tweezers. I looked like Tyrone Power (no relation) only finer, not so swarthy, higher-browed, bluer-eyed.

WHEN THE POWER Players arrived in Maryborough, the war was going badly. American soldiers were everywhere down south and causing trouble. A man named Leonski had been charged with the brownout murders in Melbourne. He'd strangled three women and was going to hang. We all talked about it, and I thought the time was right to do a Grand Guignol piece of our own devising about the wickedness of human nature. The mass murderer would be a Eurasian with impeccable credentials. He wouldn't be unmasked until the final scene when we learned that his mother was Japanese and his father was German. No-one in the troupe thought it was a very good idea. Annie Hudson, who I thought might jump at the chance to play three different victims in the one piece, said it was a particularly lousy idea. I suspected she realised that it was outside her range.

The Power Players travelled everywhere by truck. We had been allocated fifteen thousand miles annually for travel, and we had to be careful not to exceed them. With theatrical runs that were much shorter than expected we found ourselves on the move a great deal, and it's surprising how quickly we ate up those miles. Strictly speaking, it was Annie's truck. She'd paid for it with the money she'd made from her advertisements, and she'd made quite a few. They were print advertisements, mostly, and drew on her resemblance to Greer Garson — a rather low-rent version of Greer Garson, but she certainly resembled her. She'd also done a couple of radio spots. You only had to ask her and she'd tell you all about it. In 1942 she peered out at you from every magazine and newspaper you picked up. She was Connie, the bad-breath girl in the Colgate advertisement. There she was, looking all wide-eyed and lonely in the first frame and saying, 'I'd like to go places and do things.' That would be OK, she is advised, 'but first check up on your breath'. All it takes to turn poor Connie into a social success is a quick brush with Colgate Dental Cream. I'm in that ad, too, in the last frame where Connie is pictured smiling at two tuxedoed admirers, apparently breathing in the mint-masked effluvium from Connie's mouth. I'm the one with his back to the camera. The moron who managed to get his face shown pleasured the photographer orally. There are some things I won't do. It's a matter of class.

That's where I met Annie, on the bad-breath girl photo shoot. I was setting up the Power Players in Melbourne at the time, and I offered her a place, promising her all the leading lady parts. When she said that she would buy a truck, the deal was sealed. Later, though, her pointed reminders as to who owned the vehicle made me think that I had paid a high price indeed for transport. She claimed that the only reason people came to see us at all was to see her. She was the bad-breath girl and the Tampax girl ('All dressed up and then *couldn't* go! ...') and people knew a star when they saw one. I kept quiet when she was doing one of her star turns. As actor/manager I had a responsibility to the whole troupe, and part of that responsibility involved not losing the truck. We were regularly reminded, half-jokingly, that it was *her* truck and that she might just drive away in it.

The truck sat three in the front, or two if the passenger was Tibald, who weighed twenty stone at the time. The rest of the troupe rode in the back with the costumes, the props, and bits of all-purpose scenery. We wove stage magic with a minimum of scenery. It was all about the voice; my voice, mainly. Annie was at her best when looking distressed in grainy newspaper ads about her bad breath or untimely menstrual flow. There was no music in her voice. None at all. The truth is that the success or otherwise of her stage career was entirely dependent upon the reliability of her truck and the availability of petrol.

It was a cool August morning when we lurched down Ferry Street in Maryborough for the first time. My initial impression of this almost-coastal town was that it was unnervingly flat. The eye ran up and down its wide streets unimpeded by dip or hillock. There had been no attempt made to soften the brutal simplicity of these thoroughfares with trees of any kind. For a person used to the huddled houses of inner Melbourne (albeit the house I grew up in was rather grand), Maryborough's homes seemed unnecessarily generous in size, although this was partly an illusion created by the stilts on which many of them sat. The imagination of the inhabitants did not extend to their gardens. The enormous Queenslanders perched above either a riot of grasses and vines, with the odd ragged and shapeless paw paw or mango, or a blasted heath of sour and ugly earth.

We'd chosen Maryborough because we'd heard that the war had had a remarkable effect upon it. The influx of airmen and soldiers, and the shifting of industry to a war footing, had shaken it out of the drowsy torpor that anaesthetised the inland towns we had visited and failed to arouse. The awful truth — something best avoided in the normal course of events, or at any rate left undisturbed by poking at it—was that the Power Players were ideally suited to performing in small, remote places, where our limitations might pass unnoticed, camouflaged by the greater limitations of our audiences. I had ambitions or, in this context, dreams, that my own talent might provide somebody in one of those godforsaken towns with the transformative experience of art.

I was optimistic about Maryborough, prospering as it was in response to the need to build ships to keep Hirohito at bay. And build ships they did. Walkers Engineering was the pumping heart that kept Maryborough going. If ever proof was needed that war could quicken the economic pulse of a community, Walkers was it. Twelve hundred men beavered away in there, turning out

Corvettes for the navy. They travelled to and from work in a great shoal of bicycles that flowed up Kent Street each morning at seven o'clock and ebbed back down Kent Street each afternoon at four. To be unemployed in Maryborough, a man would have to be dead and buried. Surely, here *Titus Andronicus* would release its power to mesmerise and appal.

My troupe drew curious gazes on that first morning. There were few cars about, and the only truck we saw was a military vehicle. We turned into Kent Street and began looking for a suitable hotel. The Royal Hotel would have been ideal, but it was far too grand for our budget. It had obviously been built at a time when the town was flush with money from timber and gold. There were well-dressed women drinking in the lounge, looking prosperous and metropolitan, and doubtless the wives of officers put up there for the duration.

We found a place we could afford close to the river but close, too, to the centre of town. The George Hotel, on the corner of March and Wharf Streets, had three storeys that seemed to have a tentative grasp on the site. They leaned nervously away from the Mary River as if not wishing to attract its attention. The Mary River runs at speed through the town, its waters muddied by the churning drag of energetic tides. It floods with a viciousness that is almost personal. People were still talking about the flood of '37 and declaring that the town was about due for another drowning. They got their drowning all right, but it wasn't quite what they were expecting.

The proprietor of the George was a sinewy, pale-skinned man with hair the colour of copper wire and eyes of a most peculiar, insipid, yellow-flecked green. He welcomed us with open, hairy arms. Customers who stayed and paid were obviously unusual in his hotel. I wondered if the insistent wash of the Mary River, audible through the open door of the bar, had anything to do with it. There were a few men in the bar, and they looked us up and down before returning indifferently to their beer. The proprietor, who declared that his name was Augie Kelly, ran the place more or less on his own.

'The food's not great,' he said. 'I do the best I can, but there's not a big demand and there's not much in the way of decent stuff available.' As he said this he looked at Tibald, wondering, I suppose, if he was expected to provide enough food to maintain his weight. 'I'm not a good cook either,' he added. 'I had a good cook, but he joined the AIF.' Turning those unsettling eyes in my direction he explained further, moving his large hands about apologetically. 'You may not know, but the government is going to bring in austerity measures that will affect public eating houses. Three courses only, and no hors d'oeuvres.'

I did not imagine that three courses of anything had been served in this hotel for a very long time.

'It's twenty shillings a week, each,' he said.

'That,' I said icily, 'seems rather high, especially in the absence of hors d'oeuvres.'

'If you can do better anywhere else, be my guest,' he said, folding those hairy arms aggressively.

Tibald interrupted him.

'My good man,' he declaimed in his deepest Falstaffian voice, 'show me your kitchen.'

Augie was taken aback. 'Why?' His eyelids twitched suspiciously as if he thought Tibald was already on the hunt for any available food.

'If the space is agreeable and if the equipment is even a few steps up from primitive, I will cook for your establishment in consideration of a reduction in our tariff.'

'Now why would I do that? How do I know that you can even cook?'

Tibald raised an eyebrow. 'Do I look hungry?' he asked.

'Mr Tibald Canty is not only a fine actor,' I interposed, 'he is also a chef whose skills would intimidate Escoffier himself.' I took the liberty of putting my arm around Augie Kelly's bony shoulder and giving it a little squeeze. 'I can guarantee that in no time at all the word will spread that you are serving great food at the George. This will become the only place to eat in town, and that will mean a substantial increase in your profits. There must be people, even in a town like this, who like food. Imagine your dining room filled with people licking their lips and buying your booze.'

'I don't have much stuff in there,' he said uncertainly, but there was no hostility in the look he gave me. I knew we had him. If there's one thing I've learned from staying in hotels, it's that every hotel proprietor dreams of greatness. Most of them settle for squalor because after a while even that becomes a standard requiring effort.

'All right,' he said. 'Let's see what you can do, but I'm not guaranteeing anything.'

The speed with which he acquiesced was unsurprising. He could not afford to turn my troupe away. Even if we stayed for only a week, it would mean more money than he had earned in a long while.

He allocated rooms on the third floor for the men, but gave Annie Hudson a room on the second floor. It was, he said, the best room in the hotel. Not for the first time, I admired the effortless, almost unconscious, ease with which Annie subdued men.

'If business improves, you can stay for eighteen shillings a week.'

'Fifteen', I said quickly, 'and it goes down further if business really improves.'

'Show me the kitchen,' Tibald said, before Augie Kelly could object.

I followed them both down a narrow corridor. The others in the company peeled off to explore their rooms and to lie low. No one ever wanted to join me on my first excursion into a new town in search of a place to perform, which is what I would be doing after the tariff had been settled.

The kitchen was dark, filthy, and malodorous. Flies buzzed, drawn by the seductive promise of rancid fat. I thought Tibald would change his mind on the spot and express his disgust in tariff-raising eloquence. I didn't want him to do this because I had already assimilated the financial relief his cooking would provide. We would all pitch in, at least until *Titus* was up and running. I was looking forward to telling Annie that she would have to drag out her French maid's costume yet again and wait on tables. At least we would eat well. To my astonishment he didn't recoil in horror from the grim spectacle of a room that seemed to be held together by forces no stronger than congealed lard and darkness. Instead he uttered a little whoop of joy.

'It's an Aga,' he said, in a tone normally reserved for the highest expression of stage joy. 'I can't believe it. Here, in the middle of this cholera zone you call a kitchen, you have an Aga.'

'You mean the stove?' Augie said, puzzled.

Tibald looked at him with such exaggerated pity and contempt that his expression could have been seen from even the cheapest seats in the house.

'Be in the dining room at 8.00 pm,' he said imperiously, 'and if you have any friends, bring them. Now, I need the name of your purveyors. I will purchase the food for this evening's meal and I will charge it to this establishment.'

Tibald drew a red handkerchief from his pocket and wiped his mouth. It created the unfortunate impression of slobbering at the mere thought of food.

Augie said nothing.

'I presume you have preferred providores.'

'I don't even know what that is,' Augie said, 'but frankly it sounds expensive, and this new law means that we can't charge more than five shillings for any meal — not that there's a single person in this town who'd pay that much for a meal anyway. Where do you think you are? Paris?'

'Oh no,' said Tibald. 'I don't think I am in Paris, at least no part of it that's above ground. If you give me the name of a butcher and a dry goods merchant, that will be a start.'

'You can go to Geraghty's for flour and stuff, and Lusk's for meat, but you can't charge anything. I don't have an account, and even if I did I don't think I'd be sending you off to spend my money on spec.'

'All right, Mr Kelly,' I said. 'I quite see your point. We will pay for this evening's meal as a demonstration of our good faith. If it is unsatisfactory we will pay you for one night's accommodation and be on our way. You have nothing to lose and a reputation to gain. May I suggest that you shave before dinner.'

I bustled Tibald out of the kitchen and towards the truck.

'I hope,' I said with studied calm, 'that you can live up to your notices, because if this meal is a failure, we're ruined.'

'Who's going to replace me in *Titus* if I'm cooking every night?'

'Nobody,' I said. 'I'll just cut the part out. Nobody here will notice.'

I suspect Tibald was secretly glad to be out of *Titus*. My interpretation was a little too athletic for him to feel comfortable in his role. The somersaults I had wanted him to do were proving arduous and he was definitely disgruntled about wearing a leather posing pouch and nothing else.

To keep reading, buy the book at scribepublications.com.au